Are we.... LEMMINGS & SNOWFLAKES?

Mum looks sad for a moment. "Oh, Olive, you're not mad. You're just…"

"Happiness challenged?"

"No…"

"Coming down with a touch of insanity?"

"No…"

"Mentally high-maintenance?"

She laughs at that one. "Just open the door already."

WELCOME TO CAMP RESET

A ... a work
of ... real issues including
sui... ... ng
dep... discussion of sexual assault.

Those to advice and support can be found
at the back of the book

First published in the UK in 2018 by Usborne Publishing Ltd., Usborne House,
83-85 Saffron Hill, London EC1N 8RT, England. www.usborne.com

Text © Holly Bourne, 2018

Author photo © L. Bourne, 2017

Cover artwork and title lettering by inkymole.com

A CIP catalogue record for this book is available from the British Library.

ISBN 9781474933612   JFMAM JASOND/18   04434/1

Printed in the UK.

Holly Bourne

Are We All LEMMINGS & SNOWFLAKES?

USBORNE

To falling down seven times,
but getting up eight

1

There are too many people.

They clutter the pavements. They let their stupid children scream as they run under the garden hose. They chat outside until late. They play music at barbecues. They don't seem to care that they're killing me. They have loud, pointless building work done on their perfectly adequate houses. *Crash crash crash* of the scaffolding going up. Builders yelling over the blast of their radio. *Ping ping ping* goes my phone. People sharing their noise. Here's my ENDLESS NOISE. I exist. I am one of the too-many people and I need you to know I exist by screaming out my loud stupid noise.

I just want it to be quiet.

To not have to listen to the damn noise.

All.

The.

Damn.

Time.

I just need peace.

But the noise is *everywhere*.

2

A scrape of the chair being pushed back from where it's wedged under the door handle.

Mum's voice. "Olive?"

I hear the creak of her footstep on the floorboard. I wince. Close my eyes and squeeze my hands over my ears.

I feel light on my closed eyelids.

"Olive?"

Her breath hits my cheek. I'm going to have to open my eyes. I peel one open, jerking back as the light floods my vision. It takes a moment until I have the energy for the other eye.

Mum's worried face comes into vague focus. "What are you doing under here?"

If I wasn't so tired, I would probably care about the wobble in her voice. But it's like every single muscle of my body has a weight tied to it with a gift ribbon, pinning me down to the carpet.

Because I am on the carpet.

I am under my desk and my desk is covered with two duvets.

My mouth feels stitched shut. But if I don't answer her, she won't go away and leave me alone. And all I want is to be left alone.

"Olive? Please? You're worrying us sick. Talk to me."

I close my eyes again to give myself the energy required to open my mouth.

"I'm just resting."

"Resting?"

I gulp from the effort of talking. "Yes."

A sigh. It makes me open my eyes to see her pinching the top of her nose. I have let her down again. I am ruining everything again. I am so worthless. I hate humans. I hate that they're everywhere. But the human I hate most is me.

The

Human

I

Always

Hate

Most

Is

Me.

Because it makes Mum's face look like that.

"You have to let some air in."

"No…"

But she doesn't hear me whimper. Her feet pound across my room. No no no. I cower before it's even happened.

"You've got to let the world in, Olive. Look, it's your dad's birthday and you've not even wished him a happy one. Try. Please. For him. Come on, pull yourself together."

She tells me to pull myself together the moment she pulls open the curtains. She does the one thing that will ensure I do the opposite. The light hits me like bullets. She flings open the windows and the world comes rushing in – loud and brash and, God, I hate summer. I can smell the meat of barbecues. I can hear the lawnmowers roaring. I can hear the birds squawking and the buzz of insects and the fun that everyone else in the world is having. It overloads me. I desperately rummage back under my blankets. Even though the air is heavy with heat. Even though I'm sweating so much I've not needed the bathroom all day. The world is drowning me and the blankets are my oxygen mask.

"We're having your cousins round for a barbecue at six," she says. "I want you up, showered and dressed by then, please. Just…try. Please, Olive. Maybe we can do it together? How about that?"

I try to bury further under my covers but Mum claws them away.

I would cry if I knew how.

I've forgotten how.

"Olive, you're scaring me." Her voice is soft again. "Whatever is happening right now, don't let it win. Okay, darling? Come on, get up. You were fine last week."

I can't have been fine last week.

I can't remember what fine feels like.

"I'm going to come and check on you in twenty minutes."
She is closing the door. She is leaving me alone.

God, I am so tired.

A plane flies overhead and the noise of the engine makes my body feel like it's been plugged into an electric current.

I don't think I can handle this much longer.

Four hours later

Oh thank you, thank you, thank you for raining.

The sky has ripped open, chucking fistfuls of water from the clouds in giant clumps. They splatter against my head. My hair is already plastered to my face.

I've remembered how to cry.

I sob as I run through the woods up the road from our house, my gold ballet pumps slipping in the new mud. Lightning spasms across the sky and thunder belches around me.

It drowns out my screaming.

No one is around to hear it anyway. The windows are closed. The barbecues are rained off. The rain has driven everyone inside and I am the only one here in the clearing, screaming up into the sky.

Screaming because I'm so scared.

Screaming because I can't believe it's happening again.

Screaming because it's so much less life-threatening than what I really want to do.

My top is plastered to my body, my jeans are heavy with rainwater. I run and scramble and tumble through mud. My heart feels like it's been sliced down the middle and every painful thing that's ever happened is oozing out of it. Leaving a slimy trail behind me. I've got to keep moving. I've got to keep running.

Running away from myself.

Running away from what I want to do.

I keep going and going, down little paths through the trees, losing my bearings. I have to keep running. Keep moving. Until, until…

I come to the top of one of the clay cliffs.

I stop.

The drop is sheer enough. I slow to a walk, moving closer to the edge. The rain is softer under the canopy of trees. I hug the trunk of an oak tree and think about things I shouldn't.

I want to do this so much.

I want this feeling to end so much.

And I'm not sure what happens next, and I'm not sure how much time has passed, and I'm not sure of the sequence of things, but the drop is still below me and I'm crying and standing on the edge of it but I'm still holding onto the tree trunk, but then…then… Several men in uniform are walking slowly out towards me through the storm, their hands outstretched, the rain bouncing off their helmets.

And they're saying:

"Olive?"

3

Okay, so it doesn't look good.

I'm thinking of all the things I need to explain.

1. The shattered glass of our old greenhouse from where I kicked in the window
2. The blood all over it
3. The fact Mum found the blood, and the glass, and I'd vanished
4. The several eyewitnesses who saw a distressed girl running through a storm
5. The fact I was found, by police, standing at the top of a cliff
6. Because my mum had dialled 999...

"I wasn't trying to kill myself," I tell the psychiatric nurse. The adrenaline from the whole darned mess still pumps through me, making me capable of defending myself. I have to clear things up before the numb and exhaustion return

– their arms wide open, saying, "We meet again, Olive," like a James Bond villain.

Mum and Dad sit next to me in the plastic hospital chairs. Dad's leg is shaking and Mum leans forward to interrupt.

"We found blood all over the greenhouse," she says hysterically.

And a tiny part of me laughs at how middle class that sounds.

The nurse's name tag says *Jake* and he isn't impressed by my mother. Or any of us, to be honest.

"Maybe Olive should be the one to explain?" he says. I see him glance at his watch.

I sigh and shake my head. "Okay," I start. "So I kicked in the side of the greenhouse and cut my foot. But I wasn't trying to…" I can't go any further. Not with Mum and Dad here.

Jake nods his head towards my parents. "We can talk alone if you'd like, Olive?"

Mum straightens up, ripples of rejection radiating off her. "Oh, yes. Of course," she says. "Olive? Would it be easier if we left?"

An impossible situation which I'm too drained to think through properly. Mum will take it personally, but I can't say what I need to say when she's here.

I find her eyes. "Maybe, just for a minute?"

She blinks.

Dad murmurs, "Of course, sweetheart."

Jake stands as they stand. "I'll come get you in a bit," he tells them.

The legs of their chairs screech across the floor and my entire body winces.

It comes rushing back.

The noise, the endless noise of outside, of my cousins arriving, of music floating up the stairs, of people having fun while I was screaming inside.

I couldn't stand the noise any more.

"We'll be right outside, Olive." Dad's voice is gruff. I can sense his anger, boiling just under the crust of his skin. I've ruined his birthday. I've made it about me, yet again. But he can't admit he's angry. You can't tell suicidal people that you're pissed off at them for being suicidal, no matter how much that is true.

Not that I'm suicidal.

Which is what I tell Jake the moment the door closes.

He ignores me and digs in his desk drawer, pulls out a questionnaire. "Maybe just start by filling this out for me?"

I read through the familiar questions that greet me like long-lost friends. I used to have to fill this out before every pointless therapy session I had last winter.

Over the last two weeks, have you had:
Little pleasure or interest in doing things?

Not at all
Several days

More than half the days
Nearly every day

Well, I mean, how are you supposed to answer that? Last week I had ALL the pleasure and ALL the interest in doing things. Life was a basin of water to plunge my face into. I'd soared through almost all my exams, drunk till I was sick, kissed Rick Macaby at the Freedom party in the park and dragged him into a bush to do more than kissing. I'd laughed and twirled and danced and connected and treated each moment like a lemon to squeeze until there wasn't a drop of juice left and then I'd even eat the lemon rind, thank you very much, as long as I didn't have to go to bed. But then this week? This week my primary activities were burying my head under two duvets to drown out the sounds of the world existing, and staring at my hand until I wasn't sure if it was real or not. And before both of those extremes, I was pretty usual. So what the hell am I supposed to answer?

I circle *Several days* and move on.

Trouble falling or staying asleep, or sleeping too much?

Why wasn't there an e) I *would* sleep if only everyone would just SHUT UP AND LET ME SLEEP?

I pick *Several days* for most of the survey, because I know that will protect me from getting sectioned. And I can't get sectioned by someone who looks as bored by the idea as Jake.

What a job it must be, being a psychiatric nurse in an A & E department. Imagine if assessing suicidal people was as commonplace as a barista making a flat white. I push over my finished sheet and watch as he counts it up in his head. Then he puts it down and doesn't tell me my score because they never tell you your score.

"We've not got as long as I'd like, I'm afraid," Jake says. "But why don't we start with talking through your history? Your mum mentioned you've had episodes of feeling very sad before? Why don't we—"

I interrupt him. "Look," I say, "I didn't want to come here. I didn't mean to cause all this fuss. I'm fine. Really I am. Well, I'm not. Obviously. But I'm fine in that you don't have to worry about sending me home with a *not-a-danger* sticker and then I go jump in front of a bus and you get called in for a difficult meeting."

Jake makes a note of what I've just said. Because you can't mention jumping in front of a bus without them having to write it down. Even if you're promising not to jump in front of one.

"Thank you for your concern, Olive, but it's up to me to worry about you. Not the other way around. It's up to me to decide if you're safe."

"But it's not what it looks like."

"So, what is it like?"

And I tell Jake about how, actually, tonight just demonstrates how *well* I'm doing. Because me hanging onto a tree trunk is a GOOD sign. And, actually, I was only up there because I wanted to *live*. Because I was trying to protect myself.

"I did want to die," I tell him and just that is enough for the tears to come. "Because I wanted the noise to stop. But, I didn't want to die for ever, if that makes sense? I just wanted to die...temporarily? So I could have a little break."

He lowers his nose. "You wanted to die *temporarily?*"

"Look, I know that's not possible," I say snappily. "But it was so noisy, and Mum made me come down for this barbecue because it's my dad's birthday and there's only so long they can be understanding before they get pissed off. And my younger cousins wouldn't stop screaming. Then the rain started and we all had to go into the living room and there were too many people and it was so loud and it hurt my head so...so...I ran down the garden into the greenhouse. Just for some quiet."

Jake is nodding, so I plough on.

"Anyway, then I was there and the storm was there and I realized just how *not normal* it was that I'd run out into the garden. And my head felt like it was burning and screaming and full of insects that were exploding one by one behind my eyes..." Another tear bubbles up and jumps down my cheek. "And I realized that I'm not very well again," I gasp, needing more air. "And I'm not sure I can go through that again. And, then, well, I'm not sure what happened but there was glass all over the floor and I'd cut my foot and there was this big shard and I kept looking at it and thinking that I just wanted everything to go away…" I really cry then. "And thinking…"

Jake leans forward and looks the least bored he's looked since I met him fifteen minutes ago. But, even with my enraptured audience and all, I can't go there. I blink ten times, shake my short hair out and look determinedly at my sweaty hands. The thought is too big, too overwhelming…

"But I didn't," I tell him. Because that's the important bit. "Even though I knew I could. And I knew I needed to get away from the glass and away from the noise and just get away until it passed. So I went up the common for a walk."

Jake digests this. He sips a glass of water. Eventually he says, "So you were up in the woods because you were trying to save your own life?"

I nodded. "Yes! But you see, I can't explain that to Mum and Dad. I say the word 'suicide' and they totally flip out and won't listen to anything else. All they hear is me saying 'I want to die'. They don't hear me when I say, 'But I tried really hard not to.'"

He looks at my test sheet again. "Your scores are quite high, Olive."

Jake taps on his computer, pulling up my records. His fingers are clumsy and slow. He double-clicks, reads, doesn't seem to mind that he's keeping me there waiting. "So, you say you've had periods of feeling very low before?"

I nod slowly. "Yes. Umm, last winter everyone got a bit worried about me. And then a year before that. But I've been feeling okay the last few months." I think… I mean,

I'm not always like *super sane*. But then, who is? But I hadn't felt the Nothing in ages. I really thought...*hoped* it had gone for good.

Jake double-clicks and brings up a box on his screen. "Ahh," he says. "And I can see here on your records that a psychiatrist assessed you last year and said—"

"STOP!" I shout out. "Stop it, I don't want to know!"

He looks up.

"I don't want to know my diagnosis," I'm practically yelling. "That should be in my notes. Don't tell me."

He is unmoved by my outburst and scrolls down. "Ahh, yes. It does say here. I apologize."

"I don't believe in labels," I tell him. Oh God, I sound like I want to be a freaking HIPSTER psycho.

"Fair enough." Jake doesn't press the point. He asks me some more basic stuff about my moods, my behaviour, my feelings, how I rate things out of ten. I can feel the adrenaline leave my body and the heaviness snuggle back in, complaining that its spot was taken on the couch. Jake starts yammering on about how it's okay to talk about how I'm feeling, and how it's IMPORTANT to let the people who care about me know what's going on. He suggests a course of antidepressants, warning me that they take a few weeks to work.

"How do you feel about medication, Olive?"

I'm so tired now I'm not sure I feel anything. "Sure. Whatever." I blink and it takes longer than a blink should. It takes a lot of effort to open my eyes back up again.

"We can see how you get on with them. Shall we bring your parents back in? Give them an update?"

"Huh? Yes, okay."

My fingers are so heavy, my wrists are so heavy, my arms are so heavy, my shoulders are sinking down, down, down into my ribcage.

Mum's at the door. Dad is world-weary and behind her. They screech their chair legs along the floor again and I close my eyes, trying to suppress what it triggers.

"Olive is aware that she gave us all a scare here," Jake tells them. "But I don't believe her to be in any danger right now."

"How can you say that?" Mum shrills. "She tried to…"

"Olive has explained what happened this evening, and I repeat, I don't believe her to be in any danger." His stern delivery temporarily shuts her up. "You can take her home now. I've prescribed some SSRIs. These are a standard antidepressant that should help with Olive's low moods. I know she's not taken medication before, but I think, considering what happened this evening, it will be beneficial for her. Here's a leaflet about them." He hands over some brightly-coloured pamphlet and Mum grabs it out of his hands. "I'll write a letter to your GP, and you can book a follow-up appointment with them to talk through her further treatment options."

Mum is not taking this well. I can feel her angry vibes, shooting off her like arrows.

"She needs a bed," Mum says. And she doesn't mean a

nice new one from Dreams. She means a bed in a psychiatric ward.

I poke my fingers into my eyes. "I don't need a bed. I just need double-glazing."

Dad tuts. "Olive, we've gone through this. You can't shut out all the noise. You've got to learn to COPE with the noise."

I roll my eyes. "Of course, I'm sorry. I forgot. Whoopsie. Silly me. I'll just start coping now. Cheers for the reminder."

He shakes his head. "I didn't mean it like that."

It's his birthday and I'm being a dick and I've not even said sorry, and I'm too tired for this. I sink into my chair. I let my muscles crumble into dust, my brain turn off, as Jake and Mum and Dad discuss me like I'm not there. And I

Just

Keep

Wishing

That it would

Please

Stop

Happening

…

But it seems like the Nothing is back again.

And I don't have the words to tell you how much I wish it wasn't.

4

We have to wait a week for a doctor's appointment because I refuse to see anyone but Dr Herret.

Mum's all outraged. Dad is all trying to calm her down.

I'm not too bothered because it won't stop raining and therefore the world shuts up.

I start swallowing the antidepressants each morning with a glass of water Mum brings me.

But mostly I just lie in my little bolthole, under my desk. And think about
What
A
Shitty
Terrible
Person
I am.

* * *

They have me on watch.

"I told you, I'm not suicidal," I mumble, turning over to put my back to them. "Ask Jake. He'll vouch for me. I just want to sleep."

But Mum still takes time off to check I'm safe. She comes into my room regularly to shove full-fat yogurt down me or anything else I can stand to eat. Dad comes back from work and sits on my bed, the bed I've not slept in for ten days. Flutters out his newspaper and reads in silence.

The

Days

Drag

Past.

They are of nothing. Nothing but guilt and numb and wondering who let the bath plug out on the universe.

I get my period.

Which allows one emotion to carve its way through my veneer of nothing.

Relief…

I'm not pregnant.

I'm not about to have Rick Macaby's baby.

I perk up enough to eat two whole yogurts and Mum cries and acts like I'm Tiny Tim who has finally learned how to walk without crutches or something.

And then at last it is the day of the doctor's appointment.

Dr Herret has been our doctor since before I can remember.

She was the doctor who jabbed needles into my toddler arms. Who doled out banana-flavoured yellow antibiotics when I got tonsillitis. The doctor who gave me the pill… before it sent me stark raving crazy and I had to come off it.

Oh, and she's been here throughout this roller coaster of mental unwellness that, apparently, isn't going to stop any time soon.

She greets me like a friend. "Hi, Olive, sit down. Sorry you had to wait so long. I'm running a bit late today."

I shuffle over and slump into the chair, and Dr Herret's eyebrows rise when she sees Mum hovering at the door. "Do you want to come in too, Mrs Newman?"

Mum pretends to think about it while I'm already moving over to make room.

"I mean, is that okay? Olive is a bit…out of it at the moment."

Dr Herret gestures to my now-vacated chair and looks unsurprised. It's actually less tiring to have Mum here, rather than explaining every last detail afterwards.

"So, what's been going on, Olive? It says in your notes you were taken to A & E?"

I nod my head slowly. "Yes, but I didn't need to go."

"Yes, she did," Mum butts in. "The police found her out in a storm, standing at the top of a cliff…"

Dr Herret raises a hand to stop her. "Mrs Newman, please. I'm asking Olive. If you're going to sit in on this, I need you to let Olive tell me herself."

Mum twists her hands in her lap and looks down.

"Now, Olive. It looks like you've been prescribed antidepressants to help you through this bad patch. How are you finding them? Any side effects at all?"

"All she does is sleep," Mum interrupts and my doctor puts her hand up to stop her again.

I shrug. "They're fine. They're not doing much."

"It can take some time for them to kick in. And the sleep thing is quite common, so don't worry too much about that." She looks down at my notes again. "So, this is the first time on medication, but it also says here in the notes from the hospital that they recommend you get some additional help?"

"A new brain would be great, thank you."

She smiles, just as Mum tuts and says, "Oh, Olive." I'm actually pretty pleased with myself for making a joke when I feel so incapable of breathing. The doctor fiddles with her ancient computer again, reading half to herself.

"You had those ten sessions of CBT last year, didn't you? Did you find those helpful?"

"Well they can't have been that helpful because here I am again." After my second batch of Nothing, I'd been considered Nothing enough to get some therapy. I missed weeks of school, including my mock exams, waiting for an appointment. They were vaguely useful I guess, though I remember thinking, at one point, it felt like bringing a knife to a gunfight. But they must've done something because I cheered up and, after my ten allocated slots, I wasn't considered ill enough to get any more help. They shoved a sticker on me, labelled me as *Treated* and that was it.

"Hmm, well, sometimes these things come in waves…"

Mum keeps putting her finger out to punctuate the air. Shutting up is killing her.

"Well I can refer you for some top-up sessions," Dr Herret says. "But I'm afraid there's a waiting list."

"Again?" Mum explodes. "There's ALWAYS a waiting list. Can't you—"

"Mrs Newman, please, I'm not finished."

Mum apologizes, but doesn't sit fully back on her chair.

"As I was saying, there's a waiting list, and I know, from the looks of things…" She stares straight at me right then and I feel all exposed. What does she mean, *looks of things*? Do I look ill? Okay, so I've not showered for a few days, shoot me. It's not like I've been out socializing. It's fine to smell in the privacy of your own home-made bunker. "…you may not be able to hold on for that long. There's one other possibility to run past you. There's a new treatment option that's being trialled, and I've been told to look out for possible candidates. I wondered if you'd be interested?"

I cross my arms. "In a guinea-pig trial? I'm not letting you electrify me."

She has the grace to smile. "It's not anything like that. It's this new state-of-the-art treatment centre. Hang on…I'll pull it up on here." She taps away and then twists her clunky computer around so we can see the screen. I see a staged photo of a group of teenagers sitting around laughing on some lawn. Underneath it says:

CAMP RESET - THE COUNTRY'S FIRST TEEN RESIDENTIAL CAMP FOR BRAIN WELLNESS.

"Camp Reset?" I ask.

"It's a new private mental health facility, just for teenagers. They're still in the piloting stage and they need volunteers so you could stay for free." She tilts her head, smiling again. "The standard of treatment looks incredible. Participants are asked to stay a month, and receive round-the-clock care."

Mum's leaning so far forward I'm surprised she doesn't fall off her chair.

"Are you sectioning me, after all? Is that what this is about?"

"Nobody's sectioning you, Olive. Your stay there is totally voluntary. You can leave at any time."

I think about it. Stare at the screen.

Dr Herret fills the silence. "I do think it's a good opportunity…the chance to get such intense treatment… for free…you do fulfil all the pilot's requirements…because you're not considered an immediate risk to yourself, the waiting list for other types of therapy is quite long I'm afraid…"

I tune her out because something new and unfamiliar has arrived in the clotted cream of my sludgy head. Something that's not lit up in me since the horrible moment the Nothing returned. Hope. Hope this could be the last time I'm like this. The thing is, it sounds good. It sounds like it could work. I mean, a month. A whole month. Of intensive treatment. I could improve. I could learn how to not feel like this again. This could be it. This could be the silver bullet. The magic pill. The miracle cure. The thing that actually does it. And just that thought – the thought this could all go away. The thought that I'd finally be able to feel normally, as opposed to EVERYTHING or NOTHING... The thought is enough to make me smile.

"Will it be noisy in the camp?" My anxiety speaks for me.

Dr Herret smiles kindly. "Are you still worrying about noise?"

I'm impressed she's remembered since last time. "I'm not worrying about it, I just can't stand it."

"Olive, one of the things they'll be able to work on at this camp is your...umm...preoccupation with noise. And your medication may help to decrease the levels of anxiety you have about it. But let's see if we can get any more information...hang on..." She taps again. "Ahh. Okay. Each patient gets their own private room with en-suite. That should help, shouldn't it?"

It depends, I think. It depends on what the neighbours are like. It depends on how thick the walls are. It depends on when the building was made and how well insulated it is. It depends how many adjoining walls I will have. It depends if it's on a main road. It depends if it's single glazed.

Mum starts asking questions about what the other patients will be like. Are they dangerous?

"No one will be dangerous, they'll just be teenagers

like Olive. And Olive isn't dangerous, is she?" Dr Herret reassures her. "Once Camp Reset's been accredited by the right bodies, it will cost several thousand pounds to attend. Olive would be lucky to go for free."

Lucky.

Ha.

I almost laugh. You are so lucky to have cancer that we caught quickly. You are so lucky that you only lost the one leg.

"Will it work?" I stutter out. "Will this place stop this happening again?"

The doctor's eyes shine with sympathy. They always want you to hope, but not too much.

"It's worth a try," she says. "You've never had intensive therapy. And you may find it's helpful to be with other similar teenagers." She looks at her notes. "It could be that this combination of medication and residential care is the ticket to get yourself feeling like you again."

I don't know who "you" is, but I like the sound of her. I guess she means the me between the mood swings. When I'm getting good marks in school, and staging elaborate photoshoots for college, and not pissing off every single person in my year group apart from Ally. When I'm steady and my brain is quieter and I go out and do normal things like shop and chill at Ally's, painting our nails. She's quite nice, that Olive. I guess she is me... But if that's the case, I don't know where the other me's fit in. The ones who kick in the windows of greenhouses. Who ruin birthday parties, who have unprotected sex with Rick Macaby, who have no friends left apart from one.

I suddenly just want to go to sleep. Right there. On the hard chair. I answered some questions. I got out of my bunker. I got in the car. I sat here on this chair. That's more than enough for one day. I feel my head hang with the weight of itself.

"So, Olive, what are you thinking?"

A month. Could a month of this camp ensure this doesn't happen ever again? A month is nothing. It's a blink in time. Could this feeling be gone with a blink? I don't want to hope. I can't afford to hope and it not…

But what can I lose?

"When does this camp thing start?" I ask.

Dr Herret smiles. "In just over a week."

5

It's the first day of Camp Reset and I'm finally levelling out.

I can *feel* it as I wake up. My eyes actually want to open. My limbs actually want to stretch. My body is not utterly horrified at the thought of leaving bed. Which is just as well as I'm about to be driven miles away to bunk up with fellow mad people for a month.

I wake before my alarm and just lie here, trying to catch up on what I've missed.

What the hell happened?

I remember the euphoria over the end of exams, and Rick's hands on my body. But then the heatwave hit and everyone was outside all the time and I got heavy...

I lurch up in my weird cubbyhole under the desk and bang my head. "Oww," I say aloud. I stretch out my bare foot from under the sheet. A thin, red, angry cut is scribbled across my skin from the broken glass.

This can't happen again.

I roll out from under the desk, pull back the curtains and open the windows. The early morning air is fresh and sodden with dew. It blasts through my window, making my body erupt into goosebumps, waking it up. It's the first time in weeks I've welcomed the world. The antidepressants must've finally kicked in. They said they would. I stare out at the sun shining down on our little street and marvel at how a little pill can bring me back to me. Why did I refuse to take them last time? I think it was Mum who put me off. She'd read some horror story about them on the internet.

I pad to the shower for the first time in ages. I shampoo my hair twice. My leg and armpit hair clogs my razor as I shave. When I'm out and dried, I scrub a hole in the steam of the bathroom mirror.

Wowsers trousers.

I am thin. How have I lost so much weight so quickly? No wonder Mum was freaking. My already-angular face looks like it's been vacuum-packed – I could probably slice a cucumber with my chin. My bobbed hair lands just at my shoulder blades, which look like they're trying to break free from my body. And my eyes are just…missing something.

I go back to my room wrapped in a towel and look around at the state of it. There's a bundle of stinking sheets and pillows muddled under the desk where I've been sleeping. The giant photomontage I had on my walls lies ripped and littered across the carpet. I blink and get a flash of a moment of me tearing the whole thing down while crying and screaming. My walls are so naked, how did I not notice this before? I'm so used to them being covered in my photos and it really jars – a bit like seeing a glasses-wearer's face when they take their glasses off. My parents clearly tried their best to tidy as much as they could around me. The clothes I'd strewn all over the floor are all washed and packed in a suitcase for camp at the end of my bed, my running trainers on the top. I reach out and stroke my shoes, and then touch my heart, trying to push the guilt back in.

I need to apologize to Mum and Dad.

I shove on denim shorts and a floaty yellow top that brings out the natural tan in my skin and go downstairs to try and make it better again.

Dad's reading the news on his tablet and Mum is waiting for her toast to pop. I pause at the door and then decide to tap-dance in across the lino. They look up and I do a little handclap and a jazz-hands finish.

"Ta-da!" I say. "Guess who's back?"

The smile reaches Dad's eyes. Mum looks like she's about to cry. I drop my arms sheepishly. "So, yeah, sorry about scaring the hell out of you again and ruining your birthday," I say. "By the way, I'm feeling better now."

Then Mum is hugging me, so hard. And Dad is scraping his chair back and joining in.

"Oh, Olive, you don't need to apologize," he says.

"Yes I do."

I can hardly breathe they're hugging me so tight. And I hate myself for a moment. I hate myself for making them worry so much. For having to put up with me. Their one child and I'm a failure. For not being stronger. For not spotting the warning signs. For tumbling back down into the abyss. I can't do this to them again. I have to get mended. I have to get fixed.

Eventually they let go. Mum offers me toast and I realize I'm starving. I eat six slices piled high with freshly mashed avocado and savour every bite. We all sit around the table like normal, sipping coffee and behaving like I imagine a regular family does.

"Aren't you going to be late for work?" I ask Dad between mouthfuls. He owns this little law firm in town and is always stressed about bringing in new clients.

"I wanted to see you off so I cleared my morning." He smiles again in relief at the restored state of me. "How are you feeling about camp today?"

I swallow my mouthful of toast. "Good. I'm looking forward to getting better."

They share a look over the table that they don't think I notice.

"Well, let's just see how it goes." Mum sips from her thin china geese cup. She's always been obsessed with geese for some reason. "You can call us and come home whenever you want."

Dad gets out the road map and he and Mum argue about why he still doesn't trust the satnav. I wash up my plate.

Enjoying the sun streaming in the window, how it feels warm on my face. The children next door are out in the street already, circling our cul-de-sac on their bikes, singing pop songs and enjoying the school holidays. The noise scrapes my insides but it doesn't make me want to shoot them. A definite improvement. I head upstairs to see what Mum's packed for me. I add a few more tops and a strappy summer dress, and take out an embarrassing pair of knickers. I know I get a private room, but I don't want to risk the other patients seeing my novelty, period-stained Winnie-the-Pooh pair. I even dab on some make-up.

I'm delaying something.

Something I've been delaying since I woke up…

The fallout.

So, I snuggle under the duvet, take two calming breaths and turn on my phone.

Eight trillion messages and missed calls.

Loads are from Ally. Long-suffering Ally.

Where are you? We were supposed to meet at twelve.

You better not have stood me up, bitch.

Okay, so you're not picking up your phone. I'm worried.

They descend into:

So, I came round but your mum said things are bad.
I love you. Let me know you're okay.

I miss you. Sending hugs.

Oh, Olive. I called around and your mum told me about
the hospital. I know you like to be left alone when
you're like this but I LOVE YOU. You'll pull through.

I wipe my nose on the cover as I tap out my reply. I
wonder every day what I've done to deserve Ally. She's
practically my only friend – the one person who stood by
me after that ridiculous drama with Bella last year. But you
don't need more than one friend when you've got someone
as brilliant as Ally. She handles my crazy perfectly, and I
handle hers.

I punch out a reply:

ALLY, YOU ARE SO WONDERFUL. I AM BACK.
I don't know what happened there. But it's over and
I'm through it, and I'm about to go off to some weird
camp that mends crazy people so I PROMISE I won't
do this to you again. We're leaving at ten. So, if you're
up in time, come round. I owe you ALL the hugs xxx

My phone goes almost immediately.

YOU'RE BACCCCCK! I'm literally just round the

corner, walking Heather. I'M ON MY WAY. Don't go
to the loony bin without saying goodbye.

A smile tickles the side of my mouth. I send loads of
kisses back. But the smile soon vanishes when I see I have
some less-nice messages. Mostly all from Rick.

Hey. Howz it going? X

U playin hard to get or what?

Finally...

Slut.

My hands shake as I read that last one. I worry that
I'm a slut for five whole minutes and then find myself
smiling and thinking, *And thank God I'm not pregnant with
your child.*

I should really take an STI test though. I wonder if you
can get them at camp?

I go through the rest of my phone – checking tagged
pictures, trying to remember what happened before I
disintegrated. I feel like I've got away with it to some degree.
No one's sending me any abuse this time (apart from Rick);
I can't have done anything that bad. Apart from...

The doorbell goes and I hear Mum answer it.

"Olive?" she calls up the stairs. "Ally's here."

I shove my running trainers further into my suitcase to make room for more stuff, and then jog down the stairs to meet her. Heather is equally excited to see me, pulling at her collar when I arrive in the entrance hall.

"Olivio! You're alive!" Ally says, bending to try and calm her terrier down, but I just envelop her in a hug. She squeezes me back and I see Mum watching, leaning against the wall with her arms crossed, smiling.

"Thanks for coming over." I crouch to give Heather a rub behind the ears which makes her ten gazillion times more excitable. "Come on up."

"We're leaving in an hour," Mum reminds me.

"I know, I know."

When we get into my room, Ally stops in the doorway and lets out a whistle. "Woah, Olivio, shit got dark." She perches on the edge of my bed and takes in my walls.

I shrug, feeling slightly embarrassed. "I know. I'm not sure what happened."

"Let's put your photos back up. This is freaking me out."

Heather is happy enough, sniffing all the things there are to sniff, as Ally and I remake my giant montage on the wall. We don't talk at first. I think she can feel me building up to it and knows I need time. So we just show each other photos before re-Blu-Tacking them to where they once were.

"I still can't believe you convinced me to pose as a Victorian mental health patient." Ally holds up the picture I have of her in a makeshift straightjacket.

"I got top marks for that!" I say, plucking the picture out of her hands and sticking it next to a group shot I took of everyone last summer.

Ally twists to look at its new spot on the wall.

"People have been asking after you," she says quietly. "I didn't know what to tell them."

I sigh and sink back onto my bed. "Just tell them what they want to hear – that I'm an attention-seeking mental."

Ally sits down with me, both of us with our backs against the wall. She calls Heather up, who jumps into my arms and settles into a belly rub, her tongue flopping out of her mouth.

"People don't think that."

"They do."

"Well, not everyone…" She pushes her dyed black hair out of her face and crosses her eyes. "Maybe Bella and her merry band of bitches."

"What a surprise."

"Most people just found you good fun. The Freedom party was INTENSE. Dare I ask what happened with you and Rick?"

I shake my head.

"He's an idiot anyway. I tried talking you out of it." She sees my mouth fall open in surprise. "Don't worry. I knew you were too wasted to remember."

"Sorry," I say. It's what I always end up having to say. But Ally never needs an apology.

She sticks her tongue out, demonstrating just that.

"Don't worry about it. Makes us equals for that night I went off with Pete and left you without any money for a cab home."

I smile and hold out my pinkie. "Shit friends for ever?"

She laughs and we pinkie shake on it. "Shit friends for ever."

I rub Heather's belly and fill Ally in on the greenhouse and the ambulance and Jake and the antidepressants and my upcoming stint at camp. I get a bit weepy and she pulls me in for a hug. And, Heather, sensing my upset, rolls over and pushes her wet nose into my face, making us both laugh.

"Oh, hon," she says. "Heather, down…down now! Olive doesn't want your lick in her face. Good girl. Aww, hon," she continues. "I promise you, that all sounds pretty drama, but from the outside, I don't think anyone noticed too much so don't worry about that. Just worry about getting better. You didn't do anything undoable."

I sniff. "That's the thing though…I think I did."

She leaves me a silence, pushing her hair off her face again.

"My English exam." This is the first time I've allowed myself to think about it. "It was my last one and well…"

At the time, I remember thinking it had gone *brilliantly*. In fact, I think I told a lot of people afterwards that I may, actually, be a genius. But now I'm remembering what I wrote. I think I may've gone off-piste… The question was about the character of Dill in *To Kill A Mockingbird*…I remember that much. But I also remember writing over ten pages in the two hours. And that a lot of it wasn't about Dill. It was a full-on rant about the problematic representation of people of colour in the book, and how bad it is that white people always have to solve racism, and that Atticus is overrated. And I remember, at the time, thinking this was the most incredible insight the world has ever KNOWN, and the examiners will be BLOWN AWAY by my analysis.

I don't remember talking about Dill that much.

Ally pats my knee. "You did tell me afterwards that you thought you'd aced it. But, not in a normal way." She paused. "You had a LOT to say about Atticus, which would've been great, except our question wasn't about him."

I feel the tears re-emerging. "Shit! I knew it. I need to pass to do it for A level…" My stomach clenches and Ally pulls me in for another hug.

"There's always retakes, Olivio," she says. "And you still maybe passed. Knowing you, you've probably still got top marks even with answering the wrong question."

We just hold each other while I feel self-hatred and anxiety bubble up inside of me.

"I can't be like this any more," I whisper into her shoulder. "I don't want to be this person any more."

"You're awesome, Olive," she says back into my shoulder, before pulling away and holding me out at arm's length. "But if you're not happy, then this camp place sounds pretty cool. Hell, maybe I need to go too? Smuggle me in?"

And she gets up and starts climbing into my suitcase

while I laugh at her sheer bendability. I feel momentarily happier but now Mum is calling up the stairs, saying the car is packed and Ally has to go. We hug goodbye and I promise to email. And Dad packs my suitcase into the car and hugs me too and says that he's proud of me and he'll miss me but I can call any time. As he hugs me too tight, all I can think is, *It doesn't matter what happened. Because it won't happen again. You are going to this camp and you are going to FIX THIS. You are going to knock this on the head. This is your chance. You are not going to be this person any more.*

I don't know what's wrong with me but I know I'm not right, and I know this time was the closest call I've had. I hug Dad back, feeling so guilty, and I whisper promises to myself that, no matter how hard it is at this camp, I will not let myself be this person ever again.

6

Okay, so the gates of this camp are mighty gatey considering the whole *you-can-leave-whenever-you-want* thing. Mum has to pull to a stop outside this giant entrance and fuss about with an intercom until the metal bars swing slowly open.

The driveway up to the big house must be at least half a mile long, and I stare out the window feeling sick with nerves. The lawns are mown into lines that stretch out into the blue sky. I squint as I look into the distance. "Is that a... farm?" I ask, catching a glimpse of some stables and tall, white weird fluffy animals grazing next to them.

"It did say there was a farm attached. With alpacas!"

I slump back in my car seat. "Pray tell, Freud. Exactly when was it that you discovered the cure to mental illness was alpacas?" I murmur.

Mum laughs. "Olive, I don't think they're treatment. I think they're just here for the ambience."

I'd forgotten this was going to become a private clinic

until I see how good the house is. Like a huge stately home. Soon only the rich messed-up teenagers will be allowed here, as opposed to us regular messed-up teenagers – sitting on waiting lists, hoping we still have marbles left to find by the time we're offered any treatment.

I remember what Dr Herret said. *"You're very lucky."* I have enough emotions now to roll this over more in my brain. Trying to figure out if I should be pissed off or not. But then we draw up outside this huuuuuuuuge house with its giant marble pillars and marble stairs leading up to the front door.

"Wow, it doesn't look too bad actually," I say to Mum.

Then we see and hear the girl on the steps.

Screaming at the top of her lungs…

The girl's still screaming as we turn the car engine off. Mum and I look at each other, totally panicked.

They said this place wasn't for certifiables…

Do we need to help? Why is she screaming? Oh God, oh God…

The girl makes direct eye-contact with me. She stops screaming and starts to cackle with laughter.

"Ha!" she shouts, pointing at me. "Got you. I TOTALLY got you."

It takes a second or two to realize she's joking. My heart is still going berserk.

The girl jumps down off the step and rushes over to say

This book is due for return on or before the last date shown below.

hello. "Did I terrify you? Isn't it funny? I've been doing it to EVERYONE."

I shake her hand and it's warm and slick with sweat. I want to rub my hand on my shorts but I don't want her to see me do it.

I don't even understand what UNIVERSE this girl lives in if she thinks that's funny.

"I'm Gabriella." She rolls her Rs and looks very impressed with herself for doing so. She's tall and big in a way that you notice, draped in baggy clothes with long sleeves.

"I'm Olive." I can't bring myself to laugh. My heart still hasn't recovered. She doesn't seem to notice.

"Here, I'll show you where to go."

She pushes through the grand doors of the giant house. Mum and I give each other a look, and for a moment I know we're thinking the same thing.

Don't make friends with this one, Olive.

The coolness of the house collides with the warm sun still on my skin. I cross my arms and stare upwards as I follow Gabriella through a long hallway. It's a converted stately home – one where every single atom of unmodernity has been stripped out. It smells of fresh white paint and orchids adorn every black, lacquered surface. The ceilings stretch up to reveal modern chandeliers made of black glass, all weird angles. Gabriella leads us towards a tall desk where a preened lady in a black kimono uniform clacks the keys of her sleek computer.

"Grace, GRACE!" Gabriella yells. "Guess what? I scared

another one. I TOTALLY got her." She pushes me towards the desk and I look back at Mum, who just shrugs helplessly. "You lost your NUT, didn't you, Olive?"

"H-h-hi," I say to the lady who must be Grace. "I'm Olive."

"Olive Newman! Welcome to Camp Reset." Grace's face breaks into an earnest smile. She hasn't even had to look at the screen to know my full name. "I'm Grace. I'm the care manager, which basically means I'm here to help you with whatever you need. I hope Gabriella didn't scare you too much." She turns to her and says, through a very gritted smile, "Gabriella? I thought we decided to stop that joke?"

"It's funny! Wasn't it funny, Olive?"

Oh God, I hope not everyone here is like her.

"Umm. Yeah, I guess," I say.

She erupts into a triumphant smile. "SEE! Anyway, I'm going to go wait for more people."

She saunters back towards the entrance, leaving me staring at Mum, Mum staring at me. I don't care how many orchids there are here, I did NOT find that funny.

"Sorry about Gabriella." Grace reads my mind and smiles apologetically. "I've told her to stop."

"But she's not stopping."

"I'll send someone out. Oh dear, it's a shame when you have to discipline clients on their first day."

The word *client* confuses me until I realize she's referring to Gabriella. We've morphed from "patients" to "clients" with some supercalifragilistic of black orchids and designer chandeliers.

"She really did scare us," Mum says, always wanting to get a word in. "I hardly think it's appropriate... I mean... Olive's been worried enough about coming here and that didn't help..."

"Mum!"

"Well, she's bound to be scared, isn't she?"

Grace nods solemnly. "Of course, of course. I can only apologize. Hang on..." She picks up a sleek phone, presses a button, waits a second and then says down the line, "There's a client at the entrance who's causing a bit of a to-do. Do you mind sending someone? Yes. Yes... That's the one... Thank you very much." She puts the phone down and beams back at us. "All sorted! Now, Olive. Let's get you settled in. Your room's all ready. Welcome!"

Then there's a rather awkward moment where Grace calls over some security men, and they search me and my suitcase. "I'm sorry, but it's policy." They take my bag off to one side and give it a huge going-over, even checking I've not hidden razor blades in the lining or whatever. While they do that, I have to sign lots of paperwork, which I read and reread a trillion times to make sure I'm not signing over my freedom.

"It's just your acknowledgement that you're aware this is a clinical trial," Grace explains. "But don't worry. This is just the final stage of the pilot. You're hardly a guinea pig."

Mum has to sign a load of stuff too. She fires off a trillion questions about the food, the safety, the timetable, the quality of the room.

"We asked for a quiet room. Has that request gone through?" I ask.

"All the rooms are quiet here," Grace replies.

My heart goes haywire – with fear and annoyance. Because that is not the point. And other people's idea of quiet is not the same as my idea of quiet. Grace must see the freak-out on my face because she stumbles on. "Don't worry though, we noted your request. Your room is at the end of the corridor, towards the back of the building. So there won't be too much foot traffic."

The iron grip on my intestines lessens slightly, though it won't go until I've seen my room and know for sure. I mean, I may still be over the kitchen. Or I may be near an air-conditioning unit. And you only have to have one noisy dickhead through an adjoining wall to ruin your life to the point you don't even want your life any more.

Mum squeezes my hand. "See, Olive? Nothing to worry about."

"All done!" the guard says, wheeling my suitcase back towards me.

Grace hands over my key card with a stack of glossy welcome documents – all with photos of perfect-looking teenagers on the lawn.

"Clients are arriving from all over today, so you can just relax until the introductory meeting later at four. Then there's dinner and welcome games. Treatment doesn't start until tomorrow, but your schedule is here." She points to a piece of paper full of posh font. It's laid out like a spa holiday, but the words don't say things like *massage* and *manicure*, more *group therapy* and *CBT*. Grace's face is suddenly very stern. "Now, there are both boys *and* girls staying at Camp Reset and we have very strict rules. Each gender has their own floor and we discourage romantic relationships."

I raise both eyebrows. "Won't stop us lesbians then, will you?"

"Olive!" Mum says, as I burst out laughing at my own joke. "She's not a lesbian," she explains to an unimpressed Grace.

"How do you know? I might be!"

Grace coughs and changes the subject. "Anyway, you can ask all your questions at the orientation meeting later. One final thing, then I can show you your room. You need this…" She hands out a small sleek bracelet. "Don't worry, it's not been turned on yet. All will be explained later."

I hold up the bracelet with one finger.

"You're giving me jewellery?"

"Everything will be explained at the introduction meeting. Now, that's you all checked in. Do you want me to show you to your room? Or are you okay getting there on your—"

We're interrupted by Gabriella yelling, "GET OFF ME, GET OFF ME!" echoing down the corridor.

Grace scuttles off to help, and Mum and I stare at one another again. I feel very much like gulping.

"You don't have to stay," Mum says. "I can drive us right home, right now."

I hear a further kerfuffle and contemplate the offer. A month suddenly seems like a really long time, and home suddenly seems like really far away. And yet a life where I'm constantly worried that I'm going to mentally disintegrate again seems like a really, really bad life.

I actually do gulp as I make the decision. "It's okay," I say. "I want to stay."

7

My room is up a giant staircase where I imagine women used to stand at the top in Victorian clothes and prepare to make dramatic entrances to balls.

Mum and I huff over to it, lugging my stuff behind us.

Gabriella is walked past us, scowling, by two men wearing silk shirts and trousers as uniform. She's tailed by a tall scrawny wisp of a boy who has no colour left in his face. She must've scared him before the men turned up.

"Umm, where do I go?" he asks us.

Mum points him towards Grace's reception desk. We hear Gabriella yell, "For God's sake, it was funny! Fun. EE!"

My whole body vibrates on nervous alert as we go up the stairs, then steer down narrow hallways, looking for my room number. Even with my medication, my anxiety about the noise is kicking in. I hear music echo tinnily under one door and almost vomit when I think I may be their neighbour. But the hallway goes on and on and gets

narrower, almost like an optical illusion, until, right at the
end, around a corner, we see my number. Room 101.

"I don't know if that's a good omen or a bad one," Mum
jokes, pointing at the number.

"Maybe it's a good sign? I'll condemn my madness to
Room 101 for ever."

Mum looks sad for a moment. "Oh, Olive, you're not
mad. You're just…"

"Happiness challenged?"

"No…"

"Coming down with a touch of insanity?"

"No…"

"Mentally high-maintenance?"

She laughs at that one. "Just open the door already."

I was delaying opening the door, too scared about what
I'd find inside. But I sigh and swipe my card. The door clicks
open and in I go.

It's like a very posh hotel room. There's a giant double
bed, a desk, a chair, a small sofa, and a built-in cupboard. All
the furniture is black and shiny, contrasting with the silky
white wallpaper.

"Looks nice, Olive." Mum sets my bags down. "Very nice."

But I'm already pacing around it. Opening the window,
leaning out. Freaking out.

I'm looking for noise.

"Ooo, the shower looks lovely," Mum says but I shush her
as I can't listen for noise when she's talking. We stay quiet
and my ears are practically up on stalks, trying to work out

if I can hear music, or voices, or anything really. Luckily there's carpet. That's an insulator.

"Olive? Seriously, what are you doing now?"

I'm getting down onto my stomach and putting my ear to the ground, that's what I'm doing. All I hear is silence. Wonderful, hopeful, peaceful silence. I scramble up and lean out the window. Later on I may take in how stunning the view is, but, for now, I'm just scanning it for traces of noise. I listen out for distant road noise. Then I hang totally over the sill, Mum squawking behind me, and try and see what's above and below me. There doesn't seem to be any extractor fans, or kitchens, or air vents and my stomach relaxes just a little. I'm smiling as I turn back to Mum.

"It's an okay room, isn't it?"

She's watching me closely, sadly. I don't care though. Not now the room has passed the initial test. I mean, later, at night-time, that will be the real test. I won't fully relax until I've had at least three nights here without hearing ANYTHING – only then will it pass as safe. But I feel vaguely optimistic. Though, as Mum starts unpacking for me, I realize that she'll be leaving soon. She senses my panic and moves over to hug me. "There there," she says, before I've even freaked out.

"Oh God, Mum, what am I doing?"

She pats my hair. "Something that you can walk away from whenever you want."

"That girl downstairs. She was crazy! Am I crazy? Am I like that?"

She laughs into my hair. "No. I promise you."

"But you wouldn't tell me if you thought I was proper crazy, would you?"

Mum releases the hug and stares straight into my eyes. There's the murmur of tears in them. "Olive, you're not crazy. You just need to work through some stuff, that's all. And we love you. Whatever happens, we love you."

I snatch her back into a tighter hug, feeling all sorts of things.

"I'm going to get better here," I tell her. "I'm going to try SO HARD and I'm going to come back totally better."

"Don't put pressure on yourself."

But it's too late. The pressure is there. I have to do this. I have to make this work. I have to put my brain back together again. I came too close; it was too scary. And then she's hugging me goodbye and I'm too weirded out to cry. When she closes the door behind her, it's almost too quiet.

8

I pace my room. Walk, turn, walk back, turn back. Everything is new. The sheets, the curtains, the carpet, the lamps. It's the perfect place to begin this change. This shedding of my madness. It is the definition of a fresh start. I feel anxiety start to curl up in my intestines like a snake. A cobra on the verge of striking. I need to get out of this room.

If I stay, the bad will come. The snake will pounce. Just me and my thoughts is never a good idea. I check the clock on the side of the plush bed. It's only two, and the induction meeting isn't until four.

I meet no one as I walk back along the corridor. I hear TVs echo under doorways – other people like me are here. But they're not out and about. I avoid reception, not wanting to encounter Gabriella again just yet. But the place is massive and there's loads to check out. I find a fully-equipped gym with a gorgeous spa on the ground floor. Everything is black and tiled and shiny and made to look all Roman-like.

The dark tranquillity feels wrong when I know it's so sunny outside. I navigate my way back through the maze of hallways and eventually find a door leading out.

It's that perfect mix of heady sunshine and refreshing breeze that lifts my hair up around my face. The grounds are huge and sprawling, with manicured trees and manicured lawns and little pebbly paths where not one pebble has been kicked up yet. There's a wood on the edge of the lawn. I spot the farm and flip-flop over. The sun heats my face and I can just *feel* my freckles coming out, one by one, like the stars do at night. There are a few stables and I poke my head into them and find some horses utterly unbothered by my presence and there's a coop full of chickens – clucking softly and pecking the ground for things I can't see. I get a sudden urge to pick one up. I imagine how soft it will be. But then I hear the neigh of an alpaca and I'm off skipping over the lawn.

I mean, they do neigh, don't they?

God, I love alpacas. They're so WEIRD. I climb up and perch on the fence surrounding them and watch them grazing and being just generally oddball and awesome. The white one comes a bit too close and I almost fall backwards off the fence. I feel a smile break out across my face. My muscles aren't sure what's happening, but I coax them onwards. Urging my cheeks to lift, the corners of my mouth to twitch, my teeth to come out and see the alpacas. I feel a moment coming on. I feel contentment settling in. If only a snatch of it. The alpaca stares at me and I stare at the alpaca.

Me and the alpaca are having A Moment. The universe is telling me that sometimes things are okay. Sometimes you can have a quiet mind and the sun on your face and the breeze in your hair and an affinity with the natural world and...

...and then the alpaca ruins it by squatting and peeing.

The pee takes a really long time. I'm not sure what to do because I'm trying to have a MOMENT here. I wait for it to stop peeing, but it won't and I swear now the alpaca is making direct eye-contact with me. This is too weird. Do I look away? Will that put off the alpaca? WHY IS IT LOOKING AT ME LIKE THAT?

Suddenly a voice behind me says:

"Why are you watching that alpaca take a piss?"

The shock jolts me off balance. I throw my arms out but it's too late. I wobble and fall backwards with an "Oomph", winding myself quite badly, and the voice says, "Whoops, sorry." I turn onto my front, coughing. I look up to see who startled me but the sun is right in my eyes. They reach down, stretching their hand out to help me up. I take it gratefully, still coughing.

"Where the hell did you come from?" I stand and dust the dirt off my butt before looking up to see who was responsible. A guy stands sheepishly, a hand running through his longish rock-star hair.

"I was not expecting you to fall off the fence," he explains. His voice is thick and gravelly.

"You can't just sneak up on people on their first day in

a mental institution," I say. "People are likely to be a tad jumpy."

He smiles and he looks like a proud lion. His incisor teeth are too long and pointy. "Yes, well, if you want to make a good first impression, you should probably not stare intensely at pissing alpacas," he counters.

I look back over my shoulder at the offending mammal. It's finally finished and ambles off in search of more grass. "We were having a moment," I explain. "Well, I thought we were having a moment but then he pissed all over it... literally."

The boy laughs easily. "Fair enough. I withhold judgement on your sanity. At least until after we've had a group therapy session or two." He holds out his hand. "I'm Jamie, by the way."

I take it. The skin is rough and hardened in a way that I can instantly tell he's a guitar player. The plectrum necklace is another dead giveaway. "Olive."

"So, when did you arrive?"

I pull myself back onto the fence and try to ignore how good-looking this boy is. "Only, like, an hour ago. You?"

He climbs up and sits next to me, sitting so close it must be on purpose. "This morning. Did you get the screaming girl?"

I smile grimly. "Indeed I did."

"Not funny."

"Totally not funny."

We're smiling at each other and swinging our legs,

watching the alpacas. I feel a sense of unrealness, like this whole day so far is a dream. "So," I say to fill the gap that's making me nervous. "This is weird."

"Your first time in a residential unit?"

I nod. "Yes. How about you?"

He shakes his head, sending hair flopping around his face. "Nope, it's my third. This one is much plusher than the others though."

Immediately I want to know what happened to him, how mad he is and what type of madness. I mean, he looks totally normal. Not that that means anything of course, but still.

As if he's a mind-reader he says: "So, as an old-timer, my advice is that day one is *all* about making awkward conversation about why you're all here."

I raise my eyebrows, pretending I'm surprised.

"It's true," he continues. "It's like speed dating. But, instead of thinking *Can I date this new person I've met?* you're thinking *Are they going to come after me with an axe?*"

"Security made me get rid of my axe when they checked my bag," I say.

We both laugh and then we're having a moment. Just like the moment I had with the alpaca. Right away. Right then. Though this one is much more sexually charged than the one I had with the alpaca. Mainly as Jamie is not peeing. I take in his carved cheekbones, his lean frame, his black band T-shirt paired with an open waistcoat and ripped jeans. This guy is trouble. That much is obvious. I'm very experienced in having moments very quickly with boys exactly like Jamie. I am *good* at having moments with boys. I'm not good at trying to stay alive, or looking at a glass of water and saying "half full" or sometimes even getting out of bed in the morning. But boys like me and I like them. Something that makes most girls hate me, apart from Ally.

I turn away and deliberately end the moment. "I'm still not sure why there's a farm," I say, letting the tension fizzle down. It's day one, and I'm here to heal, not pull. I may even make friends – with girls – if I can tone down all my apparently-offensive-to-everyone-at-school flirting. "If it's supposed to help, it's financially hard to replicate when we get home."

Jamie grins. "This place is supposed to cost a fortune though, isn't it? If they find out that alpacas *are*, in fact, the secret to eternal wellbeing then everyone can just go out and buy their own set of alpacas."

"What's the collective noun for alpacas, do you reckon?" I ask him.

"There isn't one."

"Bloody hell, I wasn't expecting you to actually know."

He shrugs. "You can use 'herd' I guess. But there's not, like, a special collective noun just for alpacas."

I shake my head, smiling. "Are you here because you have a mental health condition that makes you obsessed with alpacas?"

"Wrong. I've got one where I'm obsessed with collective nouns."

I'm about to laugh then I second-guess it. I mean, that

might *actually* be his thing. He sees me waver and bursts into a raspy laugh. "Relax! That's not why I'm here."

"Oh."

Then WHY are you here? I think. Without wanting to tell him my own reason.

"I bet you, tomorrow in group, someone does actually say they're obsessed with collective nouns now," he says. "We'll both start laughing and everyone will hate us."

He's used the word "us" already and it makes me want to leave right away so I jump down off the fence.

"Hey, where you going?"

"I'm all alpacaed out." I try to smile. "I'm going to go unpack. I'm a hundred per cent certain I'll see you around though."

Jamie nods. "Cool. It was nice meeting you, Olive. I look forward to hearing all your life's traumas over the next month."

I feel his stare as I turn and flip-flop away.

9

I'm not ashamed to admit I'm nervous as I make my way to the induction meeting. I've never been new anywhere. I grew up in a small town. I had people saying, "Oh, that's so like you, Olive," before I could even talk. "Oh, that's so like you, Olive," when I ruined the leavers' play in Year Six. "Oh, that's so like you, Olive," when I got another after-school detention because the Nothing came and it didn't leave me any room to do my coursework. Even though there've been months and even years between my bad patches, when I've got good grades and remembered how to interact with humans normally and even held down that paper round for six months, they seem to think I'm only being "like me" when I'm being a twat.

Probably because I'm a massive twat...

I loiter at the door. There's about twenty people my age, sitting on red velvet chairs and avoiding eye-contact with each other. A man and a woman, both wearing smart suits, stand at the front. They look up, notice me standing there. "Hi, do come on in."

"Sorry I'm late. I got a bit lost."

The man smiles. He's wearing black-framed glasses and can't be older than forty. "That's okay. We'll give everyone a proper tour once this is over. Grab a seat." He has a strong American accent. I slump down into the last available chair. Gabriella waves excitedly and Jamie nods in acknowledgment. I nod back.

"Right, you're all here so I guess we can begin," the lady says, who's also American. "Welcome, all of you, to Camp Reset." She pauses for dramatic effect. She's very pretty, with red lipstick and her hair scraped into a topknot. "I'm Dr Jones and this is Dr Rossen." The man waves and smiles. "We're both clinical psychologists and helped pioneer this very exciting project. We've worked at a similar camp in America, as you can probably tell by our accents. We'll get to know you well over this next month and cannot wait to see the progress you make."

Dr Rossen steps forward to take over. "I'm sure you've all seen your schedules. If you have any questions or worries AT ALL, do tell someone. If a therapy session makes you uncomfortable, if you think you're on the verge of a mental health crisis, or even if you're just plain hungry, let someone know. You've all met Grace, right? She's on hand to help you with anything you need. The reception desk is manned twenty-four hours. Now…" The huge TV screen behind him flickers to life. "I hate to be the bogeyman here, but we're going to start with some simple ground rules. Boundaries are hugely important and we really need you to respect and adhere to these."

I raise my eyebrows. Rules. Of course there were going to be rules.

Dr Rossen points to the screen. "Rule one: nothing is compulsory." He breaks into a smile. "We know people with anxiety issues struggle with feeling pressured so we want you to know that everything is optional. If you don't feel comfortable, you don't have to do it. Obviously we hope you'll *want* to challenge your fears here, but there's no pressure to—"

Jamie raises his hand, interrupting him.

"Umm, yes?" Dr Rossen says.

"So, your first rule is we don't have to follow the rules?" Jamie asks.

"Well, not exactly."

"But if everything is optional, surely following the rules is optional too?"

I roll my eyes, along with maybe half the room.

Dr Jones's smile has thinned. "Very clever, well done."

Jamie leans back in his chair and puts his hands behind his head.

"Anyway," Dr Rossen coughs and pushes his glasses up his nose. "Rule Two." The slide changes. "This is about the devices you were given. Hands up if you've put them on already."

Everyone's hands go up, their wrists glinting as the sunlight streams through the window.

"Good, now, in the interests of full disclosure, we want to tell you how and why the bracelets are used. As you know, this is a low-security camp and we put a lot of trust in you here. None of you are considered a risk to yourselves or others – which is a strict entry requirement. You have a lot more freedom than at other facilities, and we have a lot of trust in you to behave appropriately. You're allowed to wander the grounds as you wish, but you do need to give us prior warning if you want to leave the vicinity. You will also need to be searched again if you do leave the premises before coming back in. With all this in mind, these devices measure your sleep patterns and heart rate, among other things, and we do ask that you wear them. We also ask you to fill out an electronic diary each day – letting us know your moods, feelings, any triggers you've had…"

I wrinkle my nose. That seems like a *lot* of sharing of a lot of personal things.

"All of this information will be strictly confidential of course. We are not going to share it with anyone outside of camp."

My hand is up before I even know it's up.

"Yes?"

"What do you need to know all of this for?" I ask.

The doctors share a look before they answer and I blush as the room's eyes land on me.

Dr Jones wipes away a hair that's sprung free from her bun. "We feed all the data into our computers that feed them into an algorithm we've made," she says simply.

"What algorithm?" I don't want them to think I'm disruptive but all of this feels very suss. My nose is yet to unwrinkle.

"It's just a computer program we've had made that can detect if a client is a risk to themselves. It sends us an alert if someone needs an intervention. Now…" She claps her hands to signal we're moving on and launches into the next rule about bedtime hours and then one about being quiet at night. And, even though she's just announced my DREAM RULE, I can't concentrate because I'm reeling. WHAT ALGORITHM? What's going on? How can there be an algorithm that measures probabilities of suicide? I mean, that's what she was getting at, right? *A risk to themselves.* That means suicide, surely? I don't understand why no one else in the room seems bothered by this. Apart from that pale guy I saw earlier, who's listening intently, everyone else is just fiddling with their hands on their laps. But I can't concentrate for the rest of the speech.

I don't even understand what's going on when everyone scrapes their chairs around and turns to each other. This happens sometimes. Blips in time where I seem to disappear. To get so lost in myself that it's like I've been put on standby and I miss everything until someone re-presses my power button. A girl to my right turns to me, smiling shyly, and I smile back.

Thankfully Dr Rossen claps and recaps the task.

"So, guys, I know you're probably feeling a bit shy but let's break this ice! Chat to someone next to you, and ask them for three interesting facts about themselves. Then you can introduce them and their facts to the group afterwards."

Ergh.

My partner to break the ice with is more ghost than girl. Her skin is so pale she's practically translucent, her hair is mousy and hangs across her face. Even her eyes are watery with pale eyelashes you can't see. You could poke her gently and a bruise would come up straight away.

"Hi," I say and I watch her quiver at my introduction – shyness rolling over her in waves.

"Hi," she says. Her quiet voice shakes, matching the rest of her. "I'm Sophie. I have OCD, agoraphobia, generalized anxiety disorder, social anxiety and panic disorder." She collapses in on herself at the effort of getting all of that out while I try and figure out how to respond.

I nod slowly. "Riiiight. Umm, nice to meet you. My name's Olive." I smile again and she manages one back.

"I only just got diagnosed with panic disorder," she manages to add. "That's my newest one."

I don't know what to say so I just say, "Jolly good. Umm, tell me three interesting facts about yourself then, I guess."

She stares right at me and looks like she's about to cry. "I just did."

"Oh."

She thinks her mental health diagnoses are her interesting facts?!

That is both a worry and a concern, with a side order of depressing. "Umm. I'm not sure if that's what we're supposed to be sharing yet," I say. "Do you…uh…do you have any other interesting facts?"

Her eyes widen and she looks at me in total confusion. "How am I supposed to have any interesting facts about myself with all that going on?"

I nod slowly. "Fair point. But, umm, do you do anything else with your time? You know? Apart from being diagnosed with things?"

She bites her lip, thinking about it. "Umm. I read. I like reading."

"Books?"

She nods, gaining confidence in her own interestingness, settling into talking to me. "Yes. I really like romantic books."

"That's great. Great." My voice squeaks with its attempt at enthusiasm. "Umm, anything else you like doing?"

She looks at me blankly.

"I mean, what's your favourite food?"

"I don't have one. I don't like foods to touch. It's part of my OCD. I don't like talking about me," she stutters. "Can we talk about you now? What are your facts?"

Instantly every interesting thing I've ever done vanishes into the abyss. "Umm." I try to think. *What do I like?* Memories bleed into each other and it's hard to distinguish what things I *actually* enjoy and what I get excited about when I'm on a whimsy. Baking – that was short-lived. Especially as I started with that doomed three-tier wedding cake. Ally still ate it though. "I love how much you've committed to the burning of the sponge," she'd laughed. "It's quite impressive." Urban exploring – I read a blog about it, got excited, but then only really did it once so I could be alone with Jay Nashville.

"Umm, this is harder than it looks, isn't it?" I ask Sophie. We share another smile. "Photography," I say. "I like taking photographs of things." This is true. That is one of my constants. My very few constants...

"Oh, cool, what kinds of things?"

"People. Portraits. Self-portraits. I like seeing how people react to a camera lens being on them."

I get a pang then for my school's darkroom. I was practically the only one who insisted on 35mm film rather than digital. I would lose hours of my life in there – with the soothing red light, the swish of the developing tray, the acrid scent of the chemicals. I've yet to get bored of it, which is saying something, because I get bored with practically everything very quickly indeed.

"Cool. Did you bring your camera with you?"

"No..." I reply, feeling gutted. I hadn't been able to imagine wanting to take photos over the last few weeks. My fingers were too heavy to lift the camera. I hated humans too much to want to document their existence.

"That's a shame. Oh well, any other interesting facts?"

I stretch up my arms and look around the room for inspiration. Everyone appears to be struggling. Voices hushed, no one quite making eye-contact. The pale boy I gave directions to looks like he's holding in the world's biggest wee as he speaks to his partner, his leg jerking uncontrollably. Jamie looks like he's finished already. He's spread his legs out in front of him and relaxed back into his chair. Gabriella is the only one enjoying herself. She's chewing the ear off her partner. Her voice booms around the room and bounces off the corners.

"Umm, interesting things, interesting things…" I mutter. "I guess I like running. You know? Just like really, really going for it, off on your own, pounding-the-streets type running?" I smile. "Although last year, on a run, I once legitimately fell over on a banana skin and sprained my ankle."

Sophie's tiny smile grows up at the edges. "Really?"

I nod. "Yes. It came out of nowhere! Like in a cartoon. It really hurt." Sophie lets out a small yelp of a laugh. "So, yeah, that happened. And I guess the last interesting thing is, erm…" I struggle to think of anything and we descend into silence. I'm surprised when Sophie fills it.

"So, what's your diagnosis?" she asks. "Why are you here?"

"I don't know what I'm here for," I say. "I won't let them tell me my diagnosis. I'd rather just not know."

"Oh…why don't you—"

But before she can finish, Dr Rossen claps his hands and the room falls quiet.

"It's great to see you all getting to know each other," he says. "Now it's time to share back. I know none of you will want to go first, so let's just start at this side of the circle." He points to Jamie and his partner. "Jamie? Do you want to introduce your partner for us?"

Jamie smiles easily, someone used to being onstage. "All

right then. This is Hannah." He gestures like a magician's assistant. "Hannah likes playing video games, particularly Zelda. Hannah once won a competition to meet One Direction when she was nine years old. And Hannah has kept a diary every single day since she was five."

Hannah glows red.

"Hi, Hannah," Dr Rossen singsongs and we all singsong it back, like we're at primary school, or in a cult...

"This is Jamie," Hannah tells us. She has quite a posh southern accent, and a really well-cut bob. "Jamie plays guitar in a band." I knew it! "Jamie's favourite food is pizza. And he once got to go backstage at a Mightydeath concert."

"Megadeth," Jamie corrects.

"Oh, right," says Hannah.

I feel a swell of annoyance. Did he really need to correct her? I narrow my eyes across the circle.

"Welcome, Jamie."

I guess if I'm being honest, the interesting facts everyone shares as we sweep around the circle are not interesting.

"I like to collect comic books."

"My favourite country is France."

"I once broke my leg in two places."

Gabriella's facts are, unsurprisingly, larger than life. "Gabriella wants to win an Oscar... Gabriella once pulled an A-List celebrity but she won't tell me who." She taps her nose at that one. And, "Gabriella had breast reduction surgery on her sixteenth birthday."

Jamie puts his hands around his mouth and calls, "What a shame!" and she glows in his attention.

The only fact that piques my interest is the wispy boy's.

"This is Lewis," Liv, his partner, says. "He is one of four brothers. He's a huge *Doctor Who* fan, and Lewis loves maths and thinks maths can save the world."

Lewis blushes. "Now you all think I'm both delusional *and* a massive geek," he stammers and the room ripples with laughter. This REALLY makes him blush and he looks down at his shaking hands.

I find myself smiling, thinking, *Oh, you're quite interesting. And what was that about maths? How can it save the world? I mean, you can't just drop that sort of thing in and not explain further.*

Soon it's my turn. My palms go sweaty and I take a big breath so my voice doesn't wobble. "Umm, this is Sophie, she likes reading, especially romance…" But I don't get to finish because Sophie's fled the room. She's kicked back her chair and run away like a bomb's about to explode. I jerk to a halt as Dr Jones goes after her, not sure what to do.

Dr Rossen claps to get our attention again. "Oh dear," he says, trying to paper over it. "That's fine, by the way. Totally fine. As we said, there's no pressure here. But, oh no. Olive! You have no one to introduce you."

"That's okay."

"No it isn't. We're all desperate to hear your facts, aren't we?"

Nobody says yes.

"Well, do you mind introducing yourself to us?"

"Uh," I say. "Uh."

"Go on, none of us bite."

"Well that's a damn pity," I mutter.

Only Jamie laughs. A big whoop of it which turns into a coughing fit. Half the room are still trying to figure out the joke and I start talking so they never do. "Umm, yeah, so yeah, my name's Olive. And I like photography. Portrait photography."

Dr Rossen beams at me. "Ahh, Olive, well you'll be delighted to know we've got a studio here."

"No way, really?" I feel my first stab of enthusiasm.

"Yes, for art therapy."

"That's great. Seriously. Umm, well, the other thing is that I like running and I once fell over on a banana skin."

Nobody laughs. Not even Jamie.

I scratch my head. "So, umm, yeah that happened." I feel my face turn purple.

"You've still got one more fact to share," Dr Rossen points out.

I'm not sure why I even told Sophie that I refuse to know about my condition. People probably wouldn't understand it and I don't want people to hate me.

"We only got as far as two," I lie.

"Oh, well, that's a shame." But he's already looking past me to the guy sitting on my right.

10

Sophie doesn't reappear until dinner time where she surprises me as I'm examining the food on offer.

"Sorry I ran out on you," she practically whispers, next to my ear.

"Woah!" I jump. "Where did you come from?"

She looks traumatized. "Sorry. I didn't mean to make you jump. Sorry. Sorry."

I smile back in what I hope is a reassuring way. "It's okay. But, jeez, you walk quiet. Can I make you a collar with a bell on it?" I take a tray from the stack and she copies me.

"I had a panic attack," she explains, even though I didn't ask. "A really bad one. I'm not very good at having a room full of people look at me."

"They should've called it 'exposure therapy' rather than an 'induction session.'"

"Yes! They should."

"Anyway don't worry, I managed to tell everyone my

amazing banana skin story. They were enthralled."

She smiles again and it causes creases around her eyes. She has so many worry lines already. Like a piece of A4 that's been scrunched up and ironed out over and over. I get a sudden pang of liking for her, an urge to look after her, a swell of hope that we might be friends. I'm not very good at making (or keeping) friends, but Sophie seems like a good place to start. She stands on tiptoes to look at the array of food.

"So, what's on offer?"

I pull a face. "It's all depressingly healthy looking." My appetite is back with a vengeance. My malnourished body is desperate for solid carbs and fat to put all the weight back on that I've lost. But everything is spinach, or egg-white, or fresh. Not a chip to be seen.

She pushes past me and eyeballs the food frantically. "Oh, good, they've kept everything separate." Her body visibly softens again.

I put a bottle of water onto my tray. "You really don't like food to mix, huh?"

She copies me with the water. "I can't have different foods of different colours touching. And I can't have hot foods touching cold foods. And I can't have different food groups on the same plate."

"Or what?" I ask.

"Huh?"

I take two jacket potatoes from the hot counter, the closest thing to comfort food, and two tubs – one of freshly made coleslaw, the other of grated cheese. "I mean, what happens if the foods touch?"

"They just can't."

"But what are you scared will happen?"

"THEY JUST CAN'T, OKAY?" And before I have time to process, she has slammed her tray down and run back out of the cafeteria. Everyone looks up at the noise.

I sigh, put my plate down and run after her, annoyed at myself for screwing up so impeccably so very quickly.

Sophie is crouching in a nook of the hallway, squatting down with her hands over her ears. She is crying and I feel guilty.

Bad person.

I

Am

An

Awful

Nasty

Person.

I probed her and I should've known better and I wasn't concentrating properly and I'm selfish and terrible and look what I've done now, without even meaning to. This is why no one likes me. This is why I have hardly any friends. Bad person bad person bad person.

I squat awkwardly next to her and she senses my presence. She flinches and looks up, her eyes red from crying again.

"I'm sorry," I say hopelessly. "I didn't mean to upset you."

"You think I'm crazy."

"I'm quite sure that's a requirement to come here."

She doesn't smile. "You think I'm crazier than you."

"I wasn't aware it was a competition."

I sit down next to her and stick my legs out, stretching them onto the soft carpet.

"I just really don't like food to touch, okay? I know it doesn't make sense. I'm aware it doesn't make sense. But I hate it. It makes me itchy and my throat close up and I don't care how much anyone tries to reason with me, I can't stand it, okay?"

I nod. "Okay. It's okay."

We sit in silence for about five minutes.

"Everyone's going to think I'm an idiot," she says, putting her legs out like mine. "I've run out twice now. They're all going to think I'm a freak. That I'm the freakiest one here."

"No they're not," I reassure her.

"Yes they are! You think I'm a freak too."

"I don't think you're a freak. Look, I don't understand the food thing," I say. "But I have my quirks." I turn to her and try my best to look reassuring. Her tears have ebbed slightly, but she still looks like the saddest person ever.

She twists around and asks in hardly a whisper, "Why are you here though? I mean, you don't know your diagnosis, but you, like, must have symptoms. You seem fine!"

I shake my head, thinking, *If only you'd seen me last week.*

"I can't believe you think I'm fine. I get anxious about things too."

She looks disbelieving. "Yeah, like what?"

I sigh. "I can't handle noise. Like, I really can't handle it."

"Noise?"

I nod. "Yes. Particularly at night-time, when I'm trying to sleep. I go nuts if there's noise."

"What's so bad about noise?"

I feel my skin start to prickle just at the thought of it. "It's not JUST about the noise, but also, like, the *meaning* behind the noise. If I feel people are making noise irresponsibly I find that harder. Like, I don't mind nature noises, like crickets chirping, because that's just what crickets do. They can't help it. But, like, someone plays music really loudly, I get really angry because how could they be so selfish?"

"That doesn't make sense. Noise is noise."

I feel my blood start to simmer. On a low heat, but still. "No," I say firmly. "There's good noise and bad noise. Noise where people are being careless – either by playing their music, or shouting outside my window late, or not turning the beeps off on their phone… I can't stand it!"

Sophie is quiet, digesting it. "I feel like your noise thing is on a weirdness par with my food thing," she says finally.

"Happy to help," I deadpan.

"Is that all you're here for? Noise?"

I pause before shaking my head. "No, there's other stuff. My moods are somewhat…" I reach for a word that sounds adequate. "…chaotic."

"They seem okay to me."

"You've only known me for five minutes. Give it some time."

"I guess."

I try not to get pissed off that she looks reassured by my promise of madness. Her tears have dried up though. "You feeling better?"

She starts to get up. "I'm too embarrassed to go back in."

"Embarrassed? Everyone probably thinks I'm bullying you! Come on… Let's go back in to—"

We're interrupted by Gabriella bouncing down the hall, a giant grin on her face, her braided hair whipping behind her. "WHAT IS WRONG?" she shouts over at Sophie. "WE'RE ALL TALKING ABOUT YOU IN THERE."

"Really?" Sophie's face loses the tiny amount of colour it had regained.

"IT'S OKAY." Gabriella thuds down next to her, shoving an arm around her, bringing her in for an aggressive hug. "WHAT'S WRONG? YOU CAN TELL ME."

Sophie seems to get smaller and smaller under her arm. "It's nothing. I just…got anxious, that's all."

"We were about to go back in—" I start but Gabriella is already talking.

"Oh, I get anxious too. I get SO anxious. There was this one day when my foster mum took me to see a show in London and it was so crowded on the Tube that I just LOST it and started screaming at everyone and all these guards came running at me. And then I started yelling at THEM because OF COURSE I was going to get EVEN MORE anxious with all these guards trying to arrest me and then I tried to jump in front of the train and then EVERYONE lost it and…" She runs on and on. Sophie is as bewildered as I am, just nodding at the right moments. "Yeah, and so, THEN I ended up in A & E and this drunk tramp hit on me in the waiting room…" is how she finishes. "So I totally TOTALLY know what you're going through."

There is a stunned silence. "Umm, thank you," Sophie manages to say.

We finally get Sophie back into the canteen, and even get some non-mixed food down her. Nobody talks much, but we're less icy than we were before the induction. I feel sadness creeping in around my edges. Even though I smoothed it over, I'm so mad at myself for upsetting Sophie. It's like I'm poison that contaminates everything I touch. Jamie comes and sits with us and Gabriella asks him about his band, what music he's into, leaning over the table and flirting ostentatiously. I kind of zone out. They're all talking about wifi but I'm not really listening or concentrating and I start having thoughts.

Bad thoughts.

Dark thoughts.

Thoughts like, *What the hell are you doing here?*

And, *You Are A Bad Person.*

The sadness and despair find entry points, and start filling my toes up, one by one, and it spreads up into my ankles.

When I'm knee-deep, I bow out. I pick up my tray, and tell this table full of strangers that I'm going to bed.

"But it's not even dark," Jamie complains.

"You'll miss the games," Sophie adds.

"See you tomorrow."

As I make my way up through the maze of corridors, more and more thoughts cram in. Worrying about noise that night. Worrying that someone here really is crazy and is going to go all Bertha from *Jane Eyre* and set my bed on fire in my sleep. Worrying I triggered Sophie twice today because I'm insensitive and terrible. Worrying about my English GCSE result. Worrying about missing Ally and my mum and dad and being away from them for a month. I'm exhausted by the time I flop into my room. Yet my heart picks up the second the door closes. I listen out for noise. I hear a clank from somewhere and my heart doubles its pace. *Where was that clank from? Where where where?*

No. No, no, stop it, Olive.

I need my protective kit.

I start unpacking and lift out my white-noise machine. I plonk it on the desk, and turn it up to full whack, and the reassuring hum of it helps drown out the chaos starting inside my skull. I turn the TV on, to try and distract my brain from itself, but there's nothing decent on and I give up after five minutes.

Maybe I should call Mum or Dad or Ally? Get my mind off things?

I rummage for my phone and swear when I see there's

no signal. I try and connect to the wifi, but there isn't any.

HOW AM I SUPPOSED TO TALK TO THE PEOPLE I LOVE?

My heart is in full-on freak-out mode, and it powers me out through my door and downstairs, thump-thumping back through the corridors. I see Maths Boy, Lewis, go into his room and we share a shy smile. He doesn't say hi though, just squeezes himself through the door. I hear music and TV coming from other rooms and it makes everything worse.

Grace is at the reception desk when I get there – looking as pristine and upbeat as she was when she greeted me hours ago.

"Olive!" she coos. "How can I help you?"

"My phone has no signal and I can't get wifi in my room."

I have no space for manners when I'm like this.

Grace smiles sympathetically. "Yes, the phone coverage here is TERRIBLE. None of us get any." She shrugs. "It's good though sometimes, isn't it? To disconnect?"

"What about the wifi?" I ask.

"Did they not explain in your induction? We don't have wifi here. You're all allowed an hour a week in the computer lab. But part of our ethos here is that we don't want you all switched on all the time."

What?! I do NOT remember anyone telling me that. I mean, yeah, I zoned out for the second half, but my subconscious would've certainly woken me up if it had known wifi wasn't available. Maybe *that's* what the others were talking about at dinner?

Grace is wittering on, talking about how social media leads to feelings of isolation and depression, but I'm too busy freaking to listen. As if she's reading my mind, Grace's forehead crumples up in concern. "Aww, are you getting first night homesickness? You're welcome to use the phone here to call your parents? It's always here. We'd never leave you with no way of contacting them."

For no discernible reason, pride turns up in my tortured brain, waving, and calling, *Coo-ee, wait for me!*

"No, that's fine. Thanks for the offer," I find myself saying. Because I'm an idiot who doesn't want a mental health professional trained to deal with emotional neediness to think I'm needy.

"Well, do come back later if you change your mind," Grace coos. "Or if you need ANYTHING. And don't worry about wifi. Within a day you won't even notice it's missing."

I trudge back to my room, my stomach a swirling vortex sucking in every available emotion. How am I going to get through the evening? When I finally get back in, I stop for a second. Listening out. Thankfully, thankfully, it is quiet. So, with that all sorted, I can focus on the other pressing issue, which is that I am a terrible, worthless person.

I pace my room, my brain clogging and fogging. My ego running away from me, leaving only loathing and self-hatred and terror that my brain will always be this brain. And that, even in a quiet five-star-hotel-type place, my brain can't stop hurting.

Unpack, unpack – that will keep me busy. I get out the

clothes Mum packed for me, laying them flat, then I open my cupboard to hang them and…

And there's my camera, sitting on the floor of the cupboard, with a red ribbon tied around it. And a little note.

I squat down and pick it up, cradling it in my hands. Then, with shaking fingers, I open the note.

Hi Olive,
We hope you don't mind that we smuggled your camera in. We just thought you might want it. You really enjoy taking pictures when you're going through a better patch, and we didn't want you to go without. Hey, who knows? Perhaps you can take photos of all the new friends you'll make?
We also just want to say how proud we are of you, for giving this a chance. We will always love you and we're always here for you.
Good luck at Camp Reset! Call us any time.
Lots of love,
Mum and Dad xxx

The letter sends me over the edge. I whimper as I turn the camera over in my hands. Wondering, as I always do, how it got to this. I cry for a few minutes – really letting rip with it. The snot is everywhere, my eye make-up is meshing with it, my tear ducts feel actually sore from the effort of overworking. I catch myself in the mirror and my reflection worries me again. I look so ill. I look everything that I feel.

And I get an urge then to capture it. To take this moment down. *First Night In Sort-Of Mental Institution*. The idea is like a lifebuoy and I cling to it. I open up the camera and start looking for the best shot, looking at angles of the room, figuring out what I want this portrait to say. More than anything, I just want it to tell the truth. One of my favourite photographers – Cindy Sherman – is famous for her self-portraits. Some call her the inventor of the selfie. But her portraits are all stylized, with her in lots of fancy dress or disguises – trying to look like anyone other than her. That's not the photo I want to take today. I want my raw pain, my gaunt cheeks, my blotchy face. Finally I find an angle that works, looking right up at me from below. I sit on the bed and clutch my knees to my chest because that's how I feel today. Foetal and self-protective and childlike and lost. I stare into the lens as I wait for the self-timer to go. I hear the click, the moment is captured.

I don't know what it means about my sanity that I want to capture a moment as dark as this one. But I set the timer again and take another shot, just in case the first one didn't come out. I want to confront this. This darkness inside of me and how I'm trying to find the light again. I am going to try so hard to not be this girl, and, if I succeed, it all will have started tonight, with this picture. A slither of an idea creeps into me. That maybe I should take my photo every night while I'm here? See if my journey to a better version of myself is something that shows on my face. And, with the glint of a way of making sense of all this, I manage to smile. Just about.

11

I hardly slept. My body just knew it wasn't where it normally sleeps (in a home-made bunker under my desk). I sweated and twisted in my sheets and kept thinking I heard noise and taking out my earplugs just to check.

"Why do you need to check?" the CBT therapist once asked me. "If you can't hear the noise with your earplugs in, then why does it matter that it's there?"

"Because it matters," was all I could say. Because trying to use logic to explain anxiety is like using a banana to open a locked safe.

I was staring at the light filtering under the blackout blind when my alarm went off. And now I'm foggy and heavy despite the incredible water pressure of my en-suite shower. I check my schedule for my day as I brush my teeth. I've got group therapy, something called a "core belief" workshop, lunch, art therapy, some "pet therapy" – which explains the alpacas I guess – and I've got a one-on-one session with Dr Jones to end the day. Whoop de whoop. I push my bracelet up my arm and step into a denim summer dress. They're not going to be very impressed with my sleep data from last night.

At breakfast though, it turns out I'm not the only one who had a bad night.

"I didn't sleep a wink," Sophie tells me as she removes every single tiny BIT of shell from her hard-boiled egg.

"Me neither." Hannah, the One-Direction girl, slides her tray in next to us. "Is anyone else, like, proper scared about today?"

Sophie has found her egg to be somehow contaminated and drops it back onto its separate plate. "I'm scared by every today," she says as she stares miserably at a single piece of brown, unbuttered toast. "I have OCD, and generalized anxiety disorder and—"

"Oh my God, I have OCD too!" Hannah says, beaming like they've just discovered they are wearing the same trainers.

"You do?" Sophie squeaks.

"Yes, totally. That's why I'm here."

"What sort of OCD do you have?"

"So, I hate drains. And bad smells. So smelly drains are, like, my worst nightmare. Everything has to be clean, but it's about smelling, not germs. I'm always worrying I smell basically."

I smile over at her. "You don't smell," I offer as reassurance.

Hannah doesn't smile back. "Don't. Otherwise I'll start

asking you over and over and it's just not good for me if that happens."

Fine then, you do smell, I whisper in my head, hurt at her response.

She turns to Sophie. "So, what OCD do you have?" And Sophie starts listing off her showreel of phobias. Going to parties. Having to talk publicly. Everyone looking at her. Having different foods touch. Any orange foods… I feel weirdly left out and concentrate on my coconut porridge, leaving them chatting.

Jamie arrives with a laden tray. "So, what have I missed?" he asks, unloading his towering plate of "poach-up" onto the table.

"I'm being left out of the OCD bonding," I stage-whisper and he grins.

"Aww, poor Olive! Mental illnesses aren't Pokémon, you know that, right? You don't have to catch them all."

Sophie turns her head back. "But Olive doesn't know what her mental illness is. She won't let anyone tell her what her diagnosis is," she says.

The table goes quiet, right at the moment Lewis sits down across from me.

Hannah gives me a strange look. "Is that true? You haven't been diagnosed?"

I feel my face blush, annoyed at Sophie for revealing that.

"Umm, I assume I have," I bluster. "But I don't know what it is."

Jamie grins and talks with his mouth full of egg. "You've

got something weird and new that they haven't figured out yet?"

I shake my head. "I doubt it. But I wouldn't know. I don't want to know."

Lewis – the wispy boy – talks to me properly for the first time. "Why not?" he asks. His eyes are insanely blue. The pale, icy type of blue, rather than a deep blue.

I look back at him, and shrug. Then shrug towards the whole table. "I just don't."

Jamie nudges me in the side with his elbow. "Ooo, mystery girl."

I roll my eyes again. "Hardly. It's just my choice. I mean, obviously I have issues. Because I'm here and all. But I don't want a label on me in case I use it as an excuse for not trying to get better, or for just being a dick, or…" Everyone really is staring. Oh God, have I offended them? "I mean…it's just not for me." I try to smile. "But, whatever works for everyone else is great."

Lewis nods. Jamie just looks bored and returns to his food. Sophie heard it all yesterday. Only Hannah takes offence.

"So you think you're better than us?" she asks, shooting me a glare.

"I didn't say that."

"But, like, you don't need a label, and we do?"

"You're putting words into my mouth."

"Oh, am I? I thought I was just paraphrasing your opinion that I'm only ill because I've given myself a label as an excuse."

My mouth falls open. "That's not what I was saying at all."

She screeches back her chair and picks up her tray. "I don't have to listen to this." She looks down at Sophie, whose mouth is also open. "You coming?" she asks her. "Or do you want to stay here and be judged?"

To my horror, Sophie stands up too, looking a bit confused about what to do. Then she says, "I'm coming," and turns on her heel. All I can say is, "This is ridiculous," before they both flounce off, leaving me with the two guys.

Jamie pats me on the shoulder. "Don't worry about them, Olive."

I shrug him off but still seek reassurance. "That's mental, right? I mean, I know that's the underlying theme of our stay here, but that was totally, undeniably mental, right? I wasn't trying to offend anyone..."

Oh God – why do I always rub people up the wrong way? I don't understand what's just happened. It's taken a day, less than a day, to piss people off just by being myself. I'm so awful, so completely awful, no matter where I am.

"I'm not offended," Lewis says. "I'm quite interested really. I mean, it didn't occur to me that I don't *have* to know what's wrong with me."

Jamie touches my shoulder again and I flinch. "Don't worry about them. Some people are just looking to be offended."

"Anyway, Jamie..." I decide to change the subject and yank his hand off abruptly. "You've been to this kind of place before. What's group therapy like? Do we all have to stand up and tell everyone our awful secrets?"

"Kind of." He half-nods. "It's a weird set-up, staying in a place like this. You get to know really deep things about people really quickly. Which can be great, as you feel close right away, but it can also mean that people get upset really quickly too. That's why I wouldn't worry about those girls if I were you. Someone always ends up saying something in group that upsets someone else. If you like, I'll go first today? Get the bullseye off your forehead? Tell everyone I'm a sex addict or something?"

"You don't have to say anything," I tell Jamie. "But thanks for the offer."

"Honestly, I don't care. It will be funny. Scare Hannah senseless. She was my partner yesterday and she was well up her own arse."

The thought of Hannah and Sophie hating me makes my tummy hurt. I really hoped my inability to get on with girls was just a school thing – something that only stays a problem because my town is too small and bored to forgive and forget my past dramas. But it appears I'm unlikeable just because...

Jamie looks at his swish watch and I notice his bracelet fall up to his elbow. "Anyway, it's time, guys. You ready to share?"

Lewis and I exchange a nervous smile. "I'm ready to listen to *you* share," I volunteer.

"Good enough for day one." He scrapes the last bit of food onto his fork and shoves it into his mouth. Then, with it still crammed with beans, he says, "Let's go."

12

Here's what I know about group therapy based on TV:

- The chairs will be in a circle
- There will be a depressing little table at the back with bad coffee, bad biscuits and one of those water machines
- People will get up and talk and you have to clap them and tell them they're brave
- Somehow this helps...

Things seem slightly different as I enter the room with Lewis and Jamie. The chairs are indeed in a circle. But there's a *posh* coffee machine and plates laden with fresh fruit rather than stale biscuits.

Hannah and Sophie are already seated and I sit across, giving both a hopeful smile. Sophie smiles shyly back but Hannah gives me a huge evil. Jamie notices.

"I've got you, Olive," he whispers. "Don't worry."

"I'm not worried," I lie. I go play with the coffee machine

and press multiple buttons, then way too much coffee comes shooting out, overflowing my cup and spilling on the floor.

"Shit." I grab another cup to stop the onslaught but that's already overflowing too. "Stop, stop!" I tell the machine but the coffee just keeps on coming. Then Lewis appears and the coffee stops.

"Thank you," I sigh. "How did you do that?"

"I turned the machine off at the wall."

"You're a genius." I hand out a cup. "Coffee? I've got plenty."

He smiles and takes a cup from me. "Yeah, all right then. Seeing as you're in surplus."

The room fills up. Gabriella shuffles in, a very different Gabriella from yesterday. She's not got any make-up on and she doesn't wave or say hi, just slumps down in a seat. She's wearing a big grey sweatshirt and I don't know how she's not dying in this heat. I take a small sip of coffee...mmm... coffee. I take another slurp and feel how it dances in my veins already – sending zing and buzz about me.

There's something I've been meaning to ask Lewis so I turn to him. "So, what was all that yesterday? About maths saving the world?"

He goes red and starts stammering but Dr Rossen strides in and claps for our attention. The conversations die down.

"Good morning, everyone," he says. "I hope you had a good night's sleep. Don't worry if you didn't. I'm sure you will tonight after your first full day of activities and when things feel a little more familiar." He's wearing a jumper that looks a bit too hot for the weather and there's a thin film of sweat on his forehead. He reaches into a box on the table and pulls out some iPads and hands them out. "Here are your electronic diaries," he says. "Ideally fill them in each day. They're pretty self-explanatory. They just ask you to rate your mood, what you've eaten, et cetera. They sync with your bracelets and help our algorithm. All confidential, we promise."

There's that word again…*algorithm*. I'm grasping at it, turning it over in my mind, but we've moved on. Everyone has put their diaries down and it looks like the actual therapy is about to start. I have no idea what to expect and the coffee is making me nervous. I try to catch Sophie's eye again but she won't look at me. I can't believe I've messed up my chance to make some new friends already.

"Now," Dr Rossen starts. "Group therapy is going to be a big part of your stay here and most of you are probably wondering what it means. And the answer is, it can mean whatever you want it to mean. You can talk about what you like, what you've been through, how you're feeling, any coping mechanisms you've found useful, or even just your favourite TV shows. The only rule we have is that you need to actively listen when it's somebody else's turn to talk. But, to begin. It's day one of this journey. Let's start with a goal. Just for today. You've got paper and a pen under your chair, so take two minutes to write down what your goal is for today."

I raise my eyebrows – this all sounds very *American* to me – and Dr Rossen spots it.

"That make sense to you, Olive?"

It doesn't but I nod anyway.

"Good."

Everyone is already scribbling as I suck on my pen. I mean, what's the goal for any day? I shove something down, feeling somewhat unconvinced that this is going to magically cure me of me but hey ho, what do I know?

"Right, finished? Now, let's all take it in turns to reveal our goal. Then we can all help each other achieve it."

He did not mention we would have to share our goal.

"Who's first?" Dr Rossen surveys the room. "Hannah? How about you? What's your goal for today?"

She stands and turns her paper around. "My goal today is not to apologize for who I am." She looks me straight in the eyes as she says it, getting confidence from her hatred of me.

"Woah," Lewis mutters under his breath. "You really made an enemy there."

"That's great, great," says Dr Rossen. "What a strong, powerful, defiant message."

She beams at him and I feel a flash of dislike for her. So, I stare her out. Which I'm very good at. I cross my arms and lower my chin and give Hannah my special look. Her confidence breaks and she looks away. She's staring at the ground by the time she sits down and I feel a swell of victory. Okay, so winning against someone with OCD isn't the nicest thing to do, but come on! Sophie is next. And I feel a swell of pride as she manages to stand up and talk. Her whole body shakes and she tips back her head, taking deep breaths, drawing strength from the ceiling.

"Good," Dr Rossen says. "Really good, Sophie."

Finally she looks back at us and turns her paper around. "My g-goal for t-t-today is to try and speak to p-people," she garbles out. She flushes red and I find myself clapping and everyone joins in. I notice Hannah is the last to do so. This makes Sophie go even more red, but she's smiling. She catches my eye and this time doesn't look away. I feel instantly better. Somehow this room of strangers knew what a big deal this was for Sophie and we helped her fly. I'm so buzzing that I hardly hear everyone else's goals until Dr Rossen's saying, "Olive? You with us?"

"Huh?"

Everyone laughs.

"It's your turn, Olive."

"Oh, right." I really don't want to show my sign, but no one else has abdicated.

"I...umm...this is what I wrote."

I let them read it.

My goal for today is just to get through it.

Because that is my daily goal. My goal on any day when the darkness comes – following me around like it's harpooned me and is reeling me in. Sometimes getting through a day is too big even. It's about trying to get through the next hour, the next minute. Sometimes even the next breath.

"Interesting take on this," Dr Rossen says, which basically means FREAK, FREAK. "Care to elaborate?"

"No." I sit down again.

"Well, that's your choice, Olive."

Hannah leans over and whispers something to Sophie, looking at me the whole time. What has she taken offence at now? I let out a sigh and Jamie must notice because he winks as he stands up.

"My aim for today is to try and not seduce anyone," he declares.

Laughter ripples through the room while Jamie stands there grinning, still holding his paper. "The problem is," he says, "I don't think I'll do very well, so, ladies, you watch out." Then he turns and winks at an outraged Hannah.

She gasps while Dr Rossen waves his arms, saying, "Okay, well, umm, thank you, Jamie, now who's next?"

But Jamie stays standing. "I'm a sex addict," he explains. "I'm totally obsessed with sex. Can't stop thinking about it. If I'm talking to you, if I'm even LOOKING at you, then I'm no doubt imagining us having sex. I mean, Hannah, I'm imagining us having sex right now. I can't help it, I have a problem."

Hannah's mouth goes wide open. Sophie lets out a shriek. The room has lost its control.

Dr Rossen is waving more frantically and practically shouting. "Thank you for sharing, Jamie, but this isn't the right moment and—"

"I think about vanilla sex, I think about depraved sex. I masturbate, like, fifty times a day. I've already done it twice, just this morning. I thought about some of you when I did it."

Everyone erupts.

Hannah yells, "Stop it, stop it, stop it!"

I'm just sitting there with my mouth open in shock.

Lewis, next to me, mutters, "Is he for real?"

"Enough!" Dr Rossen yells. "Jamie, did you not hear me? This is not the time."

"But I'm letting it out!"

"Please, Jamie, sit down. If you won't cooperate, I'm going to have to ask you to leave this session."

"Oh, don't give me an ultimatum, ultimatums really turn me on."

I can't help it. I let out a laugh. My first in weeks. Hannah gives me the world's biggest evil but I'm laughing too hard to care.

Jamie's really ramped it up a gear – singing Rihanna's "S&M" at the top of his voice and dancing while he removes his waistcoat. "STICKS AND STONES MAY BREAK MY BONES BUT—"

"JAMIE, THAT IS ENOUGH."

Out of nowhere, the two dudes that escorted Gabriella turn up and start gently removing Jamie from the room.

"S S S and M M M…" he's singing, still pissing himself laughing as they guide him out.

His singing fades. Dr Rossen's face is red and he mutters under his breath and pushes his hair off his sweaty forehead. The rest of us aren't sure what just happened. On the plus side, the whole affair seems to have jolted Gabriella out of her funk. She hums the Rihanna song loudly and dances in her seat, until Dr Rossen says "Hush" a bit too harshly for someone who's supposed to be a psychologist. After a further five minutes of whispers and giggling and Hannah going out for "some air", we settle once more. Lewis has gone quiet, his hands in his lap, scratching the skin around his thumbnail.

"You all right?" I whisper and he nods but doesn't speak.

I worry suddenly that he hates me too, for laughing.

I worry that *everyone* hates me.

They must do. Hannah obviously does.

And Sophie.

And

I feel myself slipping.

You're a bad person.

You're a bad person.

You're

A

Bad

Person.

But it's Liv's turn to share her goal and wrench me out of my self-loathing.

"Okay," Dr Rossen says. "Sorry, about that. We all know he was just being silly, but it's worth pointing out that having, an, er, preoccupation with sexual matters is nothing to joke about. Now, Liv, sorry to you too for that...distraction there. What is your aim for today?"

She stands up, already smiling a little as she turns around the card. She's got a really good red lipstick on that sets off her cropped hair.

"My aim for today is to try and accept I cannot always control what happens around me..." Her smile grows wider. "And I guess what just happened was a pretty good example, right?"

There's a silence before the giggles. Then the whole room starts laughing. Even Dr Rossen joins in.

My face splits into another new smile. And I think, this is a good kind of therapy. Sitting in a circle and just laughing at the ridiculousness of it all. Maybe that is the therapy? I want every moment to feel like this moment. I want to be able to laugh again and live again, without worrying I've only been given an allocated time slot of feeling normal before I lose it indefinitely. I'm going to try so hard. I can't even tell you how hard I'm willing to try.

13

I find Jamie sat on the front steps after group, smoking a cigarette and staring off into the grounds.

"Was all that really true?" I ask, squatting down to sit next to him.

He laughs but still looks away. "What do you think?"

I unfold my legs out in front of me. "I think you need singing lessons."

Another laugh that turns into a smoker's cough.

"What did those men do to you anyway? Take you away for electroshock treatment?"

He nods and turns to look at me. "Oh yeah. They gave me a full-blown lobotomy. Can't you tell?"

I smile and tilt my head at him. "Well, thank you. I *think* all that was for my benefit. Not that it worked, mind. Hannah seems to think I put you up to it."

He rolls his eyes. "Ergh, people like her are the WORST. People like her are the reason I almost didn't come."

I find a small pebble from the gravel driveway and push it around in my palm. "People like what?"

"People who can't laugh at themselves. Can't laugh at the situation. I mean, I know, I get it, mental illness sucks. I would know. But I hate it when people take themselves too seriously, you know? All quick to be offended?"

I toss the pebble up in front of my face and then catch it. "I've never met other people with mental health problems before," I tell him. "Not that I know of anyway. You lot are my first time."

He raises an eyebrow and I see him make an innuendo in his head. Oh God, is he really a sex addict? "Well, trust me," he says. "There's a certain type – who use their diagnosis like a human body shield. They think it's a reason to find offence in anything. Accuse everyone of triggering them. Act like the world should wrap them up in cotton wool and lie coats over puddles for them just because they're on antidepressants or whatever. They drive me crazy." He laughs again at his unintentional pun. He takes another drag of his cigarette and I get a sudden urge to have one too. Sensing it, he opens up his packet and flicks the bottom so one pops out. "You want?"

I nod and reach out for it. Put it between my lips hungrily and hold his eye-contact as he leans closer to light it. Then I breathe in, feeling the heat hurtle down my throat, the nicotine hitting my blood, mixing with the coffee. I let out the smoke and watch it float off.

"I dunno," I say. "I know that I'm a complete nightmare

when I let the dark side of my brain win." I take another deep drag. "I have no say in what I think or say or do…so I can't really judge anyone else. Not if I don't want people to judge me."

Although everyone does judge me, and I know I judge them. I know the names they call me at school. Behind my back. Sometimes to my face. Slut. Attention-seeking. Needy. Attention-seeking. Self-obsessed. Attention-seeking. Crazy bitch. No matter how many months I can go without accidentally flirting with someone's boyfriend, or taking weeks off school because getting out of bed is so impossible – no one ever gives me credit for it. I'd been labelled "attention-seeking" and there was no way to make them unlabel me. I guess that's part of why I'm so resistant to knowing my diagnosis.

"People like Hannah need to learn how to laugh at themselves," he says.

I smile and pat the space between us. "Like you? Is this a safe distance to sit from you, by the way? Mr Sex Addict?" I blow smoke in his direction, not sure why I'm flirting with him, but flirting nonetheless.

"The whole thing was funny, right?"

"So, you're not…?"

His eyes crinkle as he takes a final drag and grinds his fag butt into the stone steps. "No, Olive. I am not a sex addict. You're safe from me mauling you, I promise." He flicks the butt out into the gravel. "If you really want to know and all, I've got cannabis psychosis. That's why I'm here."

"What the hell is cannabis psychosis?"

Jamie plucks out another cigarette straight away and pauses while he lights it, taking in a huge drag. "It means I did too many drugs and started to see stuff that wasn't real."

"That can happen just from smoking weed?" I ask.

He stares back out over the manicured lawns again, his face unreadable. "It can happen when you smoke weed every day for two years, and also it turns out that, lucky you, you have an underlying propensity for psychotic mental illness." He pulls at his cigarette again. "It just came out of nowhere. One day, I was getting high with my band, like we always did. I hit two bongs because I was bored and it was Tuesday. We were just hanging out. Watching YouTube clips of people falling over and sharing this giant bag of Kettle Chips and then…then…" He's taking drags before he's even finished exhaling the previous ones. "Then I hear this voice in my head. A really sly one, like some pantomime villain. And the voice says, *None of these people are your friends. They are out to get you.*"

Smoke, exhale. Smoke, exhale. My own cigarette has burned down to the butt while I listen. "And the voice went on and on. Telling me I couldn't trust them. Telling me that they were going to try and hurt me. The voice told me they were jealous I was so good at playing guitar and they wanted me gone because they couldn't handle my talent…" He laughs then, hanging his head before finally twisting to look at me, the merest wisp of a smile on his face. "Because it turns out I'm not just a psychotic nut job, I'm an egotistical psychotic nut job."

I'm not sure what to say.

"Well, I admire that you were able to maintain such a high sense of self during a psychotic episode."

And, thankfully, he laughs. Sadly. But he still laughs.

"Anyway, I ran out of the garage, screaming at them to leave me alone. And I then told my parents about the 'danger' I was in and started packing to run away. When they tried to stop me leaving, I went berserk and pulled a knife on my dad because I believed he was in on it too, and ran out into the dark and…well…before you know it I'm on a ward and it takes me ten whole days to not think my friends are trying to kill me any more. So I'm like, brilliant! I'm cured! Until I got stoned again two weeks later and the whole sorry thing happened all over again. So then they sent me to some rehab place to get me all clean. But the moment I was out, I did drugs again. And I did it again…and again."

I shake my head. "So why the hell do you keep getting stoned?"

He throws his second fag butt into the gravel without putting it out. "That's what I'm here to figure out. They've transferred me right here from detox, to see if we can make it stick. Anyway, even if we can, I've still got a heightened risk of developing schizophrenia later on. Go, me!"

He stands up and I do too, wiping the back of my dress with my hands. We're so close our noses almost touch. We stare at each other a moment, then…

"Sorry," Lewis says, loitering in the doorway, bright red as usual. "I didn't mean to… It's just, they sent me out to get you. It's time for this core belief workshop thingy."

I take a step back by default. Not sure why I was so close to Jamie anyway. I nod. "Cool, thanks for letting us know, Lewis." But he's already retreated inside.

We both follow him into the air-con. We push through a heavy mahogany door, back into the room we had group therapy in. The chairs have been rearranged into lines with little tables in front. Hannah's sitting at the front with Sophie at her side. She turns and glares as we enter.

Jamie waves all over-the-top and shouts, "HELLO, LOVER!" and she turns purple. There's two empty seats next to Lewis so I ask if we can sit and he nods. I slide next to him and pick up the yellow pencil on my desk.

"This is bull," Jamie mutters to me, smoke on his breath. "I don't need a workshop to tell me what my core belief is."

"Oh yeah? So what is it?"

And there is not one atom of swagger in what he says next. Not one.

"That this is all my own fault."

He looks like he's going to cry.

14

After an hour of the core belief workshop I feel like my brain has been hacked into.

I stare at the worksheet in front of me and parts of my mind feel literally hot from overwork. The heat is so tangible it seeps through my skull and warms up my hair.

"Now," Elizabeth says. That's the name of the workshop lady, Elizabeth. She wears a long floaty skirt with lots of little mirrors on it. I dismissed her as a hippy know-nothing until she gave me the worksheet that has disintegrated my insides. "You'll probably find that you can identify several core beliefs on this sheet. But, for today, if you can, try to pick only one or two that really resonate with you."

I look down at the magic piece of paper again.

Negative core beliefs:
I am vulnerable
I am helpless

I don't fit in anywhere
I am unwanted
I can't help myself
I am unworthy
I'm not good enough
I'm not valuable
I'm unimportant
I am inferior
I can't control anything
I can't change
There's no way out for me
I always get it wrong
I am a mistake
I am unbalanced
I am out of control
I mess up everything I do
I attract trouble
I can't fix it
It's my fault
I'm a bad person
I am hopeless
I will fail
I am invisible
I don't know what is real
I am damaged
I don't deserve to be loved

On and on the list goes, lots of them twinging my brain

in recognition. It's like going to a restaurant and wanting everything on the menu but knowing you can only pick one thing. Except nobody would want *anything* on this menu.

"Core beliefs are narratives you tell yourself every day," Elizabeth says. "Things you believe about yourself that run through your brain like a broken record, over and over. So pick the beliefs that are playing the loudest right now."

The words swim before me. I blink, surprised to find my eyes are slightly wet. I look around, like I'm cheating in a test. I glance at Jamie's paper and see him circling, *I mess up everything I do.* His face is serious, the tip of his tongue poking out the side of his mouth. I go red, feeling guilty for having seen what he circled. Lewis hides his worksheet with his arms, like the good kids used to do in primary school to stop me from cheating. Diagonally, I see Gabriella circle every single one and roll my eyes.

And that.

That thought.

That snide thought.

It leads me like a golden ball of twine back to that undeniable truth.

I am a bad person.

A bad horrid messed-up selfish broken annoying disruptive awful person who does and says terrible things and ruins the lives of people around me. That's why people don't like me. That's why I hardly have any friends.

I sigh, pick up my pen and circle the words on the paper. The physical act of doing so drains me. Makes the blackness feel like it's sliding down my throat again. Then, without really thinking, I circle a second one.

I am out of balance.

Because even though I won't let them tell me the official label for it, I know this is the truth. I know it is not *normal* to swing from euphoria to suicidal in one earthly rotation. The enormity of that presses down on my skull, travels down my spine, sends tingles of dread firing out through my frail, human body. I shake my head violently, trying to dislodge it. Because I am here to fix this. I am here to balance myself out. Here to heal. Here to get rid of this. It's ruined me three times, but not any more. Not again. I will get rid of this poison inside of me.

"Has everyone circled something?" Elizabeth's voice is loud but calm. Soothing, like she sucks on a throat pastille between each intake of breath. "Brilliant. Well done. I know it's not easy."

She starts explaining how core negative beliefs become self-fulfilling. How we subconsciously make life decisions that will reinforce and validate our core beliefs. "For example, if your core belief is *Nothing good happens to me*," Elizabeth says, "then you'll probably find that you turn down a lot of opportunities. You don't try out for the school play because you're convinced you won't get a part. Then, of course, you won't get a part, because you never auditioned, and then you feel nothing good happens to you, and it reinforces that belief."

I bite my lip, silently disagreeing. Because I don't feel

like I choose to be unbalanced. It's not like I wake up in the morning and think, *Hey, I know what I'll do today! I'll lose the will to exist and build a fort under my desk.* But whatever. What do I know? I'm an unbalanced horrible person…

"So, how do you challenge these core beliefs?" Elizabeth wafts around, gesticulating so much I'm surprised she's not made a balloon model out of the surrounding oxygen. "I bet you're thinking you can't…that they're unchangeable. That you're stuck with them. But you've got to remember, these beliefs aren't true. They're just stories you're telling yourself. Over and over."

I sigh.

"Now if you turn over the worksheet, you will find the positive counterpart to your core belief. For example, if your negative core belief is *I am weak*, the positive version is *I can be brave*. So turn over your sheet and find yours."

I flip my sheet over and look for the opposite of my inner turmoil. There it is, in black and white. Comic Sans font, which kind of ruins it to be honest.

I am a good person who tries their best.

I roll my eyes at that. My body literally rejects this sentence the moment I read it.

Elizabeth notices and laughs. "So I can see by Olive's reaction that some of you aren't going to accept this new belief very quickly." My face reddens as the group turn to look at me. "And that's normal," Elizabeth reassures us. "You've been telling yourself the opposite, over and over, for God knows how long. Your brain isn't simply going to go,

Hang on a moment, okay, I'll just think this instead. Let's test this thing. Look at the positive belief and write down how much you agree with it out of ten."

I stare at it.

I am a good person who tries their best.

I am a good person who tries their best.

I

Am

A

Good…

I can think of so many things I have said and done that prove otherwise. I can think of feelings I've hurt, and feet I've trodden on, and letting-downs I've been responsible for.

I write *2/10*.

"So," Elizabeth says. "Have any of you put a number higher than five?" We sit in silence, and she smiles. "I thought not. How about this?" She turns on her heel, walks to the white board at the front of the room and she writes:

I would prefer it if…

"Why not add this before the belief. Try it and see."

I carefully copy it down and read my worksheet again.

I would prefer it if I am a good person who tries their best.

"Now, how much out of ten do you believe in this new sentence?" Elizabeth is smiling smugly, like she's got the elixir of life. I almost write *Well duh* instead of my actual answer, which is ten out of ten. Because – well duh. OF COURSE I'd prefer it if I was a good person. "I'm guessing your numbers are much higher than five now, right?"

We all nod in unison and Elizabeth beams at us. "Well, there you go. You see, the brain is not going to accept something it does not believe is true. If you keep telling yourself *I am brave, I am brave* when you believe the opposite, your brain will suss that out and press the reject button."

We all nod again, like a chorus of nodding dogs.

"But here's the interesting thing about the brain," Elizabeth says. "It tends to only hear the last part of a particular sentence. For example, if I say to you, 'At the end of the road, past the red postbox, turn left', the main message you will take from that sentence is *Turn left*. So, if you say to yourself over and over *I would prefer it if I can be brave*, all your brain actually hears is *I can be brave*, and – because you believe the adapted phrase – your brain absorbs it and takes it in."

Lewis puts his hand up.

"Yes? Lewis, is it?"

He leans forward in his chair and his voice is hardly a whisper. "It can't be that easy."

Elizabeth's eyes crinkle as her smile turns sad. "Of course it's not that easy. I'm not saying any of you are going to change your core beliefs straight away. They're no doubt very entrenched. However, just *try* repeating these new phrases to yourself whenever you have a quiet moment. If you're on a walk, if you're showering, if you're brushing your teeth, repeat over and over, *I would prefer it if I can be brave, I would prefer it if I can be brave*. See how you feel this time next week."

Jamie doesn't put his arm up before he interrupts. "So we just tell our brain something and our brain is like, *All righty then, I'll let you brainwash me.*" He sounds as sceptical as I feel.

Liv twists around in her chair. "Stop being so negative!" she says, curling her perfectly red lip.

"I can't. I would prefer it if I wasn't a negative person, but I haven't told myself that enough times for it to magically come true."

"Elizabeth! They're not taking it seriously!" Hannah whines.

"It's good to have questions," she replies. "And, Jamie, there is more to this exercise than just repeating a phrase over and over."

"I'm delighted to hear it."

I marvel at Elizabeth's ability to keep her temper. "I also want you to look at the evidence you find to support your negative core beliefs," she continues. "People tend to sift out all the experiences that don't buy into their negative core beliefs, and only hold onto the experiences that do. Kind of like the opposite of panning for gold." She smiles. "So, using your digital diaries, I want you guys to try and reverse this. Every night, I want you to note down whatever things you've done that are the *opposite* of your negative beliefs. Start panning for gold rather than silt." She claps her hands and half of us jump. "Starting now...I want you all to write down three pieces of evidence from the last twenty-four hours that support your new, positive beliefs."

I look down at my sheet of paper once more. Hundreds of examples of being a bad person are flooding my brain. The way Gabriella annoys me. How Hannah obviously thinks I'm all superior. The constant stress and worry I cause my parents. Laughing when Jamie used group therapy to wind everyone up.

I'm a bad person.

Bad person.

Bad...

I shake my head. Wowsers. This core belief really is embedded into my very...core...oh, that's why they're called that. Right. I am a good person who tries their best. A good person who tries... What have I done that's good?

I followed Sophie yesterday to make sure she was okay.

I mean, I was probably the reason she got upset in the first place, but I tried my best. I sigh and write it down. What else, what else, what else?

What other nice things have I done? Or nice thoughts have I had? I mean, I guess I didn't yell at Grace last night when she told me there was no wifi. Even though I was screaming inside. That counts, right? That I held it in? Could I give myself kudos for that?

I remember suddenly, something Mum said. About me and me losing it.

"I'm sorry," I'd sob on her, after a dark patch had passed, or a screaming-at-the-top-of-my-lungs patch, or a we-didn't-know-where-you-were-for-two-days patch. Because not only do I have my big ups and downs – "episodes" as

Mum puts it – I have little spurts of being too much one way or too much another. Little snacks of being mentally unstable. "I'm sorry I let you down," I'd say to her. "I just couldn't hold it in. I'm weak and stupid and I'm sorry." And I'd bury my face into her shoulder, getting snot trails all over her.

"Hey, hey, hey," Mum said once. Hugging me tighter, smoothing down my hair. "Olive, you've got to stop being so hard on yourself. What about the times you wanted to scream but you didn't? What about the times you felt yourself spiralling and managed to pull yourself out of it? What about all those times when you still remembered to call us to let us know where you were? Why aren't you giving yourself credit for those times?" She let me out of the hug and held me at arm's length, forcing me to look into her eyes. "Stop only apologizing for the times you lose control and start giving yourself a giant tick for the days you don't."

My heart hurts as I stumble back out of the memory, back into this strange new room. I sniff and write down:

I didn't lose it at Grace, even though I was stressed and anxious.

But I will lose it again. Maybe not then. Maybe not now. But at some point in the future I know I'll lose it again. Because I am unbalanced. My pattern seems so entrenched. Every time I think that's the end of it, but now it's happened three times. And the gap between my last two was much shorter. The record keeps playing the same album.

OLIVE'S ALBUM OF CRAZY

Song one: Everything's fine again.

Song two: I'm still fine, I'm just not sleepy that's all.

Song three: Honestly I'm fine, I just don't know what time I'll be home.

Song four: Olive? OLIVE? Stop pretending it's not happening again, it's happening again.

Song five: IFeelSoGreatWhyWon'tEveryoneLeaveMe AloneOhLookAtThatOverThere.

Song six: And now I've done something so undeniably awful I can't pretend there isn't a problem.

Song seven: I hate myself, I hate myself, I hate myself.

Song eight: I would cry but I'm not even worth the tears.

Song nine: I've forgotten what feelings feel like.

Song ten: Oblivion.

Each replay ripping a chunk out of me. Ripping a chunk out of everyone who loves me. Bite after bite gnawed out of me – bites that didn't even taste good. I don't know how much flesh I have left. How much resilience I can keep reproducing.

I'm sketching all over the page now. Elizabeth's fading to background as I let self-hatred truly engulf me.

I ruin everything.

Because I'm a bad person.

And, by the time the session is over, I've coloured over all my positive so the whole paper is grey.

15

The afternoon is mainly about photography and alpacas. Jamie delights in telling everyone about my encounter with the pissing alpaca when we get shown around the farm and taught how to muck them out. I develop my self-portrait in art therapy. This place has a state-of-the-art darkroom, which is pretty much the best thing that's happened since I got out the car. Everything is new. Each machine, each tray of developing fluid. The art teacher, some guy called Dave, ran an "introduction to photography" session but let me just get on with things when I told him my experience. I have the blissful red tranquillity to myself as the others learn about shutter speeds and f-numbers and the rules of thirds. I develop my film, dry it, and play with the photo I took last night. It's a shock when the image comes into focus in the tray. Every part of me looks lost. My eyes are hardly focused, my limbs don't seem to belong to my body. I look like a ghost. And I'm still wigging out about it now I'm sitting here in Dr Jones's office for my very first one-to-one therapy session.

"So, Olive," Dr Jones says, leaning back in her big soft green chair. "How are you doing? Your first day going all right?"

I shrug. "I guess. I like the food."

She smiles. "And the place? Your fellow campers?"

"Yeah, it's fine I guess."

"You guess?"

"I dunno. Is all this...is it really going to work?"

She makes a note in her pad before she replies. "What do you mean by 'work', Olive?"

"Am I going to get better? I mean, the food is great and I love that you have a darkroom and alpacas and stuff but, like, is that really all it takes? I take some photos? Recite a few positive affirmations? Stroke a llama? Tell you about my childhood and then – poof – no more mental health problem?"

She makes more notes, but gives a small smile and holds eye-contact as she does, which I guess is some kind of therapy trick. "What does 'better' mean to you, Olive? I'm interested to know what that looks like in your head."

I feel like that's not answering my question, but I reply anyway. "It's not so much what it looks like, but what it doesn't look like."

"I see."

"I want to go to places and not freak out if there's noise. I want days where I feel sad but it's just sadness because something sad has happened. I don't want to feel sad for no reason and then completely freak out that this sadness is the start of ALL the sadness until I get to the point where I'm so sad about being sad that I give up and slump into numb." I hardly pause for breath. "And I want to be able to go out when I'm in the mood to go out and not vanish for two days and make friends with strangers and go back to their weird houses, or drink alcohol without drinking ALL the alcohol and waking up in a bed I don't know with some guy loads older than me who is so scary in the morning I climb out his bathroom window. And I don't want to worry all the time about how I'm feeling and whether it's normal and what it all means and if I need to go back to the GP or not. And it's not like I've got a black dog following me around but more like a huge pack of them, dragging me on my stomach through some dark wood and—"

She raises her hand to stop me and I gallop to a halt. "Sorry," I mumble.

"No, don't be sorry. I just worried you needed to breathe." She smiles in a way that makes me feel safe. "Do you need to breathe, Olive?"

"No. Yes." I realize I'm practically panting. "Yes, I guess." I focus for a moment on my breathing before I launch into yet more explanation.

"Better means worrying about normal stuff, like A levels and getting into uni, rather than whether next door are due to mow their lawn again any time soon. Better means being a good person who does good things, rather than being an erratic mess who hurts people and never knowing whether that's my fault or my malfunctioning brain's fault. Better just means…not being…me any more…" I run out of oxygen again, and Dr Jones uses this opportunity to veer me off track.

"Not being 'you' any more? What's wrong with being you, Olive?"

I'm a bad person.

Although I'm supposed to stop thinking that. *I am a good person who tries their best…*apparently.

"Well not, not me. I'll always be me, obviously. But me without all…without all…the crap."

She leaves a silence at that. And the quietness does what I guess it's supposed to do. It unravels me slightly from whatever spring I've wound myself up into. Dr Jones doesn't speak again until I've leaned back on my seat and stopped jiggling my foot.

"Olive, I can't make any promises," she starts. "There isn't a magic wand I can wave to give you the life you want."

I cross my arms. "Then why the heck am I here?"

I mean, seriously? The woman has just set up a camp to make people better, and she's claiming on day one it might not work. What the hell kind of shit show is this?

"Coming here will hopefully help you understand why you are the way you are, and we can explore ways you can start challenging unhelpful thoughts you have that lead to you feeling stuck in an unhelpful pattern. Does that make sense?"

It doesn't really, but I nod anyway. I'm not sure why.

"I think we should shelve what recovery looks like for today, and just focus on getting to know each other. We'll be seeing a lot of each other over the next month and I hope you'll feel able to talk to me openly and honestly. To start with, it would be useful for me to know where this all started." She leans back in her chair, matching my body language. "Why don't you tell me what's been going on with you?"

It's all a mess but I try. I tell her about how I've always been a weird kid. That Mum and Dad tell me stories of my "moods". That I would have huge tantrums they couldn't get me out of. That I didn't sleep through the night until I was past eight years old.

"How do you know all this?" she asked.

"Mum and Dad told me."

"I see."

I can see where she's trying to go with this and I stop her.

"I asked!" I tell her. "It's not like they woke me up one morning and said, 'Hey, Olive, here's an anthology of all the times you were a total jerk as a child.'"

Another long pause. "You think you were a jerk as a child?"

"You know what I mean."

And I start to worry then. Because isn't this the most clichéd thing ever? For a therapist to try and get you to blame everything on your parents? And isn't this place supposed to be cutting-edge?

"Look, my parents didn't mess me up," I tell her, keen for her to understand this. "It's not that way around. I'm the one who's messed them up. I've ruined their lives."

I win the biggest pause of the day. If there was a Pause Olympics, I'd get the gold medal.

"That's an…interesting thing to say," Dr Jones lets out eventually. After writing half a freaking essay on her notepad.

"Look, let's not pretend that isn't the case," I say, trying to tough it out, when really my throat is closing and my lungs are shrinking and I don't like thinking about this. Although I do think about it. All the time. It's my "core belief" apparently.

"What do you mean?"

I blink three times.

One, two, three.

And then make myself say it. "I've ruined their lives because I'm a terrible person."

She doesn't react. Instead she says, "That's a very strong statement to make, Olive. Why do you think you're a terrible person?" A further flurry of notes across her notepad.

"Because I do terrible things that hurt people." And, then, just like that, my highlights reel of Terrible Awful Things I've Done starts to play in my head. Oh, here's the look on Dad's face when I ran out of his birthday barbecue and embarrassed him in front of our extended family. And here's a lovely memory of the sound of Mum sobbing in fear through the locked bathroom door because I'd barricaded myself in there and she thought I was doing something stupid. Right on time, let's welcome in the wonderful brain reflux of Ally and the countless ways I've let her down as a friend – by flaking, by leaving her alone at school for weeks, by always making it about me. And, finally, let's not forget all the sneers and wrinkled noses and whispers that accompanied me as I walked through the corridors at school after I'd slept with Bella's boyfriend.

And I don't want to talk about it any more. Because what's the point? It's all going to go away because I'm here to fix it and I won't ever be looked at like that again and I won't hurt anyone again. I notice the bracelet on my tanned arm.

"I'm still not sure what the deal is with these," I say, showing mine off.

Dr Jones makes yet another note. "I thought we explained in the induction, but I'm happy to go through it again. What questions do you have?"

"I don't understand why you need to know all this stuff."

"To help us help you."

"By knowing our sleeping patterns? What we've eaten? What our mood diary says?"

She nods. "Yes."

"But how…? How does that help? What do you use the information for?"

Dr Jones pauses for a moment and rests her notebook on her knee. "Well, in the interests of full disclosure, the main purpose of the information is to help keep you all safe."

"Safe?"

She nods. "We feed the stats we get from our clients into an algorithm that helps predict suicidal behaviour. As I said in the induction, a requirement of being here is that you're not considered a risk to yourself, but we, of course, feel you can never be too careful. The algorithm can pick up on changes in behaviour that could be seen as risky, and sends out early alerts to staff that a client may be veering in that... direction. Then we can intervene, give extra support, and hopefully help avoid a situation that's emotionally painful for everyone involved."

"So it's all to do with suicide?"

"Not all of it, but that's its main usage." She crosses and uncrosses her legs. "I know it sounds sci-fi, Olive, but it's really not that new. Lots of mental health facilities are starting to use this kind of technology. It's quite remarkable what we can do these days when we combine technology with mental health. Do you feel like it's invading your privacy? Is that your concern?"

"It's not that...maybe..." I'm not sure what it is. I'm not sure how I feel. I have a flash. Of the rain. Of the smashed window of the greenhouse. Of the screaming inside me. The voices that told me to do things that I wouldn't be able to take back. If I'd been wearing that bracelet, would it all still have happened? "I just don't understand how anyone can predict anything like that," I say. "I mean, surely it's all so sudden? And so individual?"

"It is, it can be." She wrinkles her nose and I can tell she's not happy we've gone off topic. Part of me feels I should leave it. Not waste time. I'm here to get better – not worry about how. If it works, it works. That's all I need, right?

"Look, Olive. Suicidal behaviour is a complex issue. Just like any symptom of mental illness. Although it's also a life-threatening symptom, and therefore one we prioritize. And, even though it's very complex, that doesn't mean there aren't patterns to it. Things that through quantitative analysis, we're able to see as indicators."

"I have no idea what half those words mean."

She smiles. "Quantitative just means 'looking at lots of numbers', I guess. Analysis of statistics. Through that we've been able to design the algorithm but, really, honestly, Olive? I feel like we're getting off point here. I want to get to know you a bit better. Why don't you tell me about photography? Dave tells me you've started some kind of self-portrait project? I'd love to hear more about that."

16

I think about it.

And I think about it.

And

I

Think about

It.

Algorithm…

Suicide…

Mental illness…

Technology…

My brain feels like a top quality Swiss watch – every cog turning perfectly, tick, tick, ticking towards something that feels like it could be very important indeed. I am an oyster and Dr Jones has given me a piece of grit to wriggle on, and if I wriggle hard enough I just feel it's going to turn into the most glorious of pearls.

It's a good distraction really, as things with Hannah

escalate over the following introductory days.

"That's the girl," she whispers to Liv as I come in for breakfast.

"The girl what?" I ask outright, but they twist away from me in their chairs.

Within three days, I've heard on the grapevine. Apparently, according to Hannah, I "think I'm better than everyone" and "don't believe in their mental illness", which is so ridiculous that I push it away. I pretend it's not happening, and instead I think some more about my bracelet and algorithms and what Dr Jones said. I lie awake at night, listening to the hissing of my white-noise machine, thinking about it and staring up at the freshly painted ceiling.

I think about it in group therapy, as Hannah fills us all in on which smells are and aren't okay. (Drain smells, BO smells, cow manure = not okay. She hasn't been anywhere near the farm section of the camp.) I think about it in art therapy as I take another self-portrait. I think about it as the image comes alive in the developer tray under the soothing red. Jamie comes in at one point, proudly cradling his first ever roll of developed film. "This would be a great place to…you know," he says, patting the table suggestively.

"Shh, I'm trying to think."

I think about it through lunch and the afternoon and the evening, when I say goodnight to everyone and go to bed at eight fifteen. I think about it the next day and the next day.

I feel like I'm onto something. Something huge. I think

about it as I muck out the alpacas, and I think about it as I swim twenty lengths of the swimming pool, and I think about it every spare moment even though I'm supposed to be telling myself, *I would prefer it if I am a nice person who tries their best.*

I take my morning antidepressant, which really seems to be working, and I think about it. I think about it in CBT when my therapist, Dr Nada, suggests not using my white-noise machine that night and I laugh at the sheer impossibility of that. I think about it in my therapy sessions with Dr Jones. She wants to know about my early years. How safe did I feel as a child? And I tell her over and over, I don't know and I can't remember. But mostly I tune her out and nod when I feel I'm supposed to nod because I know I am on the cusp of something and I have a feeling it's going to be really good.

The days go past in a weird blur of everyone getting to know one another. The group has divided, somewhat predictably, into quasi groups based on diagnoses. Hannah and Sophie hang out a lot with Liv, who also has OCD. They sit in the corner and share their lists of things that they can't stand, all while giving me evils, making it clear they also can't stand me and that's nothing to do with their OCD. Three of the boys, Darrell and Kieran and Alex, clump together as depressives. Gabriella comes out of her sad patch and returns with a vengeance, making friends with everyone – squealing loudly in pet therapy, forcing everyone to look at her work in art therapy. She's also developed an irritating habit of saying "Me too" whenever anyone admits anything in group.

"I have OCD about smells."

"Oh, me too."

"I self-harmed really badly during my depressive periods."

"Oh me too." And she'll roll up her sleeves and show us her angry arms that are more scar than skin.

The pale boy, Lewis, mostly floats from group to group, hardly speaking to anyone. And I'm way too busy thinking so I float a bit too. I eat with Jamie but hardly socialize. The days pass and I just think about it. Look at my bracelet and think about it. Fill in my emotion diary and think about it. And then…

Day six. It's almost lunchtime and we're doing a mindfulness workshop. It's run by Elizabeth, who asks us how our core self-beliefs are coming on and I blush because, if I'm being honest about it, I've sort of forgotten about them. I've not really been taking as much notice of camp, and all the things I'm supposed to be doing at camp, as I should. But I'm not worried because I'm quite certain that this irritating thought of mine is going to produce something great. Don't ask me how I know, I just know, all right?

"Now, everyone, take a mat from the corner. Make sure you're not too hot or too cold before we begin."

I cannot imagine ever being cold again. The August sun is honking and fat in the sky, the air heavy with humidity.

It's been killing me sleeping with my windows closed, but I do not trust there not to be noise if I open them. There's a pile of mats and I pad over and drag one to the corner, my bare feet sticking to the wooden floor. Everyone copies me and soon we're sitting cross-legged like we're about to start a yoga class. I cannot settle as Elizabeth starts droning on about the benefits of mindfulness and the present moment and the power of breathing. The thoughts that have been banging against the door of my brain feel like they're about to smash through. *Thud thud thud.* The wood is breaking. *Thud thud thud.* The defences have almost been breached.

"Now, everyone, if you could lie down on your backs, with your legs slightly apart. Yes, that's good. It's comfier if you let your feet fall out to the side."

I wiggle down my mat and lie flat but my body can't keep still. My hands tap on my stomach, my feet twitch from side to side.

"You all comfy and relaxed?" Elizabeth's voice coos.

There is silence as an answer, even though I'm thinking *no*. I look from side to side but everyone else's eyes are closed. Even Jamie's.

"Now, I want you all to start by just breathing in slowly. Feeling your chest expand as your lungs fill with oxygen."

I try and take a long breath, but I can't seem to make my lungs bigger as I do. In fact, as I breathe in, my stomach sucks in. Is that supposed to happen?

"And feel your chest contract as you exhale…"

Oh, okay, no, the opposite is supposed to happen. It takes me five or so breaths to get it right.

"Now, focus on the weight of your body sinking into the floor. Notice which parts of your body are in contact with the floor. Do you feel light or heavy today? Do you feel tired or alert? Remember there's no right or wrong, just notice…"

I feel my shoulder blades digging into the mat. They've always stuck out a bit too much. Ally finds them hilarious. Whenever I turn round, she jumps back and says, "Watch out, don't get me with your weapon." I try and focus on my feet, how they're hanging off the mat and touching the wooden floor. But I think, *How is there an algorithm to suicide? How can that even work?* And it must work because, if it didn't, then they wouldn't be using it. And if there's an algorithm for suicide and suicidal feelings are a symptom of mental health problems then…

"And I want you to start listening to the noises around you. Try not to have an emotional response to the noise, just notice."

Oh boy. Focusing on noise. Well, I'm bound to get top marks in this section of mindfulness. Right, I can hear the slight gurgle in Gabriella's throat as she breathes heavily next to me. That's quite annoying actually. Hang on, not supposed to have an emotional reaction to it… *Gurgle gurgle.* Gurgle in, gurgle out. Actually, it's more like a gurgle in and a rasp out. *Gurgle, rasp. Gurgle, rasp.* Ahh, REALLY annoying. I'll try listening to something else. I let my ears scan the room. There is a clock. A loud ticking one. I've not heard the ticks until now which is strange, because they must have always been there. *Tick tock tick tock tick... What if my bracelet could be used for something else?*

"And, now," Elizabeth interrupts, "I want you all to focus on just letting your mind go blank. Whenever you have a thought, which you will, because minds have a tendency to do that" – I can hear the gentle smile in her voice – "well, don't beat yourself up. Just acknowledge the thought and then let it go. Acknowledge and let go."

Sounds easy enough. And this mindfulness stuff is supposed to be very good for me, and I want to be better. I wiggle on my mat and let my brain go blank.

Blank.

Just blank.

Wow – look how good I am! Totally blank. I am the Queen of Blank.

Hang on. That's a thought. Shit.

I have acknowledged the thought and now I will go back to blank.

Blank.

...

...

GABRIELLA, YOUR BREATHING IS SO NOISY.

Whoops. Sorry, blankness. Sorry, Gabriella.

Blank.

How is this supposed to help my brain? All it's doing is giving it even more attention than it usually gets. Blank.

Blank.

Bl…

I don't trust this camp.

This is a thought I have. And I suddenly know it is correct and that I'm totally in the right about this.

I don't think they know what they're doing. I think they're just huge money-grabbing idiots who are going to trick loads of rich families out of their cash. I mean, I've been here a week and I've only got three left and I don't feel any different. I mean, sure the rooms are nice and the alpacas are fun and the swimming pool is nice, and dare I say it, the coconut porridge is really something, but I still don't think this is going to stop my brain grabbing the steering wheel whenever the hell it wants to and driving me into a ditch and oh fuck I'm supposed to be not thinking about anything.

Think blank.

Think blankness.

Think…

I think I'm better than this place. I think I know better. No, I know I know better. I can't explain why. I just know.

Think…

I think I am cleverer than this camp. That is the truth. I think, maybe, I've cracked it. Because…because…

"Now," Elizabeth disrupts my concentration. Again. "Just a reminder. Don't follow your thoughts. If you find yourself buying into a thought then just notice, acknowledge and then return to the present moment."

Dammit! Where was I?

I feel my chest move in and out, in and out. I hear Gabriella's gargles. I feel the warm wind gently brushing my closed eyelids as it whispers through the open window. I smell the faint aroma of lunch coming from the kitchen. I feel every limb in my body tingle as though it's charging in a battery pack, my fingers twitching, my feet wanting to tap dance...because here it is. Here's the thought. The thought that it's taken a week to give birth to...like laying a really huge important egg.

If there's an algorithm for suicide, there must be algorithms for other mental health things.

There is a formula to mental illness.

My fists clench with excitement. My breath catches in my throat. Oh God. This is something, this is something, this is something.

What if I can...*find the formula for my own sanity?*

Oh my, oh my, oh my. If I can find the formula, if I can balance the equation, I will always stay well! It's just a puzzle that needs to be solved! I sit up. I sit right up. Lurching up like I have rigor mortis. Everyone is lying like dead donkeys around me. I do not have time for this nonsense. This isn't how I get better. This isn't what I should be doing. They're wrong and I'm right and OH MY GOD I'M NEVER GOING TO GET ILL AGAIN.

"Olive?" Elizabeth whispers, crouching down next to me. "Is everything okay?"

"I have to go," I tell her. I'm scrambling up. I need to get this down before I lose it. I feel like I'm cradling liquid gold in my cupped hands but it's draining out of the gaps between my fingers. I need to get out of here. Out of this silly room, with these silly people lying on the floor, waiting for sanity to find them, when sanity is actually out THERE, waiting to be found. I need to capture this gold. I need to drink it.

I rush out of the room, jumping over bodies. I see Jamie open his eyes and give me a *what-the-hell?* look but I don't have time for him right now. I'm about to dash off down the corridor but Elizabeth calls after me.

"Olive? OLIVE?"

I sigh and stop. Each moment I'm not capturing this is a waste. But, the quicker I lose her, the quicker I can get on with this. "Yes?" I say, trying to keep my voice calm when inside I'm dancing and twirling and want to grab her hands and get her to tap-dance with me.

"Are you okay? Are you… Have you had a panic attack? Sometimes mindfulness can be uncomfortable."

"What?"

"I mean, that's fine, Olive. That's totally okay. You can build up to it."

"I'm good."

She tilts her head to one side.

No. Don't delay me. Don't try and get me into an interaction. I have no time for interactions. I have no time even for an "inter", let alone an "action".

"But you're leaving."

I'm already turning on my heel. I can leave at any time. Nothing is compulsory, they said. "Yes, but I'm fine.

Honestly!" I widen my eyes. "I just need to go to my room for a while and…"

I don't bother to finish the sentence. I run down the corridor, run up the stairs, my bare feet feel so good as they rush through the thick new carpet and I don't even know if Elizabeth calls after me and I don't even care because I've got it. By bloody ho, I've got it. And nothing is ever going to be bad ever again. More importantly, *I'm never going to be bad ever again.*

17

It's almost unbearable being in my room when I'm feeling like this. I want to run across the lawn and whoop and sing. I've never felt so much hope in my entire life. It's like someone's attached me to the end of a tube of toothpaste of it and then jumped on the tube. I rip off a piece of paper headed *Camp Reset* and start writing it down, snapping the lead off my pencil as I do. I'm too impatient to even sharpen it and just grab a new pencil out of the drawer.

I write:

Algorithm to sanity?
Maths to mental health?
Is there a formula?

Then I write:

Find Lewis...

He'll still be in mindfulness, which is unacceptable if you ask me. I'm just about to go back there and try and get him out, when I hear a knock at my door. I jump.

"Who is it?" I ask cautiously.

"It's Grace."

I roll my eyes but get up to let her in. She's standing there grinning like a maniac, like she's about to try and appease me. I tilt my head and wait for it.

"Just checking you're all right," she says. "Elizabeth says you've left mindfulness?"

"I'm fine," I reply. Because I am. "I thought they said in our induction that things weren't compulsory?"

Her smile gets wider. "They're not. But we still want to make sure you're okay."

"Well, I'm fine. I just, er, needed a nap." I step in front of the gap in the door so she can't see my paper-strewn desk.

"Well don't sleep too long. You've got lunch."

"Thanks." I want to add "Mum" afterwards, as I'm feeling a little bit checked-up-on and annoyed, but I'd rather just get rid of her so I can focus on my breakthrough. I smile and wave as she walks off and then mutter the word "Witch" after I close my door.

Waiting for lunch almost kills me and I grab Lewis to one side the moment I spot him in the cafeteria queue.

"Hey, Lewis. Let's go on a walk!"

He looks down at his tray of food. "Umm, I need to eat."

Why? Why would he need to eat at a time like this?

"Okay, I'll sit with you, then we can go for a walk."

"O...kay," he says slowly and I follow him to a table.

I watch as he takes his lunch items off the tray, which he does much more normally than half the other people here. Sophie takes about half an hour to set all her food out in the correct way; Hannah checks the smell of all of hers. She catches my eye and then turns to Sophie and whispers to her before giggling. But I don't give a crap about that right now. I'm just watching Lewis, who lifts up his bowl of soup and places it on the table, alongside a rosemary and sea-salt artisan roll.

"You're eating soup?" I ask.

"What's wrong with soup?"

"It's, like, ten million degrees outside."

"Well, I like soup." He rips his bread into chunks and dips bits into his soup. Just as he's about to take a bite, he sees me watching. "Are you not eating?"

I shake my head. "Not hungry."

"Well, can you not watch me eat if that's the case?"

"Okay okay. I'll look away."

I cover both my eyes with my hands and I hear him mutter, "That makes it worse," under his breath. I stay in the dark for a moment. It's quite nice here behind my hands. I can hear the clattering of the canteen. I hear Gabriella's voice over everyone else's. I can hear the birds outside, tweet-tweeting and Jamie complaining about the fact he can't play guitar here.

"Okay, so it was weird when you were watching me eat, but this is even weirder," Lewis says.

I take my hands away. "Sorry, I'm impatient. I need to

talk to you about something!"

He dips another piece of bread into his soup. He has a very big mouth. Big gums. Which is ironic considering he's so quiet. "Can't we talk here?" he asks.

"I don't want anyone else to hear."

Both his eyebrows draw up. "Jeez, what do you want to talk about?"

"You'll find out once you HURRY UP AND EAT ALREADY."

I tap my foot and drum my fingers and sing under my breath and nod my head to my own music until Lewis stands up with his soup only half finished. "Okay, I'm done already."

"Brilliant! Let's go."

Jamie sees us walk off and calls, "Hey, where you going?"

"For a walk."

I push Lewis's back to hurry him up. His face has gone all red as I guide us outside into the gorgeous summer air. God, it's a nice day. Not a cloud in the sky, which is as blue as a bluebottle who's the winner of a bluebottling beauty pageant.

"Shall we take a walk around the woods?" I suggest. "I've not gone into them yet, but Jamie did the other day and said they were pretty."

"Umm, yeah, okay..." Lewis's face is all blush now. It seeps up into his dark curled hair. I get the very distinct feeling that he isn't used to talking to girls. He's all stiff – no, not like that ha ha ha ha ha. But he follows me into the trees where the light falls on us all dappled through the leaves, scattering our bodies with yellow.

I find a little path and say, "Let's follow it," and run further in.

"God, this light is just EVERYTHING." I twirl and smile back at him. He returns it. The blush diminishing, him getting used to my presence.

"It really is pretty," he admits, looking up at the canopied ceiling – where the trees overlap and interlock but leave gaps to let the gold through. We walk further in – each twist in the path brings further joy to my innards. I am so relieved I've figured out what I'm supposed to do. We end up in this clearing, where a fallen tree provides the perfect seat.

"Let's sit down," I say, jumping up on the giant log.

Lewis sits down awkwardly. He's tall enough that the tips of his toes just about brush the ground. The change in tempo has stiffened him up again. His back is poker straight, but he keeps trying to make himself slump. I smile. I can almost hear him saying to himself in his head, *Play it cool, play it cool…* And even though I've not asked him out here for anything like that, I feel touched I've had that effect on him. It makes me feel all glowy and invincible.

"Thanks for coming."

He coughs, he blushes. "It's fine. Umm, what is it you wanted to talk about?"

I twist to face him and give him my most enigmatic grin. "Math."

"You mean maths?"

"Well I never know if saying it 'math' as a singular is just an American thing, and whether the English version is 'maths' plural. Or," I put on a posh British accent, "I guess I could just say 'mathematics', or…" I put on a crazy robot voice, "Mathamatica, which sounds like a kind of really awesome band, don't you think?"

"Umm…I guess…"

"You are into math, right? Or maths? I mean, I remember you saying you were."

He doesn't reply right away. He just twists his hands in his lap and says something quietly.

"What was that?"

"I said…umm…I'm just well…it's just you remembered."

I break into a grin. "Of course I remembered! It was interesting. One of the only interesting things ANYONE said actually."

He's so red now he may well turn purple. "I remember what you said too, about the banana skin."

"Well aren't we just the cutest?" I say, but this is the wrong thing to say because he is so far beyond red now that I think I may have to throw him into the ornamental pond back near the house so he can calm his face down. Anyway, we are getting off point and I'm getting impatient so I just blast through with it. "You said maths could change the world. And I don't know anything about maths, or anything about changing the world, so I was wondering if you could tell me more."

"Did you not do maths GCSE?"

I nod. "Yeah." And I was predicted a seven, and higher in all my other subjects. Oh God…my English exam…I so messed up my English exam. Nope. No-sir-ee. No time to think about that right now, thank you very much. "But I just kind of learned what I needed to learn to pass, you know?" I continue. "I never really UNDERSTOOD maths."

The corners of his eyes smile. "You're missing out!" he says. "Maths is everywhere and it's everything."

I scootch over to sit closer to him. His excitement for the subject kind of vibrates off him and it's like a magnet, guiding me in. He notices my closer proximity and gets even redder.

"Tell me all about it. Please."

He opens his mouth, hesitates. "You really want me to talk about maths?"

I nod. "Yes!"

"Nobody EVER wants me to talk about maths."

"Well *I* want you to talk about maths."

He opens his mouth again, unsure. "And this isn't a wind-up?"

I scrunch my face up. "Why would this be a wind-up?"

"Because you're a pretty girl, sitting next to me, asking me to talk about maths. This doesn't happen to me. Ever."

I raise an eyebrow. "Oh, so I'm pretty now, am I?"

There is nowhere else on his face left that isn't already red to get redder, but somehow he manages it. I smile wickedly as he stumbles and dies and essentially crawls out of his skin.

"Oh God, I didn't mean it like that. Sorry. Well, like I did mean it, obviously, but oh God, that isn't what I was trying to say, I'm not sure what I was trying to say."

I move closer so we're sitting butt to butt. This is fun. I'm momentarily distracted from my life-changing brilliant idea of brilliance. "Talk to girls much, Lewis?"

He hangs his head. "Umm. No. Is it that obvious?"

"Well, I think it's cute."

The compliment destroys what is left of him. I'm surprised he doesn't combust. I feel a flash of guilt for winding him up and sadness that he's probably never been called cute before. Because it's not like he isn't cute. He'll probably be even more so in a few years' time when he's out of school and doesn't walk like he hates every inch of his body and cuts his hair properly and gains enough self-confidence to own his shit.

He surprises me by pulling it together, leaning over and picking up a long twig. "Yes," he says, with quiet confidence. "You are pretty. And I can explain why, using maths." He draws a line in the dirt and then another shorter line underneath it. "There's this thing in maths called the Golden Ratio. It's basically the maths of beauty. Essentially everything in nature is proportioned to this ratio of 1:618. So the width of your mouth is 1.618 in ratio to the width of your nose. Or your two front teeth are 1.618 ratio to the teeth next to them. This ratio is everywhere. It's in flowers, it's in animal markings. And, generally, the more aligned you are to this ratio, the more beautiful." His voice has stopped shaking as he draws a triangle in the dirt. I lean over to look. "You can build a whole face on the ratio. Some mathematicians have even made a mask of the golden ratio and put it on top of photos of famous models. Kate Moss's face fits it perfectly." He puts his twig down and looks right up at me. He holds his finger against my face and it's my turn to go red. His touch sends tiny fireworks across my chin. Even though his face is all serious, scientific, his eyebrows furrowed in concentration. "A-ha, I knew it." He leans back. "Your face is well ratioed. I mean, I'm only measuring using my finger of course, but, still, when I said you were pretty, I meant scientifically. Mathematically. That's all. And well…" He looks down again and trails off.

I knock him with my shoulder. "So I'm only pretty because maths say so?" I tease.

He doesn't laugh, only gets flustered. "That's not what I meant. I mean, it's just maths. I mean, you're pretty in other ways too, but, oh God…sorry." He finally laughs when he sees I am. "So, umm, what did you want to talk to me about?" he asks. "What do you want to know about maths?"

I point to his arm. "You know these bracelets they've been making us wear?"

"Well, they're not *making* us wear them, are they? But yes."

I wonder why he needed to correct me. It makes me feel slightly irritated but I'm too excited to care for longer than a second.

"They're recording our eating, our sleep, how much

exercise we do, alongside all our diary entries. Right?"

"Yeeeees," he says slowly.

"And they say they're making us wear them for our own safety? So it alerts them if we're suicidal."

"Yes." I see his eyes glint, oh he's almost there. He's almost with me.

"So, don't you see?" I gallop on. "There's a MATHS to suicide. All this data they're collecting is somehow being put into some mathematical formula that can detect changes in human behaviour... I didn't know you could use maths for something like that. Did you?"

He nods wildly now. "Oh yes. This is the new big thing in maths. It's called Big Data. Big Data is the best!" His hands fly madly as he talks. "We all generate so much data now – from being constantly on our phones, from shopping with our debit cards, from wearing Fitbits. And all this data is being collected. We're literally pumping out data about what it means to be a human all the time. Mathematicians don't even know where to start with it."

I'm nodding with him. He's here, he gets this. He's essentially saying it all for me. I want to grasp his hands, press hard against his fingers. My mouth is stretched into a wide grin.

"Like, did you know food shops can tell if you're pregnant before you do?" he continues. "They have your buying habits data through your store card. They also have the data of what pregnant people buy. Combine that data and WHAM!" He claps his hands. "You buy a carton of juice or something and they can tell you're pregnant before you've even taken a test."

"Yes, yes, yes!" I say. "And that's what these bracelets do! They know we're going to have a complete meltdown before we even do."

He sits back on the log. "I guess I've not thought about it, but, yeah." He laughs up at the sky. "I'm not sure WHY I've not thought about it. It's definitely the sort of thing I think about. When Dr Jones mentioned algorithms on the first day it got my interest, but then I've been so busy with getting used to this place and working on getting better that I forgot about it. I can't believe I forgot about it."

I smile over at him but he won't smile back because he's already formulating under his breath.

"God, you're right. I mean, there's maths even in suicide! I've never thought about it. But, of course there is. I wonder what data they use... Oh God, I wonder how they even begin to make that algorithm. I guess they would need to feed age into it...and maybe geographic location...and family history and..."

"Lewis?"

"I mean...I guess they need to personalize the algorithm too. That must be why they ask us to fill in the diaries, but, oh God, the variables would be infinite..."

"Lewis?"

"What else? I guess they'd factor in previous attempts, and the mental health diagnosis...those would each have their own probabilities and risk factors..."

"LEWIS!"

He comes back to earth. This tiny bit of beautiful earth where the sun is shining and the birds are tweeting and I'm potentially about to cure myself of my broken brain.

"Sorry, I got carried away."

"It's fine. I mean, this is why I need you. I was hoping you could help me?"

"Help you what?"

I bite my lip. "Make an algorithm?"

He laughs at first, revealing all his gums. "Oh, okay then. I have a spare five minutes later, I'll just whip you up an algorithm," he says sarcastically.

"Look, I know it's not easy. But we can try, right? I'm not even sure if I *need* an algorithm, I've just got this idea. About the bracelets, and what they mean."

"What's your idea?"

I take a breath, fill my lungs, and get ready to spill it out. My magical solution. Well, not magical – mathematical. "Well, you were saying maths was everywhere, right?" I start. "So that got me to thinking, if there's a formula for suicide – which you could argue is a sign of 'insanity' – then there *must* be a formula for sanity. *A maths to not going crazy.* Don't you see? If we can crack this, we'll both get better. We won't need to be here. We won't need bracelets to alert people we're in danger, because we'll never be in danger again! We can just follow the formula and be sane constantly. Imagine that. Think about it. No relapse. No meds. No time off school. No dreading waking up in the morning because you've still got the same brain and it bullies you all day every day… Just – you know. Sanity! The end of all this."

Lewis falls quiet. He stays quiet.

"Is it doable?" I cannot bear his silence. If he says this won't work, if he says it's too hard, I'm not sure what I will do. He doesn't answer. "Lewis?!"

He looks up at me. "So, let me get this straight… You're thinking we could turn a mathematical formula into a *preventative treatment*?"

I nod so very ferociously. "Yes! Is that possible?"

He looks down for a moment, and when he looks back up, his eyes are shining. "Olive?" he half-whispers. "I think it might be doable."

"It's not too complicated?"

He chews on his lip, then shakes his head. "It won't be the easiest, but the theory behind any algorithm is always really simple. They're just a set of steps that complete a task. We use them all the time. You use an algorithm when you walk to and from school, you use one when you make a cheese toasted sandwich. They're not as scary as people think. They're just a method of getting things done in the easiest way."

I launch my nuclear smile and grab his hands between mine because I'm excited and also really feel like being touched again. "And our current task is how to stay sane in the easiest way! It's something, right?" I say.

He looks down at our entwined fingers and his face glows in the sun. He pulls away and I try not to mind. "It's going to be hard though."

"But you're good enough at math, right?"

He nods and scratches his neck. He won't look at me again. "Well I'm only sixteen. And I only came third in the National Young Mathematics Award this year," he says, bitterly. "But I can try, right?"

"Right!" I pump my fist. I feel happier already. At the hope of a cure. Maybe even *thinking* there's a solution to your mental health problem helps your mental health? Maybe they should find a way of bottling hope and selling it in pharmacies. And we could pour a dose out on measuring spoons each morning and shove it into our mouths to get through each day. What would hope taste like, anyway? Sunshine, like today. And floral scents – daisies. And honey. Hang on, getting off topic, getting off topic. Lewis seems lost too. He's picked up the stick again and is leaning over, scribbling away in the dusty ground.

I'm grinning and it's hot and suddenly I cannot stay still in this little clearing any more. I need to move my body. I need to let my energy out. I feel like running. Really far and really fast, seeing how far I can go.

I jump off the log and turn to Lewis. "Let's walk."

He scrambles to his feet and we stride back into trees, the cooler air a welcome relief. He looks at his wrist. "Lunch finished twenty minutes ago. We're late for art therapy."

"They'll cope without us." I hop over a log. "So, where do we go from here? How do you even go about building a sanity algorithm?"

He carefully steps over the log I just vaulted. "Well,

you need to feed things into it. Imagine an algorithm as an insatiably hungry monster who wants to eat data. You need to feed it data. More data and more data and more data. So, if you're walking to school, you need data about all the different routes you could take before you could build the best algorithm. Or, if you were making a grilled cheese sandwich, you'd need data about all the different types of bread, types of cheese, toasting methods, et cetera. If you keep shovelling data inside its mouth, eventually you find patterns."

"Does the monster poo them out?"

"No," he says, incapable of joking about his beloved maths. "The monster does not *poo them out*. Mathematicians have to then make algorithms that can sift through the data and find the best solution. Imagine an algorithm as a customized sieve, with a particular pattern of holes. You plunge each one into the water and each different sieve will catch different things."

"You really like maths, don't you?" I ask. Because I've never seen his face glow as much as it does now.

He holds back a branch for me, standing aside to let me pass. "I do," he nods. "I like that it always has explanations and answers. I like how it makes sense of the world. Otherwise…" He steps past the branch too and it goes flying back when he lets go. "Otherwise, I tend to find the world quite…difficult. Understanding it helps me cope with it, I guess."

"And imagine if you made an algorithm that helped keep your brain in check," I say. "Imagine how much easier it would be to cope then!"

"I guess. Isn't that what this place is for, though?"

I roll my eyes as I shake my head. "Hardly! They're just telling us to take deep breaths and whinge about our childhoods. Not really groundbreaking, is it?" Not like this. Not like a personalized mathematical formula made into a treatment plan. This is so much better. So, so much better. He has to realize this – he must! I give him my full beam smile with added eyelash flutters and wide-eyed vulnerability. "Please say you'll help me, Lewis."

He practically staggers backwards from the force of my charm. "Of course. Of course I'll help you."

The trees are thicker overhead. I think we may've taken a wrong turn, but I don't mind. I quite like it. The feeling of being lost.

"You've not spoken in group yet," I say, glancing over at him. "So I'm not sure why you're at camp."

His cheeks redden. "Same with you. Though I guess nobody knows why you're here if you don't even know."

I roll my eyes again. "Does everyone hate me for it as much as Hannah does?"

He doesn't reply straight away. "I just don't think everyone understands it." He sighs and pushes past another low-hanging branch. "Actually, the way Hannah's treated you makes me scared to talk in group."

I leave space for him to spill, sensing he won't talk if I fill the silence. Fucking Hannah! It's one thing to go after me, but if her behaviour actively puts other patients off getting help. ARGH.

We grind to a halt and stand facing each other in the dark tunnel of trees. "I have this thing called Pure O," Lewis admits. He shakes his head. "I hate that title. It sounds like an energy drink. But, essentially, I suffer from obsessive thoughts. Like all the time. One particular thought especially."

I'm never sure what to say when people get serious. I always panic and say the wrong thing because I'm a terrible person. So I find myself saying, "Ooooo, what is it?"

He doesn't laugh. He stiffens, shakes. His fists clench in on themselves. Oh God, he's panicking. "Shit, sorry. Lewis, you don't need to tell me. I'm sorry. I was trying to joke."

He keeps shaking his head and, when he looks up, I see tears in his eyes.

"Why don't we sit down?" I suggest.

We smile at each other and he squats down and leans back against the tree with me, his breath still shallow.

"You okay?"

He nods and we both quieten so he can catch up on his oxygen.

"I'm worried the others won't get it," Lewis says quietly. "Because what I have is just thoughts. I don't need to do any compulsive behaviours like with full-blown OCD. It's just the thought. It's only one, but it's so overwhelming. But I don't have to separate my food, or touch things a certain number of times, or clean everything, or line things up, or whatever it is people with OCD do. I'm just tortured by this one thought." I hear him swallow. "What if no one believes me?"

I twist to look at him and raise one eyebrow. "Then screw them?"

"What if they think I don't deserve to be here because I only have thoughts? Nothing else."

"I repeat. Then, screw them?"

He shakes his head. "You don't mince your words, do you?"

I shrug. "Never have. Look, don't let Hannah put you off. Yes, she has OCD, and yes that's very sad for her, but she's also a bell-end. I'm sure they don't shove us into group therapy just for the sake of it. Maybe you need to open up a bit? I'll be your bodyguard if you want?"

"Great...a girl as my bodyguard."

"Hey! Yes, there's no wifi here, but that's no excuse to pretend we're in the nineteen-fifties."

"Bollocks, that's a point," he says. "It's going to be harder to get all the data we need without the internet."

"We've got an hour tomorrow in the computer lab," I remind him.

"We'll have to make the most of it then. Get as much data as we can. We need to look into all the different ways people stay sane, and then combine that with knowledge about ourselves. Things that we know help us. Then we can combine the data and start building a treatment plan based on maths." He trails off and looks down at his wrist again. "Everyone will be wondering what's happened to us."

I stretch up my arms, feeling my back crunch as I do so. "You okay to go back?"

He nods and starts getting up. "Yeah, sorry about that."

"Don't apologize."

I don't want to go back to camp. I want to stay here in the woods and use Lewis's brain for solving my riddle. But I sense he isn't a natural deviant, and don't want to push him too far in one day.

We make our way back towards the house, ducking under branches, the sunlight speckling our faces. Five minutes later we emerge back into the sunshine proper. I stop for a moment, looking back at the house. Part of me really doesn't want to go in. I don't want the cool air-conditioned air, the long corridors feeling like they're holding me in. I don't want to go from A to B depending on what a timetable says. I'm enjoying being here with Lewis, on the cusp of something important – a cure as well as a potential friendship. Lewis stops next to me and I look over. He's sweating in the heat. His T-shirt sticks to his thin chest and his hair curls around his neck.

"So, what's going on with you and Jamie?" he asks, totally out of the blue.

"What?" I screw my face up. "Nothing! Why?"

"Oh, sorry. Everyone says something is going on."

I sigh and feel my tummy twist up. No, no, no. I don't want to feel bad. Not now. Not today thank you very much. I'm only just starting to feel better again. "Who's everyone?"

It's occurring to Lewis he's made a mistake and he's now sweating more than ever. "Not everyone. Well, it's just something Hannah mentioned..."

I throw my head back. "Ahh, of course! God, WHAT DID I DO to that girl?" This is it. I'm done being nice to her. I don't care how ill she is. I'm ill too.

"Sorry, I didn't mean to upset you. And, well, I did think maybe you and Jamie…"

"Why?" I hiss. "Because he's a boy and I'm a girl and we smoked together once on the steps?"

"Look, I shouldn't have said anything. I'm not good at making conversation…"

I shake my head and storm across the grass, leaping from dark green stripe of lawn to light green stripe.

He streams behind me, apologizing. "Please, Olive. Really. I was just filling the silence. I should know better. And, well, Jamie implied."

I swish around. "What did he imply?"

"He's not said anything, but he's…he's…"

"What?" I demand. We're almost at the front steps.

Lewis's eyes are wide, his voice quivering from upset. I kind of want to give him a break but I'm too pissed off. Because this isn't the first time I've been here. This isn't a new thing. I'm always in this scenario somehow. Girls not liking me because I get on better with boys. Being asked if things are going on with boys that nothing is going on with. From my side anyway. Boys do tend to like me. I give off a vibe that I wish I didn't. I think it's because I'm all angles and how you're supposed to look, and that combined with me when I'm soaring… Well, they regularly think I'm a girl I'm not. And, to be honest, sometimes I am that girl and I've trodden on a few toes but it's never been intentional and I swear the hate I've got for it is out of proportion. Ninety per cent of the time, if I allow myself to think about it, I've felt...*used*. I really hoped some girls would like me here. That the problem was school people, not me. Obviously not. And I really thought Lewis and I might be friends. Why am I SO BAD at getting on with people?

"He just said he thought you were fit..." Lewis trails off.

"Well that MUST mean we're having sex," I say. "I mean, that's really why I came here after all. To get laid."

"I really am sorry." He stops on the step and he looks like he's about to cry, which pisses me off again because *I'm* the one who's been insulted. But I remember how stressed he was only ten minutes ago and try to rise above it.

"Look, it's okay. I'm more mad at Hannah than I am at you. And I'm just...bored of not being allowed to be friends with boys without it meaning something. I mean, I'm sixteen. Surely we're too old for this?"

He's nodding. "I know, I agree. I don't know why I said it."

"Don't worry. I'm used to it." I think of the words that have been used for me – slut, bitch, psycho, snake, whore, cheap.

"Look, we all have our labels," Lewis puts forward as an olive branch. "I've been called 'creepy' my whole life if that helps?" We climb up the white marbly stairs and the cool air-con hits me. "Because I'm too shy to talk to anyone properly so I just sit on the edges and watch. Which is mysterious if you're good-looking, but I'm not good-looking so I just get called creepy."

We steer our way towards the art room and I shake my head. "You're good-looking," I tell him. "Your problem is just CONFIDENCE."

He lets out an exasperated sigh. "If I had a pound for every time someone's said that to me."

We push through a double door into the art room and everyone looks up from their canvases. Jamie's looking from me to Lewis in disbelief. Hannah is at the back with Sophie, her face all scrunched up in disgust at our late arrival. Something bubbles up in me and I can't be bothered to suppress it.

"Oi, Hannah," I call.

The whole room quietens.

"What?" she asks.

I give her my best ever dazzling smile.

"Go fuck yourself."

18

I didn't want to sit through a special one-on-one with Dr Jones today but apparently you can't go around telling people who deserve it to go fuck themselves without people forcing you to talk about it.

"...very disappointed with you," she's saying. Her face is grim and unfriendly for the first time since I've arrived. "Camp will not tolerate clients verbally abusing each other."

I lean back in my chair and cross my arms. "Well you've tolerated her bullying me, spreading rumours about me, and systematically trying to stop me from making friends," I retaliate. "So, what's that about?"

Dr Jones's mouth opens a tiny bit but she closes it before she thinks I notice. "What do you mean, Olive?"

I stand up because I've got too much juice in me, raging around my bloodstream, making it hard to sit still. I'm angry at Hannah and angry at this place and angry that I seem to keep repeating the same patterns with people. But I'm also excited about the project and feeling on the mend and alive and bright eyed and bushy tailed and I'm really ANNOYED that my anger is ruining all this.

"Hannah has been a dick to me since my first day," I say. "I don't randomly go around telling innocent people to go fuck themselves. She had it coming." I need to do something with my hands to stop them balling into fists so I go to Dr Jones's bookshelf and pick up a book, flicking it open at random, scanning the pages. She doesn't stop me, so I rant on. "She's got a bee in her stupid bonnet about the fact I don't want to know my diagnosis and has tried to make half the camp hate me for it. And now I find out she's telling everyone I'm seeing Jamie, just because he's like the only person who hasn't taken her side."

The book is some kind of big bible of psychotherapy stuff and I flick through the pages. Random words blurt out at me.

Freud!

Childhood trauma!

Psychosis!

I wish I could steal it to give to Lewis but Dr Jones is staring right at me and therefore will probably notice if I stick it down my denim shorts.

"So, you say Hannah has been causing you some distress since you got here?"

I shrug. "I mean, I don't care. But she's not been nice, no. In fact, she's been deliberately mean."

"Why haven't you told anyone this until today?"

I shrug again. "Because I can take care of things myself.

I'm used to people not liking me." And, just like that, she switches from telling-off mode into caring psychotherapist mode.

"That's a very interesting thing to say, Olive. Why do you think people don't like you?"

I roll my eyes and put the book down. I could always break into this office and steal it later. I mean, I'm sure it won't be locked. Or maybe I won't need to. Maybe I'll be able to get everything I need off the internet tomorrow. "Because I regularly do things that upset people. I mean, I get it. It's my fault usually. So it's not like I mind. But I've not done anything to Hannah, so that pisses me off."

"I'd appreciate it if you sat back down," she says, like it's my choice. Even though I think she'd disapprove if I didn't sit back down. I slump into the chair and pull my legs up to stop my toes tapping.

"Thank you. Now, what sort of things do you do that make you think people don't like you?"

I think about how I ruin my parents' lives. And I'm a pain in the arse to be around. And I go through patches in my life where I feel invincible and want to soak up every single second and experience every single experience but, unfortunately, that means treading on a few toes sometimes. Because people do not like it if you sleep with their boyfriend, or skip the queue because you're too excited to get on a ride in a theme park, or shout out every single answer to every question in school because you can't even handle how smart you are. And then they *really* don't like it when you shrivel up and go stale like cut sandwiches left out too long in the sun. They hate it when you glaze over as they talk, and resent you for not trying harder. I am many things. I am complicated. I am fiery. I am depth-ridden. I am honest. I am caring when I have the energy to be. I am different. I can make you feel more alive just by sitting next to me.

But I am not likeable.

I wonder how Ally puts up with me sometimes.

"Have you ever heard that nursery rhyme?" I ask Dr Jones. "*There was a little girl, who had a little curl...right in the middle of her forehead?*"

She raises both eyebrows and makes a note. "Yes. What about it?"

"Well, she's me," I explain. "I mean, I don't have curly hair. But there's that line – *When she was good, she was very, very good. But when she was bad, she was horrid.* And that's me. I can be great to be around but when I'm bad, I'm terrible. Unforgivably terrible. And people, well..." I think of school and the rumours and the teachers who complain I'm disruptive and all the other stuff. "They tend to only remember the times I'm horrid."

"I see," Dr Jones says. She leaves a big fat pause that I assume I'm supposed to fill. And sometimes I'm good with silences but today I'm not. I'm too impatient for them. Everything comes rambling out. I tell her about Rick and how I need an STI test. I tell her about messing up my English Literature exam, which I know I have deep in my bones. I tell her about the storm and being found on the top of the cliff by the police. I tell her about using Mum's log-in details on eBay to buy myself thousands of pounds worth of camera equipment. I tell her about accidentally sleeping with Bella's boyfriend (though he did tell me they'd broken up). I tell her about all the times I just talk and talk and talk rather than listen. I tell her about thinking I'm cleverer than other people and more than occasionally saying that out loud. She listens and she makes notes but nothing about what I tell her seems to surprise her, so maybe I'm acting totally normally for someone who has the illness that I have. Which she knows and I don't.

When I eventually run out of steam, which let me tell you takes some time, she just responds with another question.

"And do you blame yourself, Olive? For all of those things."

I slow down a little to think about that one.

"Yes," I say finally.

I want to stand up and pace to get rid of how this admission makes me feel. Stamp stamp stamp it out like it's mud dried in the cracks of a wellington boot. "Of course I'm to blame!"

Because I'm a bad horrid person.

Bad horrid.

No.

No, Olive.

You would prefer it if you are a good person who tries her best.

Dr Jones gets her very best soothing voice out of its box. "But, if you are unwell, Olive, do you not feel like maybe that can't be helped?" she asks. "That you aren't to blame?"

164

I shake my head violently. "No! I do horrible things sometimes. Really awful wretched selfish things. I shouldn't be allowed to do that and just throw my hands up and say, 'Can't blame me, I'm the gingerbread mental.' Because if you do a bad thing I think you should lie down in it and think about what you've done."

"That's quite the metaphor."

"Why thank you."

Dr Jones smiles for the first time that session. She leans forward in her chair. "Tell me this, Olive. If you ate something dodgy for lunch – bad prawns or something – and you were sick all over your friend's car on the way home, would you blame yourself? Or, if you had a broken leg stuck out in a cast and you accidentally hit your mum's prized vase off the table and it smashed, would you think that was your fault?"

"Those are some rather random examples." I'm stalling because I can see where she's going with this.

"Would you?"

"I feel like vom all over a car and a smashed vase are still pretty annoying things for someone else to have to deal with," I say.

"But they wouldn't be your fault?"

"Well, I'd still feel bad. I'd still say sorry and stuff. I wouldn't be like, 'Woah, not my fault! So how dare you get upset about the smashed vase?'"

"Yes, but you wouldn't *feel* it's your fault, even though you're sorry it happened."

A long

Long

Long

Silence.

"No," I finally admit.

Dr Jones crosses and uncrosses her legs. "So, if you are mentally unwell, why do you insist on blaming yourself for the things this illness makes you do?"

Another

Lengthy

Silence.

"I don't know," I finally admit.

She leans back in her chair and her smile oozes across her face. "Well, Olive, I think that's all we've got time for today."

I'm stunned. What has she done? My brain feels all hurty and hijacked and I don't like it but I also feel a tiny bit lighter.

"You've got a call with your parents tomorrow, haven't you?"

"Er, yes." I'd agreed to call them once a week to check in. Then, in the last week, they're due to come in for a *What next?* joyful family therapy session, which shouldn't be awkward at all.

"Brilliant, brilliant. If you want to, it would be great if you could ask them about your early years. Maybe see if this issue with...guilt is something they remember you exhibiting."

"Huh?"

"But, for now, the one thing we have left to sort out is Hannah."

19

I can't sleep.

It's perfectly quiet. The only noise is the whirring of my white-noise machine. But still I cannot sleep. I've been going over my talk with Lewis and now I'm too desperate for the morning, to see him again. To get this thing started. But sleep. Sleep is good. Sleep is important. Sleep is good for my mental health. I don't need our new supersonic algorithm to tell me that.

I lie on my back and try and breathe like Elizabeth taught us. I keep my hand on my stomach and focus on it going up when I breathe in, down when I breathe out, up when I breathe in, down when I...

Oh, this isn't working! It's so hot and I'm so excited you could shoot a tranquillizer dart into my butt and I'd still be able to do a full-on interpretative dance routine to "Bat Out of Hell". I need to tire myself out, that's what I need to do. Run around a bit, burn off some calories. Then I can get to sleep, top up my health, all ready for the big algorithm fun tomorrow. I kick off the thin sheet and lie in my bra and pants for a moment. Where to go, where to go, where to go? I know, I'll run around the fence perimeter, see how big this place actually is. I step into a tiny pair of shorts, pull a vest over my head and yank on my trainers.

I'm conscious of how loud my door is when it unclicks, of the squeaking of my trainers on the corridor carpet. The lights are motion detected and they flicker on as I tiptoe down the stairs and out into reception. I feel like I'm being naughty, even though this isn't technically against the rules. We've even been given a security code so we can go out into the grounds in the evenings. I push the release button next to the front door and it swings open. I step out into the night air. Oh yes, that's better. It's cool and crisp and the moon is out full whack – shining and showing off, and that must be why I'm so wired. I swear I'm in touch with the moon. Maybe we can build the moon into the sanity formula and that will cure me even more? I take a deep breath of clear air and…

…smell smoke.

"We've got to stop meeting like this." Jamie sits on the bottom step. He's wearing pyjama bottoms – blue and white striped ones – with a T-shirt. It's so different from his usual look – all skinny jeans and tatty waistcoats and ten million dangly bracelets made of twine hanging off his wrists. He flicks a cigarette out of his pack and offers me one.

I shake my head. "No thanks." I'm annoyed that he's

here. I want the night to myself, the air to myself. "What you doing out here anyway?"

He takes a deep drag and blows it out into the night – polluting the air. My air. "Couldn't sleep."

"I'm surprised you didn't tire yourself out, spreading false rumours about us."

He smiles, unfussed. "Saying I think you're hot is not spreading a rumour. Anyway, haven't you and Hannah kissed and made up?"

I relent, if only for a minute, and come and sit next to him. "They made us have a reconciliation session." I shudder at the memory. Hannah sitting with her arms crossed and both of us urged to use "I feel" statements. Worked fine, until Hannah said, "I feel like Olive is full of it," and I raised an eyebrow at Dr Jones, all like, *YOU SEE*.

"Are you reconciled?"

I pull a face. "As much as we can be."

To be fair, Dr Jones had done a good job explaining to Hannah that how I deal with my illness is MY CHOICE and shouldn't be used against me. Hannah even said sorry.

"How about us? Are we reconciled?"

"I'm here to get better, not get into anything," I tell him.

He laughs. "Me too!"

"So why did you say anything?"

"I hardly said anything. Hannah just kept pestering me with questions and then clung onto the one thing I did say and then told everyone."

"Argh!" I lift my arms into the night. "Doesn't everyone

have anything better to think about?" I lean over and decide to take a cigarette after all. He lights it for me and I lean away and take a drag.

"No," Jamie says, stubbing his out into the step. "Because you are a girl, and I am a boy, and we cannot be friends without it meaning anything."

"Is that right?"

"Hey don't blame me, blame society."

I want to kiss him then. Because of the way he's smiling. Because of how damn cute he looks in his pyjama bottoms. Because he told me I'm hot and I'm socially conditioned to be grateful for that even though I'm here in a mental health facility which is the last place on earth you should be worrying about whether or not boys find you hot. But the pull of the moon is not strong enough for me to act on the sudden urge. I can beat the moon. I can beat the urges. I just need to get away from his smile.

"I'm off for a run." I flick my still-lit cigarette into the gravel with abandon.

"Right now?"

"Yes."

And, before I can be drawn into further conversation that makes me want to kiss an inappropriate boy on the steps, I am thudding off across the lawn. *Thump thump thump* go my trainers. I hear Jamie's laughter echo behind me across the night and smile but don't turn back to kiss him. Soon he is a dot behind me. I run through the darkness as fast as I can go. I run in a straight line, *thud thud thud,* until, after ten minutes of hardcore running, I hit a brick wall. A-ha! The perimeter. I bloody love the word *perimeter*. Just saying it makes me feel like I'm a ninja. I turn and follow the wall around the circumference. *Circumference*. That's a maths word, isn't it? Lewis would be proud. I hit the woods but keep following the wall, skipping over branches, tearing through undergrowth. The moon is so big and shiny that it's not that dark and my body feels so good for the exercise. Why don't I exercise when I get low? Why can't I just drag my sorry arse out of my bunker and go for a run? It's so simple. I currently can't imagine ever feeling too heavy to run. But I know I must do. Run, run, run. I'm out of the woods. Speeding across the grass. I can see the main entrance gate and it's all lit up and pretty and it's getting closer and closer and oh...someone is stepping out of the little cubicle next to it. In guard uniform. And they're holding their arms out and saying, "Woah there, stop!"

20

Honestly, you should be allowed to go for a JOG without people thinking it's a sign of mental breakdown. Jamie leans against the reception desk, laughing, as the security guards deliver me to a tired-looking Grace, who's been called out.

"We found her running at the entrance," the guard says.

"I wasn't running AT the entrance, I was just running," I explain.

Grace looks from me, to the guards, to Jamie, and back to me again. "Is that true, Olive?"

"Yes! I couldn't sleep, so I went for a run."

"It's one in the morning."

I point to Jamie. "He's up too!"

He raises his hands. "Hey, don't drag me into this."

Grace smiles wryly. "I'm not dragging anyone into anything. But, Olive, can you not see how it may confuse our security team if you're running at them in the middle of the night?"

"Maybe if I was carrying a machete and screaming, 'THERE WILL BE VENGEANCE'?"

The guard's hand stiffens on my arm. "You think that's funny, kid?" he asks.

"Oww!" I pull him off. "Yes, as a matter of fact I do."

Grace sends frantic eye signals to the guard and he backs off, but I'm still rubbing my arm and thinking this is a freaking outrage.

"I think we're all okay here," Grace tells him. "Thank you for letting us know what happened."

He nods and walks back outside leaving Jamie, Grace and me in silence. She pinches the top of her nose and the sleeve of her cardigan falls down to reveal a pyjama top.

"What am I going to do with the both of you?" she says.

Jamie and I give her *Huh?* looks.

"We did say that we don't recommend clients getting into relationships."

"Jamie and I aren't in a relationship!" I say, for what seems the ninetieth time that day.

She raises both eyebrows. "So I'm supposed to believe you both coincidentally couldn't sleep at the same time? And it's just coincidence you were both outside, alone, at one a.m.?"

"Yes!" I yell, just as Jamie says, "This is ridiculous."

I was already irritated and now I'm feeling irrational and the more and more I think about it, the more irrationality morphs into ANGRY. Because this *is* ridiculous. They say we can do what we want but then pinch my arm and drag me away from my lovely jog. And judge me for even SPEAKING to someone of the opposite sex. And they buy into rumours started by a CLIENT who is here because she is MENTALLY ILL. Before I know it I have picked up the phone on the front desk and chucked it at the wall. And I'm yelling and screaming and hurling abuse and the security guys come running back and Jamie is laughing and... and...and...

21

I wake up feeling very, very, very well-rested. My bracelet beeps like an alarm clock, which I didn't know it could do. I punch the tiny button on it to stop it and I lie back into my pillow and think how very well rested I feel.

Then I remember last night.

And me losing it and throwing things across reception.

And Dr Jones turning up in her dressing gown because I started crying uncontrollably.

And the diazepam they gave me to calm me down.

Thus the well-restedness. Even though it's 7 a.m. and I've only had four hours' sleep.

I try to piece together the night and I burst out laughing, which is a rather brilliant way to start the day. Everything's sorted anyway. Dr Jones wants me to have an extra one-on-one today when I'm supposed to be mucking out the barns, so I've actually done quite well out of throwing a tantrum.

I roll out of bed and throw back the curtains. The light

rushes into my room and I can feel it's already honking hot again. I rummage through my clothes and yank out a white dress, which complements my tanned skin perfectly. I look so cute I take another quick self-portrait and skip downstairs to the delicious smells of breakfast, eager to find Lewis and get everything started.

It's pretty busy; most of the clients are already sitting down and shovelling food into their mouths. Darrell and Kieran are building a tower out of hash browns. Liv is sitting with them, laughing. I suspect she's taken a bit of a fancy to Darrell, and has crossed over into the depressive circle in order to flirt. I fill my tray with coconut porridge and avocado on toast and look around for someone to sit with. I spot Hannah and Sophie and feel like this is a good time to start anew. I *will* make friends with girls. I do have it in me. I pace over and say, "Hi, can I sit with you guys?"

Sophie looks up and smiles, then glances nervously over at Hannah. I beam back – radiating the sun and the earth and the moon and everything else you can possibly radiate through a smile.

Hannah swallows, doesn't make eye-contact, but finally says, "I guess."

"Brilliant!" I clatter my stuff down and keep beaming and beaming. "How are you both? Isn't it a GORGEOUS day?"

Hannah looks up at me warily. "You're in a very good

mood," she remarks. "I heard you got into major trouble last night?"

Just as I'm about to ask how she knows, Jamie arrives with a tray, looking much less rested. "Well look who has made up," he says all patronizingly.

I shoot him a glare which I'm not able to maintain because I'm so excited that I'm actually talking to Hannah and Sophie. Praise be to Dr Jones.

"I'm quite offended that you're so determined to keep you and me a secret," he laughs.

"You're ridiculous."

"Says the girl who went running at one a.m., and then got upset when it scared security."

I sigh and start attacking my toast.

"Did you really go running around in the middle of the night?" Hannah asks. "Why?"

"Because I'm crazy," I laugh, with a mouthful of food. "Or I just felt like a run…"

She laughs nervously and I appreciate the gesture. Sophie is silent then laughs a bit too late, but it still melts my heart that we're communicating again.

We fall into normal conversation, like none of us has ever fallen out. Hannah starts complaining about the stench of the alpacas and we talk about what the world's worst smells are.

I see Gabriella carrying her tray and feel a burst of friendliness. "Hey, Gaby! Come sit with us and tell us what smells you hate," I call over.

She doesn't hesitate. "Where on EARTH do I start?" she gabbles, plopping her tray down. "Okay, so I HATE the smell of petrol, and eggs. I mean this canteen KILLS me each morning. And I hate going into a toilet just after someone's you...you know and the air is all fuggy and..."

"Please stop!" Hannah goes white.

"Whoops! I forgot."

Miraculously, Hannah laughs. Showing the progress she's made in a week. We all laugh. We all smile at each other and laugh and continue eating and talking and I feel SO GOOD. What people don't understand about feeling such potent sadness is, when it lifts, it really lets you know what happiness means. I almost feel sorry for people who just mosey about in the middle "appropriate" lanes of the joy spectrum. And part of me thinks, *If you cure yourself, if this maths thing pays off, will you lose this? Will you want to lose this?* But a flash of Mum's face and how it looked in the hospital is enough to make me think the sacrifice might be worth it. I push the thought away and think about the algorithm and how much better I'm going to be once I've cracked it. How I'll know what I have to do not to get the Nothing again.

Lewis rocks up, big bags under his eyes but vibrating so much energy you can almost see sparks flying off him.

"Hey, Olive." He points to a space next to me. "Can I sit?"

"Sure."

Conversation has moved on from worst smells to worst foods and Gabriella is dominating again but it doesn't even bother me. Her joy is contagious, my joy is contagious.

Lewis leans over to whisper. "I didn't sleep," he admits. "I was up all night working on stuff."

I smile. "I didn't sleep either." But I don't tell him the whole story.

"How long do we get with computers today?" he asks.

"I checked. Only an hour."

He pulls a face. "Well, it will have to do. Let's try and get in early."

"I like your dedication already, Lewis."

"I like that you've given me a mathematical challenge to distract me from the bad thought that brought me here."

Gabriella notices our quietened voices. "What are you two whispering about?" she demands.

"Nothing," we both say at the same time.

"Yeah," Hannah adds. "What's going on with you two? You vanished off together yesterday too."

I don't even blink. "Oh, it's just this thing I do," I say. "I take each boy into the woods and have sex with them as a welcome." There's a stunned silence and I have to add, "OH MY GOD, I'M KIDDING!" before the table laughs, although Lewis has gone beyond red.

We eat quickly and his face still hasn't calmed down by the time we rush to queue for the computer room.

"GRACE, OPEN UP," I yell over at her.

She makes her way towards us, holding a big ring of keys tauntingly. "You're in a better mood this morning, Olive."

"It's the promise of wifi."

Gabriella, Hannah and Sophie join us, playfully pushing each other. I feel a tug at my hand and find Sophie right next to me.

"Sorry," she whispers, her eyes filled with tears. "Sorry for being so mean to you."

I'm in no mood to make her pay for it, only to get into that room and find the secret to my wellness. "Don't worry. I'm just glad we can be friends now." And her grim little face twitches up into the tiniest smile.

Grace steps forward and starts unlocking the door.

"Oww, Gabriella, that hurt!" Hannah squawks.

"Guys, guys, guys, take it easy or I won't open up!" Grace barks. "We limit wifi for your own good. Look at the state of all of you at the merest whiff of it."

The door swings open and we pile past her into a room full of computers. Like everything else here, they're all brand-new. I catch Lewis's hand and drag him to a quiet corner. Everyone's so excited that they don't seem to notice. Jamie's already logged in and has a music website up, putting on his headphones. His face is instantly trancelike, a warm smile spread across his face, his eyes closed.

"Now, we have put some filters on," Grace says. "Pornography being the obvious thing." Darrell boos and she smiles. "Any problems, I'm at the front."

I can hardly contain myself as I turn on the computer and wait for it to load.

"Where are we going to start? HOW are we going to start?" I ask Lewis.

He gets out a big notebook and flips it open to a page filled with indecipherable maths. Seriously, it's like a calculator drank too much maths and vomited it up onto the page.

"We need to add in measurable variables," he says, stabbing at his notes. "So we need to research things that are known to improve mental health generally. Then we can eventually combine it with individual factors that we know work best for you and personalize the algorithm."

The computer is on! I click on the internet straight away, so quickly that I accidentally triple click and multiple windows pop up.

"I only understood half of that," I say. "But I will try." I type in:

How to stay sane

Lewis peers over my shoulder and I can feel his smile. "Umm, you may want to type in more…er…scientific wording than that." His breath smells sweet, of the sugary tea he drank at breakfast.

"Oh, okay then." I delete it and type:

Why am I so fucking crazy?

He lets out a laugh.

"I'll behave, I'll behave," I protest as he tries to grab the mouse off me, our hands brushing.

"Good."

"You're very assertive when it comes to maths," I tell him.

"What can I say? It's my happy place." He starts up his own computer.

"So, when we build *your* sanity algorithm, we have to build in an hour a day for you to chill out with some simultaneous equations?"

He smiles. "Maybe."

I input proper search terms and start making notes. Lewis spreads out his notebook between us and we write things down as we find them.

"Mind if I put the radio on?" Grace asks and the room fills with gentle classical music and everyone is absorbed in their internetting.

"Look!" I whisper. "How about this?" I pull up a page called *Five Steps to Mental Wellbeing* on the NHS website.

"Perfect!"

I beam at him and write the five points down. "How do people even go about working this sort of stuff out, anyway?" I mutter as I read through another page.

Lewis looks up from his own scribbles. "Well, when it comes to predicting any human behaviour, it's important to remember two important things," he says.

"Which are, Einstein?"

He grins. "That human beings are both utterly predictable and yet utterly unpredictable."

I raise both eyebrows. "Well that's useful of us," I deadpan.

"It's true though! That's why algorithms based on human behaviour are so hard to build. In some instances, we're all like lemmings. We like to think we're special, but, actually, we're pretty stupid and do the same predictable things at the same predictable times. Like all get into our cars the evening of a bank holiday and then wonder why there's a traffic jam. Or, for instance, shops know *exactly* how much to put something on sale by so that we'll think it's a bargain and buy it. There are patterns everywhere. We march like ants over the same paths and react in very predictable ways to even unpredictable events."

I raise my eyebrows. "This is so depressing in a weird kind of way. And there I was thinking I was a special snowflake."

He points at me, all *a-ha*. "A-ha," he says. He actually says "a-ha". "But this is the beauty of maths when you combine it with humans. Because we're not all lemmings. We're not robots. We are individuals! And therefore you *can't* always predict what we're going to do. There's always going to be people who go against the pattern. For every person who climbs into their car and gets stuck in a traffic jam, there's the person who waits until midnight and drives through the night. For every person who says, 'Wow, twenty per cent off, what a deal!' there's someone who storms out of the shop in a huff. Maths can only predict so much because humans are, indeed, special unique snowflakes. Not one universally similar."

I smile. "So, we are all lemmings *and* snowflakes?"

He nods. "Bingo."

22

When we only have fifteen minutes left, Lewis and I decide to park our sanity-solving abilities and do what everyone else is doing – desperately catching up on all the various social networking we've missed out on. The air is quieter – just the violins and piano echoing softly out from the radio and the odd click and sigh. The occasional tapping of keys as everyone sends out messages to friends and families – reassuring them all that we're still here.

I'm surprised I have 100+ notifications when I pull up my homepage. There are lots of messages on my wall, asking me where or how I am. I get a stab of feeling that people *do* care and that maybe I *do* have friends, then realize they've probably just heard I've been shipped off to a funny farm and want to *pretend* they care so I can tell them all about it and they can carry the gossip around like a glowing pearl. I scroll through photos of parties I've missed. They all blur into one big smudge of girls I know taking multiple selfies in multiple locations wearing multiple different outfits. I sigh and delete everything apart from messages from Ally. I'm about to write a long email back when I see she's online and shoot over a message.

Olive: Hello! I've not got long. They only let me out of the straightjacket for fifteen-minute intervals.
Ally: OH MY GOD, OLIVE!! HOW ARE YOU?
Ally: I miss you so freaking much you have no idea. Everyone else I've been hanging out with is so basic.
Olive: I'm okay. Good. Brilliant actually!
Ally: That's so good to hear. So this place is helping you? X x x
Olive: Yeah, sort of. But more than that. I've found this amazing guy who is really good at maths and we're going to use maths to make me better.
Ally: What?
Ally: What guy?
Ally: And since when do you care about maths?
Olive: Since I met this guy and we're figuring out how to fix me!
Ally: Is he fit?
Olive: WHAT?? ALLY!
Ally: It's a fair enough question.
Olive: Ha. Well, umm. I've not thought of him like that. He's really into maths. I get virgin vibes.
Anyway, I've not got time for all that. I'm only here three more weeks, so I've not got long to figure this

all out. How are you?

Ally: OH MY GOD you've remembered to ask.

Ally: I'm in shock.

Olive: Shut up. I care. I ask...

Olive: I've learned to ask.

Ally: Well I'm okay. Missing you. Dreading results day! But glad that place is helping you. Don't come back too sane, will you?

Olive: I can't make any promises. I really feel I'm onto something, Ally!

Ally: Umm...please don't take this the wrong way but...this maths thing? It's not like that time you thought your photos had the power to change people's political beliefs, is it?

"Fuck you," I find myself saying to the computer screen. The whole room looks up. Grace raises her eyebrows at me and I smile apologetically. She looks tired, big bags under her eyes. My fault. Oh well...

Ally: Olive? You still there?

Ally: Olive?

I can't be arsed to reply to her any more. I'm wasting precious time chin-wagging when I could be curing myself. I've only got ten minutes left.

Olive: G2g – love you bye x x

And click off.

I hold my face in my hands for a second or two, feeling my eyelashes brush against my palms as I blink.

Fuck Ally.

Fuck her for reminding me of results day, when I've been doing so well at pushing it out of my brain.

And fuck her for bringing up the photography thing. She always teases me about that. "Remember your God phase?" she'll say, punching my arm lightly and thinking I'm ready to laugh about it. But I'm not ready. The sting of humiliation from when I stood up in my photography lesson and lectured everyone about "the power of my work" is still brutally raw. That, and I'm still in trouble with Mum and Dad for spending all that money on photography equipment.

I really believed I was doing something good at the time.

But, I guess I'm willing to admit now that the whole thing was a little bit nuts. This, however. This is completely different. It feels different. It feels special, and not in a way that's short-lived. I look over at Lewis's screen to see how he's getting on and he's engrossed in some lengthy document – leaning right over to see the tiny print better. I push my wheelie chair over so I'm right up close to him.

"Whatcha looking at?" I whisper and he jumps.

"Olive, look what I've found. There's so much data to read through," he whispers back.

"Didn't you want to email your friends or anything?"

"Look." He points to the screen. "They've already begun to organize different mental health conditions into

CLUSTERS. So much work has been done for us. But, woah" – he jabs at the screen – "is it trippy. They work out what 'cluster' you're in and can essentially work out what mental health recovery journey you're going to have based on which cluster you're assigned. It's like the Sorting Hat but for mental health problems."

I take the mouse off him and scroll to the top. "Hey, let me see. What does *payment by results* mean?"

Lewis leans in closer so our cheeks are almost touching. "I'm not sure…hang on…" He scrolls. "I think the health service gets PAID based on how quickly and efficiently they're able to diagnose someone into a cluster and get them better?"

"So patients are, like, factory chickens?"

"I guess…"

I scroll madly, trying to find anything of interest. Yikes it's a scary document. There's even a "decision tree" for confused psychiatrists which they can use to help figure out how to diagnose someone, like it's the same as doing an internet quiz with a mate.

"Five more minutes, people," Grace says to a chorus of moans. "I know, I know."

"We don't have much time," Lewis hisses. "Quick, we need to get down those criteria." His pen is blurring across his notebook, stopping only to smack my hand when I scroll too quickly.

I'm reading a list of symptoms and, without meaning to, ticking some off in my head.

Overactive, aggressive, disruptive or agitated behaviour due to any cause...non-accidental self-injury...problems with depressed mood...strong unreasonable beliefs that are not psychotic...

I mutter some under my breath and, even though I know it's a bad idea, begin to work out which cluster I might be in. I mean, I think it's fair to say I have problems with depressed mood. And my obsession with noise has been considered "unreasonable" by quite a few people, though I feel like they're the mental ones for not being bothered by something so obviously bothering.

"Stop moving the screen," Lewis complains and I realize I'm scrolling back and forth between care cluster five and care cluster six and nodding and biting my lip and thinking, *Oh yeah, there's something in that.* Then I see a phrase underneath care cluster six:

Course: The problems will be enduring.

It's like the plug has been pulled on my bathtub full of hope. I grab the mouse to see if I've made a mistake but Grace yells, "Okay, folks, time's up. Log out of your networks, embrace the real world, live for the now, not for the likes."

Enduring? Does that mean everlasting? If I'm in care cluster six does that mean I'll always be like this? Hang on...I just need a few seconds more.

"Even you, Olive," Grace instructs. "We've made enough allowances for you for one twenty-four hour period."

And, before I know it, the screen's black and so is my soul.

189

Lewis doesn't seem to notice. He's babbling excitedly next to me. "I got so much stuff! I just need to work out how to combine it with data, and then you need to tell me your own individual variables, and we can start trialling different things and see how they work and…" His voice fades out because all I can hear is a voice in my head.

The problems will be enduring.

The problems will be enduring.

The problems

Will

Be

Enduring.

"Olive?"

Enduring?! What sort of defeatist attitude is that? How are these people who made those clusters even allowed to work in mental health if they don't think they can make it go away? You wouldn't want a freaking FIREFIGHTER to think a FIRE was enduring, would you? I mean, what do they know? With their stupid mental health cluster tree of madness? What was it Lewis was saying? How you can't predict all human behaviour? Maybe most lemmings will find their problems enduring, but maybe I'm a snowflake? Maybe I'm not even in cluster six anyway. And even if I am, I'm more bad-ass and determined than all the other suckers who are in cluster six.

"Olive?"

And if Lewis and I could just scoop out time alone to really get this project started we could…

"EARTH TO OLIVE."

"Huh?"

I look up and the room is empty. Even Lewis has buggered off. It's just me and Grace, who is looking pretty fed up to be honest.

"Olive, isn't it time for you to ring your parents?"

"Oh yeah. Where's the phone?"

"It's in my office. Wait for me to lock up and I'll show you."

I hang about the door, pondering and fretting. I'm not even sure if I want to talk to my parents right now, not when I'm like this. They'll want me to be all cheery and I'm-feeling-so-much-BETTER, which, to be fair, I was feeling fifteen minutes ago. Now I'm not sure I have the energy to play happy face.

Grace fiddles with the lock and then turns to me and says, "Shall we, then?"

We walk the short distance to her office behind the reception desk.

"You feeling any calmer today?" she asks.

"I didn't mean to cause such a fuss."

She smiles in a way that shows it's genuinely not a problem. "I would *not* be doing this job if I had problems with people who cause the occasional fuss. I just hope you feel better today."

She pushes through a frosted glass door into a sleek little office made of shiny black furniture. Grace picks up the phone, which is one of those fancy jobbies where it doesn't need a receiver – it's just a thin black expensive oblong. "Here's the phone. You just dial nine to get out. You can take as long as you want. I'll be outside."

The phone feels cool in my hand and I pass it from palm to palm. "How do I know my parents will even be in?"

"Oh we let them know you're ringing." She's already on her way out, clopping along in her black heels.

"Did you tell them I got into trouble?"

Grace pauses and pulls an *Oh honestly* face. "No, we didn't. And you didn't. We don't like clients to feel like they're ever 'in trouble' here. You just…had something to get out is all."

Is that what this is? Is my mental illness just a lifetime case of emotional hiccups?

The problems will be enduring.

ENDURING.

No, no, no, no, no. I won't let it, I won't let it. I can mend this and be a better, likeable person who doesn't mess everything up.

"Thanks, Grace," I call after her as she pushes the door shut.

I sit in her comfy office chair and make myself smile, because humans can tell if someone is smiling when they talk, even if they can't see them. My fingers shake as I punch in my home number and I hear the tinny noise of it ringing all those miles away, where Mum and Dad will be waiting next to it – waiting to hear if their precious baby is well again yet.

The problems will be enduring.

Mum picks up on the first ring. "Olive?"

"It's me," I say. "I'm so glad they're letting me say goodbye before the lobotomy."

"Oh God, Olive. You're always so dramatic! Hang on, your dad wants to get on the other line. Nick? NICK? YES, IT'S OLIVE. PICK IT UP IN THE STUDY."

There's a clattering and fuss on the line, then Dad's voice echoes down my ear. "Hello? Olive?"

"Hey, Dad," I say. "It's me. Your long-lost daughter."

"Oh, Olive, it's good to hear your voice."

I feel the emotion well up inside of me – pushing against the lining of my stomach, scalding up my throat, making my eyes prickle.

"How are you, darling?" Mum says. "Is it okay there? It's so weird not to be in touch with you."

"I'm good. It's good. The food is nice."

They both laugh down the line. "Well, that's the important thing, right?"

I make myself smile wider. I mean, anyway, what does a stupid weird prescriptive mental health cluster sheet know anyway? I have a maths genius on my side. I can be cured. I can TOTALLY be cured. The smile works on me then, not just them. Of course I'm going to get better! Of course I am! I'm more dedicated and more clever and more just…special than most other people. No one else is using MATHS to cure themselves. It will be fine.

"It's going really good here, actually," I tell them. "I really feel like this is going to do the trick. You won't recognize me when I'm home. It will be like having a brand-new daughter. A really, really sane one. You'll go to dinner parties, and the Watsons will be all like, 'How's Olive coming along?' and you'll be like, 'Oh boy, she is so sane these days, can you believe it?'" I trail off before I get too excited and tell them about the formula, just in case they go blabbing to Dr Jones. I don't want them thinking this maths thing is just another one of "Olive's ideas" like Ally obviously does. Okay, yes, so I've had projects in the past that haven't worked out. But this is different. I can just *feel* that it's different. I'll show them.

"It's great that you're feeling so, umm, positive about things, Olive," Dad says. "Really great."

"It's not just positivity. I'm certain this is going to work."

"Hmm, yes," Mum interrupts. "How are your sessions going with the therapists and stuff?"

"Yeah, they're okay, I guess. They're obsessed with talking about my childhood."

Dad laughs. "Is that right? And they claim this place is state-of-the-art."

I nod triumphantly. "I know! They're like 'Tell me, Olive, were there ever moments when you were young when you didn't feel safe?' and I'm like, 'I can't remember, I was an infant, duh.' So, do, please, share some occasions where you accidentally left me in a shopping centre or something." I laugh. "Please, give me TRAUMA. It will make Dr Jones so happy." I stop laughing when I realize it's not being reciprocated. "Guys? Everything okay over there?"

Dad's voice is gruff when he responds. "Yes, still here. Sorry, love, I'm just…I think the line cut out a bit there. Did it for you, Carol?"

A delay, then, "Yes, Olive. What about the art facilities there? Are you able to do any photography?"

"Yes. I'm taking a self-portrait every day," I reply, feeling all funny. If the line really did cut out, then why didn't they ask me to repeat what I'd just said? But I humour them because I don't want to get in a row when I probably won't talk to them for at least another week. "I thought it would be interesting to see if I look different leaving compared to when I arrived."

"That's such a good idea," Mum coos. "You're so creative."

We chat a bit longer – them telling me about all the news I've not missed out on. "Uncle Frank's built a new shed. The neighbours have put their house up for sale." They check I'm still taking my antidepressants.

"Yep. Every day. And I'm still un-depressed."

They ask if I've managed to gain any weight.

"A couple of pounds. I told you the food was good."

And it's nice to talk to them and all but I don't feel any better. I love them but talking to them is distracting me from finding Lewis and working out how we can put our research into action.

"I better go, it's almost time for my one-to-one," I say.

"Oh okay, sweetie, we miss you," Mum says.

"We do," Dad echoes. "And we're so proud of you for

trying this out. We're here no matter what. You can call us any time. We can't wait to see you in a few weeks."

"Okay, thanks. Bye, I guess."

"Bye."

I sit back in the posh chair for a while or two, because Grace doesn't know I've finished yet and it really does recline in the most marvellous way.

My tummy hurts.

It's doing that thing when it tightens like someone has clamped it between their fingers and squeezed down hard. I know I won't be able to eat anything until it passes. My tummy hurts because I miss my parents. My tummy hurts because there was something I said about my childhood that upset them. My tummy hurts because I read earlier that my potential mental health condition will never go away. My tummy hurts because I don't want an extra hour of therapy today, with Dr Jones prying and prodding into my brain like she's got a giant sharp fork. I make myself take a big breath the way Elizabeth told us to do it. And I tell myself:

I am a good person who tries her best.

I am a good person who tries her best.

And I will try my best now. I will fix this formula. I will get better and be better and feel better and look better, but right now I can't do that without Lewis.

So I push myself out of the chair and go looking for him.

23

So, Lewis says that in order to make a personalized algorithm, you've got to imagine it as a two-layer cake – like banoffee pie. Mmmm, banoffee maths pie. The first layer of the cake is the Lemmings layer – STATS and DATA that work on everyone. In terms of "staying sane", here's what we found out works for most people:

- Connecting with other human beings
- Being active
- Learning new skills
- Giving back
- Being mindful
- Being outdoors
- Getting enough sleep
- Eating carbs
- Smelling flowers, hanging out with happy people, having healthy and safe sex with someone who respects you, giving money to charity, etc., etc., etc.

Then, on top of this, you've got the second layer of the sanity cake. This is the special snowflake layer. The personal layer. Things that Lewis and I figured out that make me, Olive, happy. Things that improve my wellbeing that are more unique to me.

- Quiet – too much noise makes my brain go all bo-jangly but in a bad way. Whereas quiet, calm environments usually calm me down and make me happier.
- My period cycle – Lewis looked like he was going to EXPLODE when I told him this. "I'm sorry, but it's true," I said to him. "For weeks one and two I'm a fun force to be reckoned with and then I ovulate" (Lewis shuddered) "and BOOM, out come my friends, misery and despair." After his initial combustion, Lewis, to his credit, got me to guestimate my cycle and we started looking into ways I could counterbalance it in The Bad Weeks.
- People being people – I don't like people very much, usually because they don't like me very much.

"So how do you plan to turn your hatred of people into a positive thing that helps your mental health?" Lewis asks. "I can't just write *Avoid all humans* into this. It's not realistic."

"Isn't it?"

And he laughs.

* * *

Over the next week Lewis draws up a schedule for me that incorporates all the things that are scientifically proven to make me saner and I start to put it into practice. Oddly enough, it's not too far off the general Sanity Camp timetable, which I guess means they do vaguely know what they're doing here. We fold ourselves into corners, working on tweaks. Lewis, of course, wants to sort himself out too so he starts copying me. His special-snowflake happiness triggers are: *Doctor Who* fandoms ("You don't understand, Olive. It's the purest form of love there is. And the…relief you feel when you're in a con full of people who just Get It…"). Maths, unsurprisingly is also in there. His final personal input into the happiness algorithm is, "Talking to people who don't make me feel like a freak."

"Who makes you feel like that?"

"Basically everyone."

I scrunch my face up over my notepad. "Who the hell are these everyone? Point them out to me so I can beat them up for you."

He blushes and smiles. "You see, that's why I like hanging out with you," he says quietly. "I think you're the first girl in history who can talk to me without making me feel like a freak."

I blush too. We've been spending a lot of time together just us two. And we haven't told the others about our project yet. I tell Lewis it's because they won't understand, but, selfishly, I want Lewis and his brain to myself. I want to get my algorithm sorted before he starts helping everyone else.

Because he's nice and kind and will no doubt help anyone who asks and we're not here for very long and I NEED to get it sorted.

But it's working, it's working. I can feel it working.

I've not felt low for DAYS. Not since that weird call with my parents. I fill out my mood diary each night smiling. I am swimming fifty lengths of the pool. I am using photography to be creative and also combining that with CONNECTING with people. I am learning through all my maths lessons with Lewis. I am actually taking our mindfulness class seriously – lying spread-eagled and dutiful on my yoga mat each day, letting Elizabeth's soft voice coax me into a state of breathing in and out. I'm giving back by being nice to everyone. I found Sophie crying in the hallway the other day and I totally looked after her. She was a weeping mess because Dr Rossen had made her do all kinds of hardcore exposure therapy in her one-to-one and it had cracked her open.

This could be it, I think, as I walk through the woods. Scrunching through fallen twigs, feeling the dappled light decorate my face like intricate lace. How I feel now could be how I feel all the time. Zingy and fresh-out-the-box and grateful and energized and positive and exactly the sort of person I want to be. I feel so proud of myself. For crawling my way out of the chasm again. It's okay to fall over seven times as long as you get up eight. And I got up and got here and found the secret to not falling down for an eighth time. As long as I can keep this delicate balance up. I will be okay then. As long as I can always live somewhere quiet and always have time to do the algorithm…I will be fine. Better than fine. Jolly. Even. Steady. Cured. Normal.

Some people, however, have noticed that I'm not quite keeping up with the camp schedule.

"How come you never come to group therapy any more?" Jamie asks me one lunchtime as we settle to eat with the others.

"Yeah," Hannah says. "You've not been all week."

Lewis and I share a look over our spaghetti bolognese. I'd decided that it suited me better to spend the daily group session going on a really long walk outside, so I've been skipping group to match my sanity formula better.

"No reason," I say, innocently twirling pasta around my fork. "I just like to go for a wander then."

Jamie elbows me playfully. "But you're missing all the juicy details about our traumatic pasts. Aren't you curious?"

Is it bad that I'm not actually? I mean, I like Jamie and Gabriella and Sophie, and even Hannah sometimes. They're okay enough and seem to have formed a little clump of friendliness. But I'm too absorbed in this formula and sorting myself out to be that bothered with them. Okay, that is harsh, but I'm only here a month and we're two weeks in already. I need to focus on *me*.

"I guess." I take a mouthful of food and talk through it. "What did I miss earlier?" I ask the table.

Gabriella lifts up a spoonful of today's "healthy rice pudding", looking distinctly unimpressed with it. "Today we talked about everyone's progress."

I raise both eyebrows.

"And? Is everyone cured?"

There's a rumble of laughter laced with sadness. I look round the table and really take them all in for the first time in a while. Hannah and Sophie are practically joined at the hip, sitting next to each other at all times. Gabriella seems to be having one of her calmer days – though yesterday she went berserk when Kieran accidentally hit her with the Frisbee on the lawn.

"I've been told I have to try and sit and watch the alpacas being mucked out," Hannah starts in her plummy accent. "And the thought of it doesn't make me want to leave a cartoon-like Hannah-shaped hole in a nearby wall. So I guess that's something."

I nod, impressed. Remembering how, on the second day, she ran off crying when they'd even mentioned muck-out duty. "Cool."

"And this is my third day in a row I've felt confident enough to just come and sit with you guys at lunch," Sophie squeaks, making my heart flood with warmth.

Hannah turns and gives her a hug. "Because you are totally welcome, babe."

She starts to glow. "Thank you."

I tilt my head at Jamie. "How about you?"

His eyes go dark and he shrugs. "Still a useless addict."

I get a jolt of feeling sorry for him, and I'm about to ask more questions, when Darrell and Kieran and Liv all join us.

"Liv, your lipstick is ON POINT," Gabriella says. "Do you

think it would suit my skin colour?"

The conversation fragments into different clusters. The girls start talking make-up, the boys start discussing football – like someone has just painted a gender-cliched line down the middle of us. Lewis and I share another look, silently passing our secret back and forth. He's more of a conformist than me and hasn't been missing group. He says it's "helpful", but I'm unconvinced. It's great and all that everyone seems to feel slightly better, but I can't help thinking that I'm betterer. They've made teeny tiny steps, whereas since I've adopted this formula, I feel like I'm Queen of the Universe. I've never felt so sure I'm on the right path. I've never felt so full of hope. I really, truly think I've cracked it and the thought is so overwhelmingly magical that I don't even think I can stay sitting on this chair for a minute longer. I want to go outside and cartwheel across the perfect lawn.

I really do feel bloody great, so it's kind of surprising when I'm mid-cartwheeling and Dr Jones comes out and asks me in for a "special" session.

The "special" part seems to be this man in with her. Who's all tweed and beard and coffee breath.

"Hi, Olive, nice to meet you. I'm Dr Bowers."

I don't take his hand, I just look at him with a *What the hell are you doing here?* face.

Dr Jones jumps in. "He's going to sit in on our session today, Olive. Is that okay? He's a psychiatrist."

I raise both eyebrows.

I flop into my chair and cross my legs. My toes want to dance in my trainers, so I tap my foot to let them get it out.

"Why is he here?" I ask, feeling panicked he'll make the session longer. I don't want to be late for photography because that is my creative outlet and outletting creativity is an important part of my sanity formula. "I'm feeling fine. Great even. I've been telling you as much."

The two doctors don't look at each other, and yet I sense that they want to share a look. "Well, firstly, Olive, I want to know why you've missed group therapy every single day this week."

Not this again! I cross my arms. I'm feeling twitchy already. She is messing with my formula. She is making me feel like a bad person rather than a good person who tries their best.

"I thought everything here was optional?"

"It is." She pauses. "And you're not in any trouble, Olive. I'm just interested to know why you've started skipping it."

Because that is my outside time. That is the only time I get in my day to go on my long walk in the woods that I know helps me.

"I just felt like it, that's all," I say.

"Do you find it hard to hear the experiences of the other people here?"

"It's not that it's too hard," I tell the doctors. "I just have more important things to do."

She nods slowly. "More important things?"

"Yes. That's when I go for my walk in the woods. Nothing wrong with that, is there?"

"No, there's not. But you can learn a lot about your own mental health from listening to your peers, Olive. Sometimes it's comforting to know other people are going through the same thing."

"I spend all day with these people, I know they're going through stuff. People don't save their talk just for group anyway. We talked about it just now, over lunch!"

Dr Bowers comes in, his voice all deep and authoritative. "But that's different from a safe, supervised group therapy session."

I shoot him a look. "And who the hell are you again?"

"Olive!" Dr Jones's voice is strict. "Please try not to be rude."

"It's okay," Dr Bowers says. He looks totally unoffended. "We've not really explained to Olive why I'm here. I'm sure she's not that comfortable with my presence."

"Yes, why are you here?" I ask them both. "I told you, I'm feeling good. Camp is working! You should be happy!"

Dr Jones leans over a pile of papers and picks up the top sheet. "Yes, Olive, and we're very happy to hear that, we really are. But some of your readings are concerning us, and we just need to check in."

"Readings from my bracelet?"

"Yes, combined with the data you've been giving us via electronic diary."

I scrunch my nose up. "I feel really happy. I'm not suicidal at all. Why is it alerting you?"

"The bracelet shows that you've not been sleeping as well as you did your first week here."

I raise both eyebrows again. I mean, this isn't news to me. I am me. I am aware of my sleep. Or my lack of it. I have twisted and turned in my sheets and counted sheep and recited the alphabet backwards and swum twenty extra lengths in the swimming pool so I'd be more tired at bedtime. It's the one key part to my recovery that I'm lacking. That said, I'm not missing sleep. I don't feel that tired – just annoyed at myself. Because if I could sleep eight hours, eight blissful hours a night, I could feel even better. But my body won't oblige.

"I know I've not been sleeping," I tell both of them.

"And, well, there's no easy way to put this, Olive," Dr Jones starts, looking at the other doctor. "But your behaviour this past week has been somewhat erratic. We're a bit concerned about you."

"Erratic how?"

"Well, you've started to miss group therapy. You seem very, umm, full of beans. You've taken a lot of photos in art class. Which is great but, still, it's a lot. Dave tells me you've developed over two hundred photos. You've used up all the photography paper. We've had to order more."

"I'm making a montage. You need stuff to montage. Look," I sigh, because it's so much easier when Dr Jones just says what she wants to say, rather than trying to get me to figure it out, "what are you getting at? Why is he here?" I point with my eyes towards Dr Bowers.

He coughs to assert that he's about to take over proceedings. "Olive, what Dr Jones is trying to say is that we've been alerted to your behaviour by a number of things, and I was asked to review your progress. You don't appear to be adapting to camp as easily as some of the others, and it's...well...some of your behaviour is symptomatic of the start of a hypomanic episode, and this has worried me about your meds."

"What's wrong with my meds?"

"I obviously have not been the person to diagnose you and I know your diagnosis still isn't set in stone..." And before I can stop him, before I can shout out "NO", before I can wave my arms in the air and scream "DON'T DO THIS", he says, "but in my professional opinion, you may have bipolar disorder and..."

And I zone out because I'm screaming inside and my fists are clenched and tears are in my eyes and I can't, I can't, I can't undo this. I can't unhear what I've just heard. It's like hearing a spoiler for your favourite TV show but so, so, so, so much worse. Dr Jones has noticed me screaming, even though I'm very quiet, and she's clocked on.

"Albert!" she interrupts quickly. "Olive didn't want to know her diagnosis."

His face falls. "Oh no, Olive, I'm sorry."

"IT'S IN MY NOTES!" I scream. I actually do scream. "YOU'RE MONITORING MY FUCKING HEART RATE AND YET YOU DON'T READ MY NOTES." And I'm up and the chair has been kicked across the room and I'm quite sure it was me that did it because they're calmly telling me to calm down and I totally zone out for a moment or two. I only remember blackness and crying and the word:

Bipolar. Bipolar. Bipolar.

A label. A diagnosis. Who I am boiled down to a catchy title that will probably be called something else in fifty years' time because eventually, with time, all titles get politically incorrect. They pick up the chair and sit me on it and keep saying, "Sorry, sorry," but it's not like saying sorry undoes anything.

Here's a life tip. Never do anything that requires you to say sorry. Because it's too late then. Sorry isn't a magical eraser. Sorry doesn't get the stain out. Just don't shit the bed in the first place, rather than apologize for the stain I now can't wash out.

Dr Jones is kneeling next to me, her hand on the arm of my chair. "We are sorry, Olive. For what it's worth, what you've not known by refusing to know your diagnosis is that we're still not completely sure what your diagnosis is. So please try not to get too upset by Dr Bowers's slip up. Nothing is concrete yet."

"But you think I might have bipolar?"

She shakes her head. "We don't have to go into this if you don't want. You've had a shock today."

I cling to the arms of the chair and use them to push myself up. "It's too late now, you may as well go on." Because now I know I need to know everything. And this was my concern. This is what I was trying to avoid. Now I have a sticky-note on myself, I want to know everything about it.

Dr Bowers does look really awful to be fair. He keeps pushing his head into his hands and letting out these sighs that make the coffee breath float towards me. "It's so important to stress here, Olive, that I've not formally assessed you. I've only looked at your file and your meds and come to a few hypotheses. You've not been formally diagnosed with bipolar for two main reasons. The first, your age. You're only sixteen and we don't like to jump the gun on this sort of thing. But it's clear you do have mood cycles." He smiles. "But then so does every teenager – that's what makes your age-group so fascinating. But it also makes things a little harder to diagnose."

I find I'm laughing again. "You don't know which cluster to put me in? I don't fit into your diagnostic tree!" I giggle at that. Oh God, I am a special snowflake after all!

"How do you know about mental health clusters?" Dr Jones asks.

"I looked it up."

"That's interesting. Why did you feel the need to do that?"

I guess I could tell them – about all the stuff I've been doing. Then they'd realize that I'm not blowing off group or getting hypomania or whatever it is they say I'm getting – they'll realize I'm just *helping* them do their job. Like an animal sidekick in a Disney movie or something. But Dr Bowers looks like he takes himself way too seriously to appreciate a young lass like me helping an old bloke like him.

"Just interested."

"Well, yes, in your case, we are having some internal debate about where to place you," he says. "And this leads me to concern about your medication. It says in your notes that this is the first time you've been medicated for your episodes of low moods?"

I nod. And also feel a tingle of anger. So he read that much in my notes but not the part about not telling me my diagnosis? I really don't trust him then. This thing. This whole thing is a clown operation. I'm doing a better job getting myself better than they are. I just need them to think I'm okay enough to let me stay – because the food is good and Lewis is here. Plus, the swimming pool is quite handy, and all the photography kit. But I'm done listening to THEM thinking they know what's good for me, when they can't even agree what's wrong with me. I do not trust any of them at all.

"And the hospital put you on a standard antidepressant, is that right?"

I nod. "Very standard. Tesco own-brand."

Neither of them laugh.

"This is my concern." He draws himself up in the chair so we're the same height. I want to stretch my neck up so I'm even higher but I need to act normal enough to be let out of this room to get back to my project. "If you *do* have bipolar, and not just depression, being on an SSRI antidepressant can trigger hypomania. This could be what's happening to you now."

"Or I could just be in a good mood?"

Dr Jones smiles in the tiniest way. "Perhaps. But your lack of sleep is a worry, Olive. We don't want you to crash."

"But I've never slept much! If I hadn't had a label like bipolar stamped onto my forehead, my lack of sleep wouldn't be freaking you out."

Dr Bowers coughs to get the attention back onto him again. "I would like you to try some mood stabilizers, alongside your other meds, Olive," he says. "Have you heard of lithium? You're in a safe environment here. It's a good place to be monitored, see how you take to them."

Lithium… A mood stabilizer… I instantly reject the idea. It's so clear this supposed doctor doesn't have a clue what he's doing. I bet this project doesn't even pass the pilot. It won't if I tell them that they accidentally told me my diagnosis. Especially if my diagnosis is a fucking…fucking… SHRUG!

"But you don't even know what's wrong with me! And I'm supposed to start taking serious drugs on what? Your whim?"

I can hardly compute everything that's just happened. I'm so angry. So confused. So pissed off that I was in such a good mood and now they're ruining it and making me not trust it any more and definitely making me not trust them any more. I don't like the idea of these meds. I don't like the idea of them just shoving them on me based on a random guess. Maybe I don't want my moods to be stabilized. Who would I be without them? Everyone has moods, right?

That's just a side effect of being alive.

"We could just try," he urges. "If you don't like them, you don't have to continue taking them."

I sigh and stretch my legs out. They're sore from all the swimming I've been doing but I've only just noticed. "Look," I say, "I think this place is helping. I don't feel manic, I just feel better! It's quiet here, and there's art class, and I'm learning a lot through therapy…" Sucking up to Dr Jones is bound to help. "I'm swimming and making friends and everything about this place is what I need. I'm just thriving, that's all. I don't need drugs on top of that."

Dr Jones makes a note of what I've said. You can tell when you've said something significant because she writes it down. She takes over again. "It's really great camp is having this effect on you, Olive," she says. "Really, it is. We aim to make this place a safe, restful place and it's brilliant you feel better." She pauses, gives the other doctor a look. "But this camp isn't *real life*. Unfortunately, much as you might like to, you can't stay here for ever. You will be discharged in two weeks. Are you not worried about your ability to cope in an uncontrolled environment?"

"What do you mean?"

"Well, what if you get home and it's noisy? Or you're too busy with school to fit in photography? Or someone is unkind to you? This camp is supposed to help you rest, yes. But you can't hide from the world, Olive. We want you to build your resilience while you're here, so you can cope with the world better once you leave us."

I shake my head. "So you're going to build my resilience by medicating me?"

"Not just that, no. That's just part of a number of things we try here. And you don't really appear to be willing to try lots of things we're offering."

I throw my head back, in frustration, in boredom. Just for something to do. I think about what she said. I didn't think about how I'd transfer living by this new equation into my other life. She sort of has a point… But I just can't believe that the only way to deal with the world is to dope me up so I don't feel the pain so much.

"What if I'm not the problem?" I ask them both. "What if the world is the problem? I mean, surely you shouldn't need to drug me to cope with the world? Surely that's a sign that the world should be drugged or something…" I trail off when I see them give each other a very small look of concern. Uh-oh. I've started down the *The world is evil, it's all a conspiracy* route. They'll definitely want to drug me now. I need to shut up and backtrack. Talk to Lewis. Figure out this kink in the road. And, in the meantime, get Dr Bowers and his guestimation drugs prescription off my back.

"You know what? I'll think about it," I say. "But this is a lot to take in. Can you give me some time?"

"Of course, Olive. Of course."

"Thank you for talking it all through with me," I say. Because gratitude gets you everywhere – even out of sticky sessions with psychiatrists who want to drug you up.

"Any time. Let's review this in a few days."

I only have a few days.

To do what? I'm not sure yet. But I don't have much time to figure it out.

24

It's later and I can't sleep. Again. The air is so muggy but I'm too scared to open the windows in case there's noise. And that hurts. That even after days of doing Everything Right according to maths and science and biology, my brain is still worried about noise. In CBT, Dr Nada asked me to try a night or two without the white-noise machine and see how I do. I'm trying it now but my stomach is flip-flopping with nerves and I HATE THIS! Will I ever stop being worried about noise? I cannot imagine a day when I hear music echo through a wall and just think, *Huh, there's some music playing*, rather than dissolving into hysteria. I writhe in my sheets – my brain playing its favourite game of replaying bad memories like a broken record.

Bipolar.

Bipolar.

They think I have a label and they think that label might be bipolar.

"How are you going to cope in the real world, Olive?"

Because the world *is* messy and loud and chaotic and unkind and unrelenting and unfair and…well…loads of words with "un" before them. They're right. I can't lock myself away from it. I can't live in a bunker my whole life – tempting as that may be. Even then I would have to get a job first before I can save up the money to buy a bunker and how am I supposed to get a job when I'm so messed up? And…and…

Okay, breathe, Olive. Breathe. Get out of this room and breathe.

Before I know it, I'm padding barefoot around the empty corridors, trying to remember exactly which room is Lewis's. There are two doors to choose from and, for a moment, I think, *What the hell am I doing?* It's gone one and Lewis will definitely be asleep and I could easily pick the wrong door. But I find myself eeny-meeny-miny-moing and knocking on one at random. I knock lightly. Nothing. So I knock again. Still nothing. So then I knock out the rhythm of "Happy Birthday" and I'm just getting really into it when the door opens and a very confused, sleepy Lewis sways at the opening.

"I got the right door," I say.

He rubs his eyes, like a toddler does when they've just woken up from their nap.

"Olive? What's going on? Is there a fire?"

I love that he thinks there's a fire. And, if so, that instead of setting off an alarm they send another client round door-to-door to personally wake everyone up so they don't burn to death.

"There's no fire. Can I come in?"

"Umm, is that allowed?"

"First rule of camp is, you don't have to adhere to the rules, remember? So, can I come in?"

"I guess."

I'm already stepping past him, into his room that looks just like my room. Except it smells like boy, even with the window open. I flop down face-first on the bed, letting up another big waft of boy scent, then roll over to look at him.

Lewis stands by the door. It's then I notice the TARDIS pyjamas. It makes my heart warm in a way I don't quite understand.

"So," I tell him. "Apparently I'm bipolar."

He closes the door quietly as his face screws up. "What?"

"In my one-to-one today, they brought in some drug-toting psychiatrist who accidentally told me I have bipolar. Well, they *think* so anyway. They're not entirely sure."

Lewis looks panicked about where to sit so I roll over on the bed and pat the spot next to me. It's still warm from where he was sleeping. He perches on the edge like I have a contagious disease. "I can't believe they did that. You should sue or something."

"The thing that really gets me," I half interrupt. I've been wanting to talk to someone about this since that stupid session ended – spitting me back into camp, right before dinner and everyone laughing about the meatballs and then card games in the common room. No time for me to digest, or allow it to sink in or work out what the hell it means. "...is that they're NOT SURE. I always kind of trusted that they knew what was going on, you know?" My arms flail around the bed so much I almost knock him off. "Do you not find that strange? That there's no, like, test for these things? It's not like diabetes where they can count the insulin in your blood, or a tumour where they can shove you in an MRI scan and bulgy bits all light up. How do they even decide on this stuff? I mean, the whole idea of bipolar was decided by what? A bunch of men in a room wearing white coats, VOTING on what symptoms make it a condition?" That's when I start to cry. A big booey haw-hawing like a donkey. Because I don't know what any of it means. And the people who are supposed to know what it means don't know either. And maybe I should feel like a special snowflake, but I'd really give anything to be typical right now. Boring. A round peg in a round hole.

Lewis pats my shoulder nervously and says, "There, there," and I cry myself out quite quickly, but still feel quite a lot like shit.

"You're shivering," he says. I look down and realize I'm wearing next to no clothes. Only a tiny pair of pyjama shorts and a crop top. No wonder he looks freaked out. I've essentially booty-called him but swapped the sex for crying about my mental health. He grabs his sheets and bundles them around me so I'm in a little cocoon.

"Do you think I'm crazy?" I ask him, with only my face poking out.

He winces and grabs his white dressing gown off the floor, shrugging himself into it. "In order to think you're crazy, I'd have to understand what sanity actually means."

"Never a simple answer with you, is there, Maths Boy?"

"It's true though. Sanity is an idea that changes over time, isn't it? I mean there are loads of things that are considered 'normal' today that used to be considered mentally ill. Like being gay, or being a confident woman who flaunts her sexuality." He smiles. "I'm a man of maths. I will not build my opinions on sand."

I gather his sheets further around me and flop backwards on the bed, staring up at the ceiling. "Oh, tell me about maths, Lewis," I say. "I just want to spend some time pretending I live in a world where two plus two equals four."

He smiles and lies back with me. "Two plus two DOES equal four."

"Isn't that beautiful?"

He leans up on his elbow. "Are you taking the piss?"

I roll over so he can see the sincerity on my face. "No, I'm not. I'm starting to like how maths always has an answer for everything."

"Well, it doesn't always. There's lots of maths that even the top mathematicians can't solve."

I smile. He never lets a glib comment go. Especially if it's about maths. I'm starting to really like that. "For example?"

I watch his face as he starts telling me about prime

numbers. Numbers that can't be divided by anything other than themselves and one, and how mathematicians STILL can't figure out a way of easily working out if a number is a prime number or not. "They've come up with short cuts," he says, rolling onto his back, our heads sharing one pillow. "There's no easy formula. The only way to find out if a number is prime is to painstakingly go through all the possible multiplications. We just don't understand them. They remain very elusive. Although, we *do* know that no prime numbers are even. Except for the number two, every single prime number is odd."

I feel sleep slowly creeping in on me – my limbs getting heavy one by one, the breeze from the window gently tickling my skin, my head fugging, but not enough to not appreciate what this boy in his TARDIS pyjamas is telling me. I think about the word "odd" and all the different things it means. Strange and unusual. Something that doesn't happen often. Something that won't divide. An odd one out – something missing its pair. I have been called "odd" many times in my life. As a child, when I wouldn't stop playing a certain game and would scream if you tried to make me. At school, whispered by other children, when I refused to stand in line or go somewhere else just because a ringing bell told me to.

"Am I odd?" I ask him sleepily.

"I would say so, yes. But in a good way."

We're smiling at each other with our eyes half closed.

"Maybe people like you and me are just prime numbers,"

I tell him. "We don't neatly divide into a world that demands order. And they keep trying to find out why, and what makes us the way we are, but they can't."

"They keep trying to divide us by two," he adds, his voice heavy with sleep.

"Yep, and call us crazy when we don't. And give us therapy and meds and freaking alpacas until we can be moulded into something that can at least pretend it divides nicely into the world."

My eyes keep closing, my lids dropping. Closed, flicker open. Closed, flicker open. His room is quiet, even with the window open. It's kind of nice actually, hearing the breeze of the night blow gently through your space. Maybe I could open my window a crack?

"Sometimes I like to think of myself as an X-Man," Lewis admits. "That my brain and how it plays up is a mutation, but that maybe it makes me a superhero? I just need to stop calling it an illness and work out how I can harness it into something that will save the world."

Saving the world.

I think about that as my brain finds sleep, as Lewis's snuffles become snores and yet that noise doesn't particularly bother me.

You can't adapt the whole world to fit your mental illness.

That's basically what Dr Jones was saying. And I guess it makes sense but it still strikes me as wrong somehow. Though I'm not sure how. My breathing gets heavier and I pull the sheets up over us and I think about prime numbers.

How they don't bend and shape themselves just so they can divide nicely into the world. They stand strong and unmalleable and refuse to have a pattern to them. They are snowflakes and the rest of the numbers are lemmings.

And I sleep.

Just a little.

Not for very long.

When I wake up I think it must be morning, because it normally is when you wake up. It takes me a while to figure out what's going on. Then I hear a grunt and find Lewis asleep next to me. His snoring has gone up multiple notches and probably woke me. I find myself smiling as I watch him gurgle. It's only just on the cusp of dawn. A hint of purple nudges at the curtain to let me know the night is almost over. I feel like I've slept for a thousand years, rather than just a few hours. His clock says 5.02 a.m.

I know what I need to do.

I need them to think I'm not manic. That I'm not bipolar. At least for now. Because I know I am onto something and maybe it's morphed a little but I'm not sure where yet. If I crack it…if I crack it…it feels huge, and I can't have them telling me this X-Man-type mutation is a problem, not a superpower.

Because what if it's a superpower?

Maybe I'm a superhero. One with a maths genius sidekick. Who turns over onto his back, releasing the sheet over him…

… A sidekick who has a sizeable erection in his sleep.

He stirs as I shake the bed with my badly contained laughter and vow to never, ever tell him what I just saw.

The cool air from the morning dew blows through the window, and makes my skin goosebump. I need to get back to my own bed. I write a note to Lewis, so he doesn't think it's anything to do with him when he wakes up.

Couldn't sleep. You snore. Thanks for letting me in though. Love, your favourite Prime Number x

Then I slink around the door, closing it gently behind me.

25

I have a plan.

It is not fully formed yet.

It's good though.

I can sense that much.

But, in the meantime, I need the doctors to lay off.

So my plan is to comply. To eat my breakfast dutifully and to go to group therapy and to remain calm at all times and to do what they tell me to do and to hide myself from them until I know what to do next. I'll have to adapt my schedule and I'll have to ask Lewis if we can swap bracelets at night so it looks like I'm sleeping better than I am.

I'm the first in at breakfast, even though I went out and did my big long walk in the woods beforehand. It was even prettier in the early morning. Dew suspended on each leaf in a webbed collection of teardropped patterns, the call of birds that are too shy to chirp after the sun has risen properly. I will go to group and see what the big fuss is about.

Jamie is the first down and finds me shovelling eggs into my face.

"Coffee," he announces, instead of hello. "I need coffee."

He returns with a mug full of it, sipping slowly. He looks rough. Big bags under his eyes, stubble all over the shop, his hair greasy and lank.

"You all right, Jamie?"

He mutters into his cup. "No, I'm too sober for all this shit."

"Camp getting to you?"

He puts his mug down on the table. "Yes, yes it is. I mean, we've been here two weeks and do you feel any better?"

"Umm, yes actually, a bit," I admit and his face drops. "But not because of camp I don't think," I rush on. "Lewis and I have been working on, like, our own programme and I think that's what's been helping, rather than this place."

"Ahhh, so *that's* what you two have been scurrying about doing? Thanks for letting me in on the secret."

I think he was supposed to say it all jokingly, but it came out fractured and hurt.

"We were going to tell people," I protest. "We're just trying to figure it out. Anyway, Dr Jones thinks the whole thing is just me going through a manic episode."

Jamie picks up his cup. "Ha, you're LITERALLY a manic pixie dream girl."

I shove him, and his coffee spills down his chin.

"Dammit, Olive." But he looks a bit more cheered up.

More and more people trickle in, grab trays of food, disperse themselves around the tables.

Sophie comes up alone, holding her tray. "Can I sit with you two?"

"Of course."

She breaks into a beam and lowers her tray to the table. "Oh my God – thanks, guys! Guess what? That was my homework for today, and I did it!"

"Your homework was to ask if you could sit with us?" Jamie asks dubiously.

She nods a thousand times. "Yes!"

"Well congratulations," I say. "I can't believe we're that scary."

Her hands are actually shaking as she picks up her spoon but she's smiling. "I have this thing, about being socially rejected."

"And what would've happened if we'd said 'Piss off, we don't want you to sit with us'?" Jamie asks as I thump him.

But Sophie takes a big breath and says like she's reciting lines for a play, "Well then, I would've said, 'It's your loss and I can't make you like me.'"

I find my heart smiling at how far Sophie has come in the two weeks we've been here. I may not trust their methods, but at least they're helping her. Hannah comes up with her tray and settles herself down between Sophie and me. We start trading tales of our individual progress, and there are all sorts of things this lot have done that I hadn't even realized.

"It's because you keep blowing off group," Hannah says disapprovingly.

"I'm not today," I tell them. "I'm coming today. Dr Jones is all in a huff with me."

Just then, Lewis makes his entrance. He looks pretty damn tired, even though I can verify one hundred per cent that he got more sleep than me last night. He stops, sees me, and goes bright red for some reason. Then heads over to get some food. I sense Jamie noticing but he doesn't say anything. I look down and feel myself blushing, which doesn't make any sense. Nothing happened. It's Lewis! I don't mean this in a nasty way, but I doubt he's even kissed anyone, and I certainly need to kiss people who have already kissed other people because I find that kissing is only the start of it when I'm in the mood and I need someone who can keep up and hang on…what were we talking about again? Oh yeah, group.

"So what's it like?" I ask. "Do you all know each other's deepest secrets?"

"It's just…sad," Sophie says, surprising us all by talking first. "I mean, it's useful. But, it's sad."

"Sad how?" I ask.

But Lewis interrupts with a bowl of porridge and a luminous face. "Morning, everyone," he chirps. "I overslept. Thought I was going to miss breakfast." He goes even more red and I bite my lip. I suddenly have a worry. A worry that last night and me turning up in next-to-no clothes meant something to him. And I feel guilty.

Because I am a terrible, shitty, awful person.

No, no, no, Olive! You are a good person who tries her best!

Jamie, again, seems to be the only one who notices the awkward – looking from my face to Lewis's and back again. Breakfast continues without incident – except that Gabriella hasn't shown up. I think I've got away with it until Jamie catches up with me on the way to group.

"You need to be careful," he murmurs, as I follow the others clattering down the corridors.

"About what?" I ask all brazen, even though I know what.

Jamie steers me into this little alcove where there's a giant ornate vase stuffed with lilies. He looks at me seriously. "God forbid you lose your temper at me for making assumptions, but what is going on with you and Lewis?"

I feel my temper being lost and Jamie sees it and raises his hand.

"Hear me out!" he says. "It's not just that you're a girl and he's a boy and you're hanging out together and that always has to mean something. But, you are spending a lot of time just you two and…well…I'm a guy, and I can see the way he's started to look at you."

"Started to look at me how?" I snap.

"He looks at you when he knows you're not looking at him. Once I started noticing, I couldn't not notice. Any time he gets the chance, he's looking at you, Olive. Not in a sleazy way… I think…I think he likes you."

Uh-oh.

Uh-oh, uh-oh, uh-oh.

"I've not done anything," I protest. "We're just been working on this project together."

"Hey, I'm not having a go," Jamie says. "I just like Lewis, and I don't want to see him get hurt. It's like kicking a puppy or something. I just wanted to give you a heads-up in case you hadn't noticed it yourself."

"I've not been flirting," I say, almost to soothe myself rather than defend myself to Jamie. "I really haven't. I mean, he would KNOW if I was. I'm not the most subtle flirt."

Jamie raises his eyebrows. "I can imagine."

"Well, that's the only way you'll experience me flirting with you, Jamie. In your imagination."

He laughs, unbothered. "You see! This is why I'm asking you to be cautious. You are spiky, and boys like me can handle you." I roll my eyes. "I know you know what I mean! But, well," he scratches the stubble on his neck, "I get the impression that Lewis hasn't had a lot of experience with girls. You may be showing him more interest than any girl has before and he may be a bit...fragile. You don't want to hurt his feelings."

I sigh and lean against the silky wallpaper. "No, I don't. Why does this ALWAYS happen?"

Because it does. Again, I know it sounds awful, but I do get a lot of boys randomly deciding they're in love with me and it's bloody tiresome, let me tell you. I find notes in my locker written by dudes I chatted to ONCE in the queue to get chips in the school canteen. Or get stopped on the way home by stammering boys I hardly recognize who claim we had a moment when I was sitting next to them on the bus or something. I'm not sure HOW it happens. Maybe, now I have a name for it, my hypomania makes me hyper-attractive to a certain type of guy who feels *carpe-diem-ing* is something he needs to be dragged into by someone else, rather than discovering it himself. And, before you get all jealous, like the other girls at school – the ones like Emily, who whisper that I'm a bitch just loud enough for me to hear – it's never the boys I like who like me. I mean, I only tend to like the boys like Rick, who hate me but have sex with me anyway, which is messed up, I guess. But hellllo, I'm in a residential camp dedicated to mental illness.

"*I'm* not in love with you, if it's any help?" Jamie offers.

"That's brilliant, cheers, Jamie."

"I mean…I would…but, like, I wouldn't want you to label it anything afterwards."

You see, Jamie is *exactly* the sort of person I normally end up with. But not here. Not with new Olive. So I just tell him he's gross, push past him, and stalk after the others.

"You know I was joking," he calls. "I'll let you be my girlfriend, Olive, if it means that much to you."

"Jamie, please kindly go fuck yourself."

His laughter follows me all the way into group therapy.

26

The air in group is like walking into church. Everyone is quiet and still in a circle. Lewis sits and watches Jamie and me laughing as we stumble in.

I see what happens to his face.

Oh bugger.

But I don't have much time to dwell on it because we're the last ones in and Dr Rossen claps his hands when we sit down.

"Good morning, everyone," he bellows. "Now let's begin."

The mood has shifted drastically from breakfast. We've morphed from a bunch of lively chatterboxes into a sullen group of teenagers having a silent competition over who can stare at the floor more intently.

"Now," Dr Rossen says, all soothy soothing, "yesterday we talked about our childhoods and I want us to pick up where we left off. Does anyone want to go first?"

I'm scared Dr Rossen will make me talk if I make

eye-contact. And I really don't feel like talking. It's enough I'm here, thank you very much, when I could be doing a much better job mending my own mental health.

Darrell raises his arm and I'm temporarily safe.

I've not paid much attention to Darrell until now. Is it bad that I only know him vaguely by his diagnosis? (Depression and anxiety.) That, and the fact he regularly steals the only cereal with chocolate bits? Seriously, he eats bowl after bowl of that stuff, without even THINKING maybe some of us want sugar crystals in our milk too. He stands up and wraps his arms around himself.

"So, er," he starts, "all I can remember from being a young kid is my parents fighting. They argued about everything, and they didn't even try to hide it. I'd hear them screaming while I was put down to nap. They'd have big barneys in the car park of the supermarket that everyone would watch. When they FINALLY got divorced, I thought things would get better but they just got worse." He takes a long breath in and glances up at the ceiling. "Mum and I had to move into this tiny flat and we had next to no money. She got a job working at the post office but we were poor. All our food was the really cheap stuff that's about to go off. And I never had trainers like the trainers you're supposed to have at school. In winter we couldn't afford to have the heating on much, so when we washed my clothes they didn't dry properly and they smelled funny..." He trails off for a moment, lost in his unhappy memory. "So, of course I got bullied at school." He raises both eyebrows. "I mean, the poor kid in the wrong trainers who smells funny? Oh, yeah, and my mum's black so that was extra fun. Because what's a bit of bullying without some added racism, you know?" Then, it's like he runs out of fuel. Or just his ability to share something so sad and personal. He laughs – weirdly, loudly. "So, yeah, that's my happy childhood. Who else wants to share?"

Dr Rossen smiles that proper therapy smile – all warm and beamy and *Well done you.* "That was very brave of you to share, Darrell, thank you. Do you ever think about how your childhood could have impacted on you now?"

He smiles. "Well, I always eat nice food when I get the chance." He laughs again while I slink down in my chair and feel like the world's worst human being for getting all bitchy about the cereal. I'm a bad person. Horrid, awful, terrible, selfish person.

No, no, no, Olive.

You are a good person who tries their best and didn't know young Darrell couldn't afford nice cereal.

"Anything else?" Dr Rossen prompts, which pisses me off some as it's obvious Darrell is done with dredging up his stuff.

"Well, it seems clichéd to think that a not-so-great childhood could've caused all my problems now, but I guess it makes sense?" Darrell asks it like it's a question.

"Good, good." Dr Rossen nods then looks around at the rest of us, eyeing up his next victim. I'm struggling to see how Darrell was helped at all by the last five minutes but hey, I'm just here to show my face and get doctors off my back, not to judge. "Now, who else wants to share? Maybe if…"

Gabriella stands up before he's finished his sentence. She looks all…off. She didn't come down to breakfast and she's wearing a grey hoody with a hole in the sleeve. Her hair is all fuzzed out – rather than pulled into one of her normal intricate hairstyles. "I'll go," she announces, jerking her chin up, daring one of us to say we want it to be our turn. Then she launches right into it. "So I was abused by my dad from, like, the age of two. In all the ways you can abuse someone, I guess. Physically, emotionally, sexually. Mum never did anything. She was fucking useless. Sometimes I can even understand why he hit her."

My mouth is open, eyes bulging in horror. What? I mean WHAT? I look up to see if anyone else is reacting like me, but they're not… Has she mentioned this in group before? She must've done for everyone else to be acting so complacent.

"Anyways," she breezes, like she's telling us a story about when she first learned to tie her shoelaces, "EVENTUALLY school got suspicious, I got put into care. Got abused there too, of course. I remember this really, really good day, when the social worker took me out to McDonald's and let me get two Happy Meals. Then they found me a family, but they couldn't cope with me – because I kept screaming and trying to run away. So they found me another foster family. My current one. They're all right. Though they struggle with my moods. I think this place is my last shot to sort my shit out. So, no pressure or anything." She smiles at Dr Rossen, who smiles back warmly, like she's just told a clever joke. She pushes up the sleeve of her hoody absent-mindedly and I can't help but look at her scars. Really look at them. It is not a normal arm. There is essentially no skin left on it – but scar tissue built on more scar tissue from old fat honking scars that sit out like lumps on her skin.

"And how do you feel about your childhood, Gabriella?" the doctor asks her.

She shrugs. "Well, I didn't really have one, did I?" She doesn't seem that fussed, or that angry, or even sad. Just matter of fact. The voice of someone who has told this horrible story many times before – each time hoping the act of telling it will magic away all the damage it's caused.

I shake my head very gently, almost as if I'm trying to dislodge what I've just heard because my brain finds it too sad. And I feel guilty once more. Terribly, terribly guilty. For the fact I kind of take the piss out of Gabriella. Or judge her. Or find her attention-seeking or annoying or overdramatic. She launches into a very graphic story about her dad and the room tenses as she starts to describe an incident from when she was five. Even Dr Rossen seems a little bit unsure about when exactly to interrupt her. Each word hits me like one of those bullets that explode out on impact. Because the thing is, you know there's bad in the world. You're aware of it. You switch on the TV, or scroll through a newsfeed and there's doom and there's gloom and there's unfairness and there's horror but you don't always really take it in. But sometimes the world forces you to listen. Sometimes you hear something so awful that you can't scroll past it. And Gabriella's story is chilling my bones so cold I'm not sure they'll ever warm up again.

"It's great that you want to share so much today," Dr Rossen interjects, just as Gabriella pauses for breath. "But maybe we can go into more detail in your one-to-one session?"

Gabriella pulls down her sleeves and says, "Oh, right, sorry." Then she sits down and pulls her hood up.

"I didn't say that so you felt you couldn't share any more," he says kindly.

"No, whatever, I'm cool."

I think he's not going to leave it, but he does. He says, "Thank you again, for being so brave. Everyone say, 'Well done, Gabriella,'" and we chant it at her like we're kids in primary school. She doesn't even look up.

That

Is

When

I

Have

The

Thought.

The big thought. The thought I've been incubating but I didn't know what it was. Because my throat is tight and I'm looking at Gabriella and kind of wanting to cry and kind of thinking that's totally inappropriate because she isn't crying and she's the one it happened to. And I think of those scars under the thin material of her jumper, and of the list of diagnoses she has: borderline personality disorder, bulimia, depression… And my thought is.

My

Thought

Is:

Maybe she wouldn't have all of these problems if she hadn't had all that horrid stuff happen to her?

And Darrell, maybe he wouldn't be depressed if the world was equal and fair.

This is what it is… This is the thought:

We. Are. Not. The. Problem.

The WORLD needs to change, not us.

Because if the world wasn't so messed up, maybe there wouldn't be mental illness. Maybe there wouldn't be low moods, or scars hidden under jumpers, or being too scared to leave the house.

I'm wriggling in my chair. I can hardly stand it. This electricity.

It's someone else's turn, and Hannah stands up and talks about how her parents are divorced too – which seems kind of trivial after Gabriella's big share – but still, that sucks. And maybe Hannah wouldn't be all ill upstairs if her parents hadn't got divorced. And maybe, just maybe, none of us would be here if life had been easier or fairer or righter or happier or less scary. And maybe it's not about how to mend us now we've all gone mad, but about figuring out why we've gone fucking mad in the first place. And then MAYBE society should ensure that sort of thing doesn't happen again. Because it's all very well training psychologists to sit us down and get us to talk about our awful backgrounds, but why aren't we trying to stop awful stuff? I mean, I guess society TRIES to stop bad things happening, but they're doing SUCH A BAD JOB AT IT, JUST LISTEN TO WHAT'S HAPPENED TO GABRIELLA. And…and…

Oh God, I can feel this thought blooming. Like on those nature programmes when they shove a camera onto a flower seed and show the footage of it growing really, really fast. I feel the roots go into the earth and I feel the stem start to grow and I feel the leaves unfurling and the petals turning pink one by one.

Hannah is tearing up, her voice catching as she talks about her dad and how she hardly gets to see him any more, and I should be listening and nodding and digesting but instead I'm fizzing and onto something and oh God…I can't stay. I can't stay in this room when my body and brain are overspilling with so much energy.

And I'm up. Halfway through Hannah's speech, but I'll have to say sorry later because I cannot control all this energy. This feeling. This amazing feeling that I'm onto something even bigger than what I was already onto.

My feet thud against the floor as I dash out. I feel everyone's eyes on my back. Hannah stops mid-sentence to watch my exit. I'm guessing maybe I'm the first one to take up the *You can leave at any time* rule of group. But I don't care. I'm rushing through the corridors now, finding my way outside. Because I just feel the NEED to see the sky. I call "Hi" to Grace on reception to ensure I don't send off suspicion vibes, then I push through the double doors and fresh air and sunshine and oxygen all pour over me. I throw my head back and let the heat hit my face. The fizzing is too much though, I cannot stand still. I throw myself across the lawn, running across the manicured grass, heading for the woods. It feels good to run, the way it hurts your lungs almost instantly. Makes your body know it's ALIVE and CAN DO THIS and, and…

I'm almost at the treeline when I hear my name being called.

I halt and swivel, and see who's followed me out. And there, back by the house, is Lewis. Of course it's Lewis. A little dot of him. He waves both arms over his head, signalling that I should wait, then he takes off over the grass towards me. He runs funny, bless him. All limbs everywhere, his scrawny arms kind of just flailing across his body.

"Olive." When he reaches me he has to bend over to catch his breath. There's sweat on his brow, his back heaves with each pant. Whereas I could run for miles and miles and miles and still not feel tired.

He straightens himself back up. "Are you okay?" he asks. "You just ran off? I was worried about you. And, this morning. You…you weren't there."

There is a tiny voice in my head. A voice that is saying,

Remember what Jamie said, be careful be careful, do not break this boy's heart. But it's just a whisper. Whereas the voice of my groundbreaking idea is bellowing and shouty and CAPS LOCK, so I grab Lewis's hands and squeeze them and say, "Lewis, I've had a thought! A really good thought."

"What? Seriously, are you okay? I mean, I know you're not used to group, but Gabriella kind of really went for it today and…"

I wave my hand to stop him. "Oh God, it was awful, wasn't it? I feel so guilty. I had no idea. But she's the one who's actually made me realize something. Our algorithm, Lewis, it's the wrong thing to do," I say.

His eyebrows draw down in confusion. "What do you mean?"

"It's selfish," I explain, wishing I could just download my brain into his to save the time of explaining it. "And short-sighted and too personalized and impossible to roll out on a grand scale and we need to change what we're doing and do it for good and…"

It's his turn to raise his hand to interrupt me. "But you say it's been helping you feel better? It's working…I mean…"

"It might be working," I say.

Although another tiny voice in my head, a voice very similar to Dr Jones's, whispers, *Or maybe you're just manic again, Olive,* but I ignore the voice and carry on.

"But I just realized in group that it's bigger than that. That I shouldn't be focusing on just me and my little life and

240

just my broken brain. Because all of it is part of something bigger. And I'm being self-absorbed and we're using this idea and your brilliant genius on a tiny thing – making one person feel better – when we could be working to make EVERYTHING better."

I grin at him but he isn't there yet. He's still looking at me like I'm mad, which I'm pretty used to, to be honest, but not from Lewis.

"Okay, I'll try and put it simply," I relent. "Think about it. We've been working out what we can do to make someone, specifically me, sane again. But then I was listening to Gabriella and thought, everything that's happened to that girl was preventable. Everything. And maybe she wouldn't have ended up in here if it had been stopped." I take a breath and accidentally scrape my hand on a stray branch from all my enthusiastic waving. It doesn't even hurt. "It got me thinking. I've always just thought that mental illness was something that happens to you. Like God has gone eeny-meeny-miny-mo, pointed at you when he says 'mo' and then, TADAA, you get a mental disorder. But it's more than that. Being here and having to listen to everyone's childhood and how damn horrible their lives have been has made me realize that. What if we change our focus to what makes people *insane*? What creates mental health problems in the first place?" I grab his hand out of pure excitement. "And then we can stop it happening! We'd help so many people, we'd nip so many things in the bud. Rather than slapping a bandage on the oozing bleeding wound that bad childhoods create, why don't we stop the wound happening in the first place! What do you think?"

Lewis looks down at our hands. He is too quiet for too long. I can't handle it. Then he says, "I don't want to be a buzzkill, Olive, but aren't people already doing that? I mean, isn't society always trying to stop bad things happening to people?"

No.

Why is he being so difficult? Doesn't he see?

"Not doing a very good job though, are they? Look at Gabriella and everything that's happened to her. Look how badly she's been failed by, well, everything."

"And you think we could do something better? You think we can be better than, say, social services? Or the police?"

"YES!" I have no doubt that we can. Because I am special and Lewis is special and we've already made a whole sanity algorithm in just a week. And, at the very least, we should try. Because what if I can do something that stops people feeling like I feel? How amazing would that be? How much comfort would that give me? I just really feel like I'm the only one who knows how to stop this. Maybe I'm not a bad person, maybe I am a good person who tries their best. Maybe all of this, my mind being what it is, maybe that's what's NEEDED to work out a way to change things. Really, *really* change things.

"This is too big, Olive," Lewis says to the leaves on the ground. He is not with me yet. I can tell he wants to be with me, but he thinks I'm being overdramatic. Okay. I will make it into bite-sized pieces for him. I will try and start us small. He isn't in my head, he can't see all the glitter.

"Look, I know it seems a bit dramatic," I start, even though I don't think it's dramatic *at all*. "But it can't hurt to try, can it? We can at least get some people together, see if they have any ideas? I mean, you and I made a whole algorithm in a week. That's pretty big, and we did it."

Lewis starts to smile. I still get a whiff of a vibe. A vibe that maybe he's only going along with this because he likes me, but he's still smiling.

"So you want to assemble a group of people with mental health problems and see if together we can change the world?"

"I mean, essentially I'm asking you if you want all your comic book dreams to be realized."

He laughs with all of his gum. "You're just asking me if we can build a team of X-Men? And together we'll fight the Magneto of mental illness?"

I smile at him. "If that's how you want to put it, that's how we'll put it. Let's get the word out, see if anyone's interested in some extracurricular world-saving alongside their CBT and group therapy?" I pause, and remember what Gabriella said and feel like my stomach has been taken between two hands and twisted. "Is it weird that I feel guilty, about what happened to Gabriella?" I ask him, almost not sure of my words as they're falling out of my mouth. "I mean, clearly she has a reason that she is the way she is, and maybe if we look into it, there'll be a reason I'm the way

I am. But, like, I've never had to go through anything like she has... Why am I still ill?"

Lewis bites his lip. "I don't think it's as easy as that. I don't think mental illness is as simple as one plus one equals two. But, I do think you're right. There will be common patterns that cause common things."

"The lemmings pattern."

We grin at each other.

"Yes, like lemmings. But I don't think you should feel guilty for not having something traumatic happen to you and still being the way you are. I'll have a look at the data we collected and start looking at causes of mental illness, if you like...but don't beat yourself up, Olive. It may be, in your case, you being you is just...well...you being you."

"I'm just a special snowflake," I tell him in a high silly voice. "I have lived in a happy family and wanted for nothing and yet I still have a misbehaving brain because I am soooo special."

"Well, I think you're special," Lewis mutters.

The comment flops out, bounces a bit on the grass and lies there dying. He goes bright red, and it makes me go red too. Because I can't deal with this right now. We have to get on with things. We have to recruit and get a plan together and save the goddamn freakin' world and oh no, he looks like he's dying. I have to say something. I have to, I have to.

"Well, you're quite snowflakey yourself, Maths Boy."

There. That was okay, wasn't it? A compliment back? But a matey one? Lewis seems as unsure about how to take it as

I am. He blinks a few times, like the act could help him work out what I mean by it. I can almost see him trying to search for a formula to crack the comment, one he can feed through his internal *Does she like me?* algorithm. Bollocks, Jamie was so right. I need to be SO careful about this. I shouldn't have gone into his room last night. I should've picked up on the signs earlier. I'm a bad, terrible, awful person… No…I am a good person who tries their best and TODAY I'VE REALIZED I'M GOING TO WORK OUT A WAY TO STOP MENTAL ILLNESS SPREADING AND THEN ALL OF MY PAIN WILL HAVE BEEN WORTH IT.

I cough even though I don't need to cough and change the subject back to the matter at hand. "So, do you reckon people will want to help us?"

I could crack an egg on Lewis's face and it would cook in an instant. But he manages to pull it together and says, "There's only one way to find out."

27

Gabriella pushes her sunglasses down her nose. "Exactly how I pictured the start of the revolution," she deadpans. "Scooping up alpaca poo."

"Think of it as a metaphor," I say, as I hand out the shovels. "The purpose of this meeting is all about how to shovel shit out of the world."

Jamie rolls his eyes. "Can you just tell us why we're here already?"

Okay, so turn-out for my first meeting about How to Save the World is not encouraging. We quietly put the word out that Lewis and I were starting a side-project for some kind of social revolution, and we have four takers. Just four. The other "clients" just looked at me like I was crazy, which, considering we must all be a little crazy to be in here in the first place, I think is a little bit rich and don't-throw-rocks-if-you-live-in-a-greenhouse. Hang on. Where was I? Oh yeah. There are four other people here – just four. Lewis and I managed to get us all assigned to the same stable so we can talk without suspicion.

It's me, Lewis, Jamie, Gabriella, Sophie – and, surprisingly, Hannah, who is perched high up on the fence as she finds the smell of the alpacas too triggering.

My crack unit.

My collective noun of superheroes.

Oh dear…

No. It's going to be fine. Amazing. World-changing.

"Thanks for coming, everyone," I start. "I really appreciate it, and I hope you'll hear me out."

I lean on my shovel and then get bored doing that so lean off it again. "So, umm, Lewis and I have been working on a project while we've been here. Basically, I started thinking about how our bracelets are being used as a suicide prevention device, and that made me think about algorithms for mental illness, and we've figured out you can use maths to make an algorithm that can improve mental health. Lewis? Would you care to explain?"

He looks like he's about to keel over, his face practically green as he steps forward. He steadies himself on his pitchfork and then he starts to talk about maths. He tells them about algorithms, about patterns, about our formula, about Big Data and how you can "mine" it to find answers to life's biggest problems. And even though he's talking about MATHS, he's holding their attention. His love for it is so intoxicating. He should totally be a maths teacher, although I don't think that's the sort of thing people like to be told. Once he's done, Hannah's hand shoots up angrily from her spot on the fence.

"So, you, like, have known about something that, if we work it out, could make all of us better, and you've just kept it to yourselves?"

I nod. "Yes." There's no point denying it. "And I'm sorry. But I'm a selfish cow sometimes. I got self-obsessed and wrapped up in only my own pain and mending only me, and I'm sorry for that." I swallow. "But that's changed now. I don't want to be selfish any more. I want to be a better person – not just better mentally, but better in my soul. I reckon one can help the other, and I've been thinking about how far Lewis and I have come, just the two of us. And now I've realized that we're focusing our energies on the wrong thing. We need to look at the whole of the world, at the whole of society, and what's causing people to get mentally ill in the first place. Then, I want to think of something to do that might stop it. I want to do something that makes not just me saner, but the whole world saner. If we really look at what causes mental illness, and can think of some way of stopping these things from happening, think about all the pain we can prevent…"

I realize I'm rambling. Most of them are nodding a little but also pulling confused faces. Lewis looks all proud.

"I'm not saying you sack off camp; I'm not saying this will definitely work. I just really wanted to try and do something that isn't about me, that is about fixing more than me, and I could really do with some help. So, if any of you want to be a part of this, please put your hand up. I just thought we could at least try..." I finally trail off.

Lewis raises his arm. Of course he does. Gabriella puts her arm up too but tentatively. "I'm not *not* in," she says. "But it all does sound a bit nuts. It also sounds like it could be fun."

Sophie looks at Hannah. "Do you really think we can do something that helps stop mental illness?" Sophie almost whispers. "I mean, we're just a bunch of teenagers."

"Hey." Gabriella points at her. "Never underestimate what a bunch of teenagers can do."

I wink at her. "True," I say. "Jamie? What do you think?"

He's leaning against the stable, his arms crossed. Looking kind of bored throughout my inspirational speech.

"You in?" I ask.

"I don't know yet," he admits. "I mean, I get what you're saying and all, and I'm not denying the world is a messed-up place, but I don't think it's the world's fault that I'm ill. No offence, Olive, but that's a bit overdramatic..."

I feel a flare of temper ignite in me. I have to stretch out my fingers to stop them clenching into the balls of my hands. *What do you know?* I think. *What the actual fuck do you know?*

He must see my face, because he says, "Don't get all pissy. I'm allowed to disagree with you. I'm only saying it's my fault I'm a stupid addict. It's only my fault. I don't want to blame the world because I don't think that's helpful."

Lewis steps forward, eager to defend me. "We're not

trying to say that the world is totally to blame for EVERYTHING."

"Well good, because that's what it sounded like. The reason I'm in here is because I smoked too much weed and that's my own fault."

"But WHY did you smoke all that weed?" Hannah asks him.

"Because I'm an idiot!" he shouts.

"But WHY are you an idiot?!" Hannah shouts back.

At that, he bursts out laughing, leaning against the stable door to hold himself up. "I don't know," he says almost hysterically. "Maybe I was just born this way."

"Look," I say, carefully weighing up each word I say before I say it. I realize that maybe the idea is too big for them to get on board with right away; they don't have the clarity of mind I have. I can't blame them for that. I have to get them to my point slowly. Carefully. "Jamie, no one here is doubting that you were born an idiot." We all giggle. He doesn't. "But there might be other things going on too." I sigh. "Look, Lewis and I did some research about mental illness the other week and we've made a list of all the causes we can think of – like the things people talk about in group. Can we just start by looking at it and see if we come up with any ideas?"

Jamie's bad mood radiates off him like a skunk smell. He chucks his fork into the hay. "Oh yeah? So what are we going to do, guys?" he asks, all taking the piss. "Just, like, solve poverty before dinner and then stop people abusing children in our free time tomorrow?"

"We're not at that bit yet," Lewis replies quietly. "You've got to understand a problem before you can solve it."

"But you still think we can just CURE the world of abuse and poverty and all the other things that screw everyone up? Us lot? When, like, the government and police can't even manage it?"

"Hey!" Gabriella says, pointing at him. "As a victim of abuse, I know too well how hard it is to CURE abuse. But, you know what, arsehole? After listening to what Olive has said, I want to at least TRY to do SOMETHING that might help. What do *you* want?"

Jamie shakes his head and won't look at us. His mood has swollen, like a storm forming at sea. "I DON'T KNOW, OKAY?"

"Then stop being unhelpful," Lewis practically yells. "You don't have to stay."

Jamie picks up the fork just so he can chuck it back into the hay again. "You're right," he admits. "I don't." His fists clench and unclench. "I don't *need* your research anyway. I know what got me here already. SUBSTANCE ABUSE."

Gabriella, unbothered by his anger, steps closer to him. "But WHY did you start abusing substances, Jamie?"

That's when the top blows off his volcano. "BECAUSE I'M IN A BAND!" he shouts, and Sophie squeals. "I'm not traumatized or poor or abused, okay? I just smoked a shit ton of weed because I'm in a band and that's what people in bands do. I'm just a selfish idiot addict. How are you going to save the world from selfish idiots? Because I'll tell you what…" His voice lowers to almost a growl. "I don't think absolving myself of all responsibility for the bad decisions I've made in my life is going to make the world a better place. In fact, I think it's going to make it a worse one. Yeah, shit happens, yadda yadda. But *I'm* the reason I'm here. *I'm* the reason I'm like this. And I'm the reason the moment I'm out of here I'll probably go straight to my dealer and buy an ounce, smoke it and probably start tripping out again. Letting people off is not the answer." He shakes his head and I really think he's going to punch a wall or something. He shoves a cigarette into his mouth and tries to light it but the lighter keeps sputtering and won't catch. "Fuck this. Fuck all of this," he shouts, before stalking off, leaving only a big pile of dung behind him.

We all stand in stunned silence for a moment.

"Shall I go after him?" I ask.

"Don't bother," Gabriella says. "There's no point until he's calmed down."

We all look at each other in that kind of stunned embarrassment you get when a human being has not acted in the appropriate human being way. Though considering our location, we should be used to that by now.

"Is he right?" Sophie asks. She looks like she's been slapped. "No offence, Olive. But this does all sound a bit… big. And, like, maybe Jamie's right."

She looks so upset, her shoulders all hunched. Lewis gently rests a hand on her shoulder. The gesture seems to settle her and seeing him touch her makes my tummy do something.

"He's half right," Lewis says. "Maybe we've not explained it properly. Like, maybe to some extent, we are born this way. Maybe part of it is biology and genetics and chemical imbalances. But WHY are our brains like that?"

I can't look away from Lewis's face, from the passion he feels. I made him believe this. I made him feel like that. I am good, I am good, I am good. And I can hopefully make the others feel like that too. Like there's something to fight, something worth fighting for.

"Brains don't just randomly develop chemical imbalances," he continues. "Witnessing a traumatic event can rewire your brain, not being fed the right food can rewire your brain, chronic insomnia can rewire your brain, being abused can rewire your brain. Don't you see? It's everything and nothing. It's really simplistic but it's also complicated."

Hannah raises her hand from her spot on the wall. "Is it just me, or is this getting a bit out of hand? Yeah, Jamie's being a dick, but he's right. There's so many variables, we won't be able to do anything big."

"So?" I ask.

"So, what's the point?" She shrugs.

It's my turn for my fists to clench. "We've got to do SOMETHING." Anger zings through me. It's only our first meeting and everyone's already saying, *This is too hard*?

"Look!" Lewis waves both his arms like I'm a bull to

tame. Maybe I am. "Can you please just listen to me? As I said, we have to understand the problem BEFORE we can mend it. We're just jumping the gun. Can we please at least talk about the research Olive and I found? THEN we can freak out about how insignificant we are."

Somehow Hannah calms us all down by reminding us that we really should probably muck out the stables at some point. We allow a time-out and start cleaning the place up, while she stays perched on the wall, looking mildly ill.

Jamie shuffles back and murmurs an apology.

"What was that, Jamie?" I shout.

"Piss off." He picks up a shovel and starts scooping up some mess.

"So, you in?" I ask.

He shrugs. "Anything that will take my mind off how much I wish I wasn't sober."

I shovel and rake and the mundanity of the work feels good, especially combined with the conversation.

When the poo has all been shovelled, Lewis finally gets out his list.

MENTAL ILLNESS RISK FACTORS:
- Doing badly at school, or pressure to do well academically
- Being abused or neglected as a child
- Chronic insomnia

- Chronic pain
- Being born a premature baby
- Abusing drugs and alcohol
- Being exposed to violence and trauma
- Family conflict
- Being lonely
- Being poor
- Having a physical illness
- Having a neurochemical imbalance in your brain
- Having parents with mental health problems, or parents who are addicts
- Grief
- Having bad social skills
- Reading disabilities
- Being on social media too much
- General "stressful life events"
- A bad diet
- Being discriminated against for the colour of your skin, or your sexuality, or your disability

We all peer over the notebook with grim expressions on our faces.

"So," I say. "Who can tick off any of the following?"

There is a lot of nodding happening around me.

"I think I actually have a full house," Gabriella says. She puts both hands round her mouth. "BINGOOOOOOOO!" she yells. "I'm the craziest!"

Sophie's pale face is peering at the list intently, mouthing along with the words as she reads them. "Guys?" she says, her voice quivering. "I think I've got an idea."

We all turn to look at her and that's when it happens. She starts shaking at becoming the centre of attention.

"What is it?" I ask, trying to be supportive.

"I'm just looking at all these things and thinking what might mend it…and…and…" Her head collapses down onto her lap as she bursts into tears.

Hannah's instantly soothing her. "It's okay, Sophie, it's okay. Breathe, breathe."

It takes me a second to work out what's going on, then Sophie looks up and gasps, "Sorry, it's just you're all… looking," and I realize she's having a panic attack. She starts gasping and spluttering, her hands shaking, her whole face white. "I…I…" she stumbles, her eyes bulging, tears running out of them. I see her look at us desperately and get redder and more short of breath.

"We're not looking," I say, and I make everyone but Hannah turn around quietly. "It's okay, Sophie, we're not looking. We're turning away and you can take your time." I have no idea if I'm doing or saying the right thing as I turn my back to her. I can hear her wheezing behind me as Hannah makes cooing noises.

"So…embarrassing…" Sophie manages to stutter out.

"Don't be silly," Hannah says.

"Have you not SEEN my behaviour here?" I hear Gabriella say to my side. "I overshare more than I freaking breathe."

"I've had at least twelve hissy fits in the last ten minutes," Jamie adds. "So I cannot judge."

"Sophie," I call over my shoulder. "I got SEDATED after running into the security guards in the middle of the night," I remind her.

Her sobbing is interrupted by a giggle. Then laughter. Then full-blown hysterics. You can feel the anxiety subside as it makes room for her giddiness. We all turn around at the same time to find her still crying, but with a grin across her face.

"You're right," she gets out. "You all get it. I don't know why I get embarrassed."

"We can turn away again if you like?" I ask and she snorts.

"No, that's very kind. I don't know where that came from."

Hannah nods. "Hey, sometimes they just sneak up on you."

Sophie sniffs. "I thought I would be okay because I've been doing so much better, but, like you all turned and looked at me at exactly the same time and it… I sound crazy." She lets out a crack of laughter but none of us laugh back.

Because it doesn't sound crazy. Or illogical. Or weird. Or any of the other words she's worried we're thinking. Because all of us here, in this little stable, holding pitchforks and mucking out alpacas, we all know it doesn't have to be logical, know that logic has nothing to do with it.

Is this the start of a proper friendship? I ask myself. Realizing that for the first time ever, when it comes to me and this demanding head of mine, I don't feel so very alone. *Could this little group be something?* I reach out and gently squeeze Sophie's knee. "You don't sound crazy, we all get it. Now, do you want to tell us your idea?"

Sophie gulps and wipes her eyes with her sleeves pulled over her hands. "It might not be anything but here goes." We all settle around her like it's story time. "Okay, so I kind of agree with Jamie."

Jamie shoots me a *See!* grin and I stick my tongue out.

"He's right. I don't think we can just magically solve poverty, or abuse or malnutrition or all the other huge risk factors that cause mental illness. I mean, the government are trying, and even they're not doing a very good job. But, I was just thinking, what *small* thing could make a difference? What tangible thing could we all do that might help others with their mental health?" She pauses to take a breath, looks around our little circle of misfits, sitting in the dust. "And, you guys have totally just demonstrated this." She pauses again. "Kindness," Sophie says. "The world needs more kindness."

We all look around at each other as her words sink into us like raindrops into grass.

"Kindness?" Gabriella repeats, just for something to say.

Sophie nods. "And compassion. Aren't a lot of those horrible risk factors somehow linked to a lack of compassion? Poverty is a sign of a broken society that doesn't care about looking after the needy. Understanding abuse, and how to stop it, takes time and compassion. Or just, like, how *mean* everyone is to each other these days. What if an inherent lack of kindness in this world is changing our brain chemistry too?" Her pace is getting slower and it's like watching a plant grow towards the light – I'm mesmerized by Sophie's transformation. "I don't know," she says, "but I feel like out of all the things this world values, kindness is very far down the list. When it's the one thing that could help all of us thrive."

There's a silence while we all digest what she's said but Hannah surprises us by shaking her head. "It's not that simple," she says. "Sorry, Sophie, but I don't think it's that simple. Kindness can't be the plaster that mends literally everything."

"I'm not saying it will mend everything," Sophie squeaks back, just as I was about to jump in and defend her myself. "But it will help. And that's another thing. If people were kinder in general, wouldn't that help people who already have mental health problems, as well as prevent them? I mean, look how quickly I recovered from a panic attack just now. Because you were all understanding and nice about it. Whereas, if I'd felt you judging me or getting irritated, it probably would've been much worse." She turns to Jamie, who's leaning against his fork, staring out at the white alpaca that's grazing to the side of the stable. "And what about kindness towards yourself?" she says to him. "How much quicker would we recover if we were compassionate towards ourselves? If we forgave ourselves? If we cut ourselves a bit of slack?"

Jamie bristles as he turns to face her. "You're saying I need to forgive myself for being a useless weak addict?"

And, remarkably, Sophie doesn't crumble under his glare. In fact, she grows. I see her visibly expand, the space between each vertebra of her spine rising up, making herself taller, taking up room. "Yes," she answers simply. "You do."

And I think he's about to kick off but he doesn't. He just looks at her, then he makes this weird noise, like a deranged hiccup.

He's crying.

Jamie is crying.

None of us know where to look – as this boy essentially falls apart in front of us. I think we're all in shock for about thirty seconds, until Sophie's words kick in.

Be kind. Be compassionate.

Then we all shuffle over to comfort him at once.

"Are you okay?" I put my arm around him and bring his head into my shoulder.

"I'm not crying," he mutters into my collarbone, even though my collarbone is now very wet indeed.

"Of course you're not," I tell him. "You've just got multiple things stuck in both eyes."

"Your ego?" Lewis suggests and Jamie's cry turns into a hack of a laugh before he cries again. He cries for maybe five minutes while we all stand around and pat him. Eventually he emerges from under my arm.

"Are you having a breakthrough, J?" I ask.

"Shut up…maybe. I dunno, argh!" He throws his hands

up in the air. "I still think I'm a selfish twat. I knew that drugs were bad and I did them anyway. Because I wanted to be cool, because I liked them. And now look what I've done to myself. I'm so...angry at myself." His hands bunch into fists again but he lets out a deep breath and unravels them. "But, maybe you're right, Sophie. Maybe I do need to forgive myself."

A spark has hit me.

A lightning bolt.

It is raining in glitter.

Because this is it.

This.

Is.

It.

Look! Look at what's been achieved in just half an hour's kindness. Sophie got through her panic attack, Jamie cried, but a good cry. OhmyfreakingholymolyJesus, Sophie has got it! We need kindness. We need to kill with kindness. Cure with compassion. It is the glue we have forgotten. It's the skill we've all neglected. And we are eating ourselves because of it.

I'm not the only one buzzing. You can feel it in the air around us. Everyone is smiling at each other and fizzing with the thought of it.

"This is something," I say, stating the obvious. "You know that, right?" I see Hannah open her mouth to object. "Yes, I know, we're not going to cure the world with just kindness, but it can at least help. Think about it. Think of every single horrid moment of your life. Now, imagine how different things would've been if someone there, in that moment, had been kind to you. Like, they didn't laugh when you fell over, or interrupt you when it took you too long to get a sentence out, or push a spliff into your face and make it clear it was what you needed to do to fit in." I think of my own life, it spins and spins towards me and I grasp at the memories. "Think about how much easier it would be if people weren't constantly judging you for the mistakes you make, the people you kiss, the moods you go through… If they just tried to understand and be compassionate towards you, rather than sneering or judging or being cold or mean or bitchy or…"

I trail off. Because I feel it would've helped. I know there are all sorts of reasons why I am the way I am. Some of which aren't my fault, are just in my genes or from experiences I can't even remember. Lots of things about me are my fault too. Because I do make decisions that I know hurt others. I am not a kind person who does kind things, but I'm trying to be, and maybe this is the start of all that. And even though I've probably deserved all the shitty things people have said and done to me, it would have been nice to have had some kindness along the way. It is so hard being me and kindness won't change who I am, but it will make it a hell of a lot easier.

"How do we make everyone more kind though?" I ask the group. Because, from what I know of people, it's not something that comes naturally to us any more.

Lewis steps forward into the circle.

"That, I reckon, is what we need to use our spare time here to do. Together we MUST be able to think of something."

"So you want us to form a group?" Gabriella asks. "Like a crack unit?"

"Like superheroes?" Sophie adds.

Lewis and I look at each other. "Like X-Men," he confirms. "We're the mutants who can use our power for good."

"Can we call ourselves the X-Men?" Gabriella asks.

"I was thinking we could call ourselves the Prime Numbers," I tell everyone. And I explain how they don't divide neatly into the world and there's no way of easily telling if a prime number is a prime number. "Just like with mental illness," I explain. "On the outside, we probably look like your regular run-of-the-mill bunch of teenagers, but as we all know, it's quite the opposite."

The group smiles at me.

"The Prime Numbers," Hannah repeats under her breath. She looks up. "I like it."

28

It is Saturday.

Free(ish) day.

Most importantly, the first day of us all trying to be kinder.

Here's the mission – try to do one thing each day that's truly kind, and see what happens. We're reporting back after the blessed internet hour for a Prime Numbers debrief.

How to be kind? How to be kind?

I've looked for opportunities everywhere this morning. I let Liv take the last muffin but I'm not sure if that counted. So then I asked Darrell if he wanted me to refill his coffee cup when I was doing mine. He looked slightly confused, said yes, and I did it, but I'm not sure it's changed his or my life in any significant way. I shouldn't really have had two cups of coffee. I am filled with fizzing and whizzing and my feet won't stay still as I stand here in line, waiting for Grace to open the computer lab.

The usual clump of us jostle for room while we wait. Darrell and Alex are discussing fantasy football leagues while Liv pretends to be interested. Gabriella and Jamie are focused on an elaborate thumb war. And Hannah and Sophie compare notes from their CBT with Lewis. Lewis seems a little pissed off this morning and I can guess why. He asked me last night, "So, shall I expect another late-night visit?" hardly able to keep the hope out of his voice as we walked back to our rooms. And, with Jamie's warning still loud in my head and my promise to be kinder, I'd only replied, "It's okay, I'll leave you alone, I promise. Though can we swap bracelets?" His face fell and I felt like total crap, even though saying that was the kinder, harder, thing to do.

Grace laughs as she arrives with her big bunch of keys. "Well, well, well, look how excited you all are to get online. Aren't you finding it *nice* not having your phone go off all the time?"

"No," we all reply at the same time.

She opens the door and we surge in, running to get the computers near the back. "Honestly," Grace mutters.

We have an hour. One precious hour. But, rather than look at all my accounts, I find myself doing more research. The last time I was here, I was trying to figure out how to stay sane. But now I'm, admittedly, obsessed with this idea that mental illness is preventable...and that our little gang may be able to do something about it. I jab the power button and drum my hands on the table while I wait for the computer to load. I ignore my inbox and start googling right away:

Main causes of mental health problems
Is mental illness preventable?

God, it's fascinating. And depressing. I find this incredible document by the World Health Organization and tumble through it, wishing I could print it all off, but instead cramming as much of it as I can into my already-bursting brain. I click and scroll, click and scroll. The room is silent apart from tapping and clicking and Gabriella's weird heavy breathing. Certain key phrases jump out at me:

Mental disorders are inextricably linked to human rights issues.

There are current limitations in effectiveness of mental health treatment. The only sustainable method for reducing the burden is prevention.

I knew it. I knew it, I knew it, I knew it.

I knew I was right. I'm always right. I may come across as crazy, but I'm never actually wrong. Can kindness fix this? Is this little plan of ours big enough?

"Ten minutes," Grace calls, way too quickly.

Lewis and I both look up at the same time, our eyes meeting. He smiles and retreats back behind his screen before I've even had a chance to smile back. I feel a pang. The way he's started to look at me is more discreet, more hidden. It's so subtle I'm not sure even he notices it, or if I'd have picked up on it if it wasn't for Jamie. I don't know how I feel about it. I finally find myself logging into my email.

Two emails.

Two confirmations of love.

266

One from Ally, being lovely and telling me all the good gossip I'm missing. Rick apparently got with Bonnie the other night and I sigh in relief. He will leave me be now he's got someone else to play with. Though, from what I remember about Rick and our totally not-special-in-any-way night together, I feel sorry for Bonnie. I also feel guilty for ending my last conversation with Ally so abruptly. I tap out a reply full of *You're great*s and *I love you*s and then I click off, wanting to read my other emails before I run out of time.

Then I see it.

The second one. At first glance I'd thought it was from my parents. But it's from just Dad's email address.

Sent yesterday. He never emails from just him. In fact, I'm quite sure Mum writes all the emails and he just adds his name. He's better than most men, my dad, when it comes to sharing the odd emotion here and there. He's capable of hugging me occasionally and stuttering out "I love you" once in a blue moon. But he's never emailed just from him.

My heart trampolines through my ribcage now and I click to read it.

Olive,
It's gone 11 p.m. here on Friday night and your mum is asleep upstairs. I've just been sitting here in my study, with a glass of wine, looking out of the window and thinking about you. In that place. And

how scary it must be, but how proud I am that you're trying so hard to get healthy again. You know we'll always love you whatever, right?

I feel a film of tears collapse over my eyes, the tug in the corner as my ducts struggle not to let go of their load.

Anyway, I know you get internet access tomorrow and your mother and I have been talking all week about some of the things you brought up over our phone call. You see, you asked us some difficult questions, Olive. And we weren't entirely open with you. Your mother went through a lot after you were born and doesn't like to talk about that time. I've respected her wishes up until this point, but if your doctors feel you knowing is important, then I feel I should tell you. Anything that may help you recover is worth the pain. Though I'd appreciate it if you could try not to get angry at your mother or judge her in any way for not telling you all this. It came out of love. She doesn't want you to think she doesn't love you very much, because she does. We both adore you and you're the best thing in our lives. She's asked me to send this email because she finds talking about it too hard, but has told me to say how much she loves you.

What we've never told you, Olive, is how difficult your birth was. You were an undiagnosed breech

birth, which means you were born upside down.
I don't want to upset you with too many details, but
a number of terrible things happened during your
mother's labour. Mainly, at one point, they thought
you were suffocating and that we would lose you.
But also, your position and how quickly the labour
went, meant there was very little time for medical
intervention. It was incredibly painful for your
mother, but it was also hugely stressful and we had
no idea what was happening to her, or you, and the
medical team seemed chaotic. In short, what
should've been a beautiful moment was very
traumatic. Your mum needed reconstructive surgery,
and you were rushed away from us to be
resuscitated.

When we were allowed to take you home, a week
later, everyone kept telling us how lucky we were.
We did, of course, feel very lucky, but your mum was
never quite the same after your birth. She would
have nightmares and wake up screaming. She told
me she couldn't stop reliving the labour and that
memories of it would hit her out of nowhere. And it
wasn't just that. She was obsessed with keeping you
safe and became convinced that something terrible
would happen to you. I'd find her most nights, just
leaning over your cot, making sure you were still
breathing. The nights she wasn't having nightmares
that is. She kept thinking you were ill and taking you

to the doctor to get checked. On top of this, she
would mention sometimes how she didn't always
feel like you were hers. This kept building up, until
eventually, when you were about one, she just kind
of switched off. She...there's no easy way of putting
this, Olive. But she started rejecting you. She
stopped wanting to take you to playgroup and
would ask me to instead. She wouldn't pick you up if
you were crying. And I was so stupid to let it go on
for as long as it did, but I wasn't sure what to do.

I clutch at my tummy, because suddenly it feels like bits
of it are falling out. That my guts are exploding and spilling
out of my belly button.

"Two minutes," Grace calls and everyone in the Prime
Numbers looks up at each other, panicked, like we're almost
at the end of an exam. But I'm not panicked for the same
reason they're panicked. I can't skim read this. This grenade
of an email. But I have no choice. My breath is coming fast
and short but I scroll and try and get to the end without
vomiting.

"Blah, blah, blah," I mutter, scanning through, thinking
if I tell myself this doesn't hurt then it won't hurt.

She wasn't right for at least two years, Olive. She
never really got help either. I once made her go to
the GP but they just gave her some tablets to help
her sleep. To this day she's never received any

counselling and I still worry about her. In fact, this is the first time we've ever really spoken about it as a couple. Nothing bad happened to you during this time, Olive. Maybe that's why I've never told you. And maybe none of what I'm telling you has any meaning, but I thought your counsellors might find it useful. Plus, your mum got better. It was when you were four actually. You got really bad tonsillitis, so bad your throat almost closed up, and she had to call an ambulance to take you to hospital. You were fine – well, apart from the fact you don't have any tonsils any more – but it was the shock your mum needed I think. Having more children, however, was never in the equation. I don't think either of us wanted to go through all that again.

So, that's all, I guess. I'm sure this may come as a shock but I hope you'll find it more helpful than upsetting when you talk it through with your counsellors. I'm going to ring your camp tomorrow to let them know I've sent this email, so you won't have to process it alone. We just, both of us, wanted you to hear it from us first. I cannot stress how much you are loved, Olive. We've had our ups and downs, haven't we? But, despite everything that happened, despite how traumatized we both were, taking you home was still the happiest day of our lives.

One tear slowly leaks from my eye and I wipe it away

with a finger before anyone sees.

"Thirty seconds," Grace announces all dramatically. "Update those statuses quickly, folks."

> Anyway, do ring us whenever you want. We're
> always here. You can talk to us any time and we'll try
> to answer your questions. We hope you're doing
> okay and are looking forward to discussing this more
> in our family therapy session in your last week.
> Get well soon, poppet.
> Dad and Mum xx

"And time's up," Grace says as the room echoes with protests and groans.

I hear everyone packing up and logging off and complaining about how much they miss the internet. But my head is so heavy all of a sudden, like the thoughts swimming around in there have physical weight. I rest it in my hands, and my arms struggle to hold it up.

"Come on, Olive. Time to log off," Grace chimes over at me.

I don't want to move. I'm too busy digesting.

My fault, my fault, my fault. All of it, it's all my fault. I made my mum sick. I was difficult and complicated and fucked things up before I was even born. I couldn't even come out of her womb without ruining everything. I'm a terrible person and I made my mum sick and maybe that's made me sick and, you know what, maybe all of this is just what I deserve. I don't want to look up, I don't want to make eye-contact with anyone, I don't want to talk to the Prime Numbers about kindness. Not yet. Because my dad has just shown me what's behind the curtain. And it's not some cute little old man who's going to jump out and give me a heart and some courage or whatever. It's just pain and grief and nowhere for it to go so it stays inside, rotting and decomposing and releasing toxic energy.

"O-liiiive," Grace sing-songs, thinking I'm just being silly, thinking I'm just trying to post one final update or something that will get me enough likes to temporarily validate my existence.

"Relax, I'm going," I mutter, switching my computer off without logging out. I see the group waiting for me, hanging back by the door. We have an hour of free time now, which is usually when everyone chills out in the common room and plays cards. We're supposed to have our meeting but I can't. Not right now. Not when I feel like someone's peeled back the top of my head, poured in a bucket full of difficult emotions, then slammed the lid shut again. I need to get this out. I need to process. I need, I need, I need...

I need to work on my photomontage!

That's right. That's what I need to do. I've not developed my last three self-portraits and I really think I must do that right now. I've been thinking of using this dodging and burning technique, to add extra exposure to my eyes, so they're clearer and darker than the rest of the self-portrait. Then, when I put them all together at the end, it will be the eyes that draw you. That's a really good idea actually. I need to do it right away.

"See you later, guys," I call at the Prime Numbers.

"Olive? Where you going?" Gabriella calls and I find myself literally running away from them, as fast as you can run in a corridor. They call my name and it pelts off my back and I run and run and run.

I get to the darkroom and it's blissfully empty. The red light glowing and soothing, the sharp tang of the chemicals hitting the back of my nose. I grab down a box of photographic paper and take out my negatives. I start tap-dancing as I hold each one to the light, looking for the shots I need. From the outside I may look euphoric, tap-dancing in the dark, but I'm anything but. I'm just this ball of feeling and energy and I can't believe my parents never told me any of this. Why didn't they tell me any of this? I mean, surely it's quite fucking RELEVANT? I pick a neg, wind it into the machine and turn the lamp on so I can make sure it's focused. This photomontage is going to look amazing once it's done. That's the important thing. It could even win prizes! And then Mum won't hate and resent me because I'll be a prizewinning photographer...

Why the HELL didn't they check my mum's pregnancy before I came out the wrong fucking way up? And why didn't the GP give her some counselling or something after BOTH OF US ALMOST DIED? But, no, just focus on the photo for now, Olive. Look how well you've framed it. Look at how your eyes look in it. They are practically burning through the negative. I just need to get the aperture right, and the length of time… Maybe I'll start on a low light and leave it for a minute to give it a really detailed exposure? It will be okay, fine, fine, fine. It will be fine.

I hear the first door open and shut. Someone is coming in. I swivel and wait to see who dares break my concentration. The door clicks, the door opens and in comes Jamie, face mildly worried but mostly unbothered.

"Hey, you all right? You just kind of ran off and everyone's looking—"

He doesn't get to finish what he's saying because I'm kissing Jamie. I've crossed the darkroom and put my arms around his neck and my lips onto his and Jamie isn't hesitating or pulling away or asking me what the hell I'm doing. Just like I knew he wouldn't. Jamie knows how to kiss a girl, just like I always knew he would. He wraps his arms around my back, digging his hands into the pockets of my denim shorts, grabbing my arse through them. He kisses with hunger and rage and soon he's taken over the kiss, he's leading it, even though I started it, and I do not mind at all.

He pushes me backwards and we stagger across the darkroom until I hit a desk. He's grinding his crotch into me now and starts kissing my neck and shoulders. I can hardly make him out in the red lighting. My body is singing. My body needed this. Every atom of my skin is awake and alert and alive and dancing in tune. This is just what I needed. And it doesn't mean anything. That's another reason why kissing Jamie is so great, because *he* knows it doesn't mean anything. He knows this is just what it is. Two people wanting to get lost in touch and closeness but only physically. We can take off the emotions and dump them on the floor, along with his jeans and my shorts which have shed to our feet. He groans and lifts me up so I'm sitting on the counter and he pulls down my bra to kiss me there and I'm loving every single second but also impatient for what's coming next so I tug on his boxers and he starts kissing my mouth again – his tongue fat and heavy – and he pulls them to just below his arse. Just as impatient as me it seems, and I angle myself right and this has all come out of nowhere but it really is a good idea, I'm sure of it, my body really, really wants this and I close my eyes. He's right there, this is about to happen. I don't even care if anyone walks in. I really don't. They can freaking watch if they want to. Jamie whispers in my ear and I don't quite catch it. His breath is hot and wet.

"What?" I ask, laughing giddily, high on the fact that things can escalate so quickly.

"I said, are you on the pill?"

Shit.

If I say no, he'll stop. And he can't stop. This is too good for it to stop. I'll just lie and say yes and figure it out later.

I swallow. "Of course."

But my voice is a bit too high-pitched and I hesitated for maybe a moment too long because he's not doing what I hoped he'd be doing. He's pulling away from me instead.

"You sure?" He must see something on my face because

he yanks away further. "You're not, are you?"

No, no, no. This can't stop, but Jamie is already looking indignant and pulling up his boxers.

"No…okay, so I'm not…and I don't…but we can still…" I try and pull him back but he goes all rigid, his eyes wide.

"What? No way! I mean, I know you're fucking crazy and everything, but you are fucking crazy!"

"Don't you have a condom?" I ask.

He just shakes his head, still looking at me like I'm crazy.

I pull up my bra straps and put my boobs back into it. "Suit yourself," I say, when all I really want to say is, *NOOOOOO, COME ON, WE HAVE TO DO THIS.*

Everything's very awkward as we get dressed again. The electricity we made is still humming in the air but it has nowhere to go. The atmosphere crackles around us. It's all wrong and I'm starting to feel slightly embarrassed. More frustrated than anything. I'm wondering if there's any way to reignite things. We don't have to do it. There's things we can do that will still…help…that won't get me pregnant, if he's sooooooo worried about that.

There are no clothes left to put on. There is just me and Jamie, standing in the darkroom, pretending we weren't just about to have sex.

He coughs. "Well, I was just looking for you." He still has an erection. I can see it straining against his jeans, trying to make a bid for freedom.

I giggle. "Well, you found me."

He laughs too. "I certainly did."

The laughter diffuses some of the energy around us, though I still think I'd get an electric shock if I touched his hand. I remember my physics GCSE and labelling a diagram of a ball balanced on a high shelf, saying it's got *potential energy*. Unspent energy from the fact gravity really wants that ball to come down off the shelf, but the shelf is having none of it. That is what this room is flooded with. Potential energy.

"Are you okay?" he asks, almost at exactly the same time as his jean bulge goes back to normal. Fact: it is impossible to feel sorry for someone and to get horny over them at the same time. "I didn't mean to call you crazy, I was…I'm just…frustrated."

I shrug. "It's cool. I shouldn't have lied. I don't think an unplanned pregnancy would help either of us." I smile. "Plus, Dr Jones would explode."

"And Lewis would hate me."

I groan and throw my head back. "Please, don't remind me. Not today. I already feel way too guilty about ten million other things." I wrench my body away from Jamie's and focus on my photo again.

"Do you want me to ask you about it?" Jamie asks, while I bend over to check it's in focus. I hear the zipper of his jeans being pulled back up.

"Nope." Okay, that's just right, much clearer. Good. I put the photographic paper into position. I've adjusted to the fact the sex isn't happening and am now quite glad because I really wanted to get this photomontage done. That's why I came in here. Not to have ill-advised sex with Jamie.

"Do you want me to go?"

"Just don't open the door until I get this exposed," I say with my back still to him.

I switch on the light and the image projects onto the paper. I love the science of black-and-white photography. How the paper is now reacting to all the different shades and patterns of light on it. I guess it's how life works. You start as a blank piece of paper, expose it to different shades of dark and light and "yourself" starts to develop. The timer clicks and the light comes off. Jamie is watching over my shoulder which is annoying, quite frankly.

"Are you pissed at me because I wouldn't have unprotected sex with you?"

I sigh. I've practically forgotten. And not in a passive-aggressive trying to pretend I don't care way, I really have almost forgotten. I just want to get the perfect shot developed.

"No. I'd rather you didn't tell anyone though."

"I won't. There's nothing to tell really, is there?"

I switch the projector on again but use my hands to burn in around my eyes. Ten extra seconds should do it. Eight… seven…six…five…

"Well I'll let everyone know you're okay."

Four…three…two…

"Suit yourself."

One…the projector goes off, just as Jamie's about to open the door.

"DON'T," I call. "You'll let the light in!"

He waits impatiently as I plop the paper into the developer tray and start rocking the chemicals around it gently. I bend down and watch my face slowly emerge in the fluid. Jamie, for want of anything better to do, crouches down next to me.

"Cool," he says, as my eyes appear on the paper first.

I rock the tray again, watching the chemicals swill over my portrait. The edges of my face are coming in now, the outline of my short hair. I rock and swill, rock and swill.

"Woah, you look intense," Jamie adds.

And I do. I mean, all of these portraits are quite intense, as I'm staring right into the camera in most of them. But this one, this latest one, I'm quite…something to look at. I almost want to look away, even though it's me. My face. The reflection I see when I look in the mirror. Although it's not. Because I swear I don't look this lost. But in an angry way. The rest of the image fills in, I've got my timings perfect. Technically, everything about this shot is perfect. I leave it in for ten more seconds, then pick it up with the tongs and place it into the "stop" tray to prevent it going any darker.

I finally look up at Jamie once I've plopped it into the fixing agent, where it has to stay for ten minutes. "Do I look that mad in real life?" I ask him.

He dips the tip of his finger into the tray, says, "Ouch, burny," then goes to suck the end of it.

"Don't do that, stupid." I pull off a paper towel and hand it over. He thanks me, wiping his finger.

"Do I?"

He throws his head back. "Olive. I once full-on hallucinated that I was being chased by purple ghosts wearing clown masks."

"So?"

"So, I'm in no state to judge who is mad or not."

"I get that," I say. Why is he being evasive? Why won't he tell me what I suddenly desperately need to know. "But still…"

"Well, I've only known you two weeks and you seem a bit different this week than you did the first week. I mean, Olive, we almost had sex. And you DEFINITELY initiated that."

"I was horny."

"You hardly know me."

"Hardly seems fair that you're judging me when you were totally up for it too, Mr Double Standards."

He throws his hands into the air like he's pissed off. "I KNOW that, I'm not judging you. It's just…well…do you normally try and have sex with people you don't know very well?"

"Yes, actually, sometimes."

"Well then, that's normal for you then. Nothing to worry about."

I point to the tray of chemicals and my portrait floating in it. "So, I normally look like that?"

"Yes, no, I don't know." He sighs and sits cross-legged on the tiled floor. "I wish I hadn't found you now. Too much has happened in ten minutes." He looks up, eyebrows drawn and grinning. "You're messing with my head."

I get down on the floor with him. "I'm messing with my head too."

"What's going on? Why did you run away from everybody?"

I gulp, wishing emotions didn't have to hijack my body so utterly. Making my tummy hurt and my throat smaller and my hands shake. "I got an email from my dad... He told me some shit about my childhood. It wasn't..." I pause, I swallow. "It wasn't a happy email."

Jamie raises an eyebrow. "So you CAN blame everything on your childhood?! Lucky! I still only have *I'm-a-dick-with-an-addictive-personality* as my excuse. I wish I could blame it all on my parents."

I shake my head at him, smiling. "I don't want to blame it on my parents. I don't blame them anyway...I blame myself."

"Original," he remarks and laughs as I go to playfully slap him. He catches my hand and I try with the other but he catches that too. I jerk about, trying to free them but he holds them tight and we both laugh as we tussle. Then we're kissing again, right there on the floor. All hunger and anger and passion and none of it meaning anything, but it's still what I want and need and I'm trying to pull up his only-recently-replaced shirt but he stops again.

"No, Olive," he moans, his mouth close to my ear. "Let's not start something that we can't finish."

I let out a groan and kick myself back. "You're killing me."

"*You're* killing me."

"We should get out of this darkroom together."

"That is definitely a good idea."

We scramble upwards, readjusting the tugged parts of our clothing. At least my photo will be ready to dry now. Jamie tucks his shirt back into his jeans and grins at me sheepishly. "I really need to stop doing this."

I pause, my print held in mid-air. "You mean you've done this with other people?"

He scratches at his chin again. "Gabriella," he admits. My mouth drops open. "A few times." My mouth is now fully wide. He nods towards me. "Now, she had the common sense to bring condoms with her."

I can hardly talk. "You've had sex with Gabriella?"

"Only a few times."

"A few?!"

"Yeah, what's your problem?"

I'm struggling to digest this. I peg up my photo before I drop it to the floor. "Well. Do you really think that's ethical of you?" I ask pointedly.

Jamie's face screws up. "Excuse me?"

"Dude, did you not hear her in group? About what happened to her?"

"What are you trying to say?"

"You know exactly what I'm trying to say!"

We square off. I can see the anger seeping off him now, the wobble in his jaw. "Well you can stop. So, she's sick. So what? I'm sick too. I'm not in here for fun! Also you weren't asking yourself all sorts of ethical questions fifteen minutes ago, were you?"

"That's different," I say.

"How?"

"You KNOW it's different!"

"I'm not an arsehole," Jamie says. "I'm not, like, preying on vulnerable girls, for fuck's sake. If you must know, Gabriella started the whole thing, and I even freaking asked if it was okay and she got pissed off at me for it!" He takes a deep breath. "Look, all of us are messed up in here. That's the given, right? I don't think you have the right to judge who is or who isn't the most messed up or the most damaged. And you hardly know anything about anyone here anyway, do you? You don't even bother coming to group!" He shakes his head. "Anyway, you can hardly talk. Do you think it's fair how you're treating Lewis? Leading him on?"

"I'm NOT leading him on!"

"Aren't you? He told me about your late-night visit. Did you not think something like that would be a huge deal to him? Do you not think he's quite vulnerable?"

"You're crazy."

"Right back at you."

There's silence, just us looking at each other. Two messed-up teenagers who have no idea what the hell we're doing or why. Pretty much like every other teenager. Except, somehow, our particular combination of not knowing what the hell we're doing or why is diagnosed as a problem that needs to be treated.

"I don't want to fight with you," I say. "I'm too damn busy."

"Well I don't want to fight with you either."

"So, let's stop fighting then."

"Okay."

"Okay."

I look down at my portrait again. Those eyes... Are they really what mine look like? Maybe it's because I've dropped the ball the last couple of days. I've stopped following my algorithm so closely. I've got obsessed with saving the world rather than looking after myself. Because I'm fed up with being selfish. It didn't serve me well, it never has. This is the new answer. Putting others before myself, proving that I'm of worth, that's what will really help. It's got to help; if it doesn't help then I don't know what I'll do, but it will; it totally will, it...

"I'm going for a run," I announce suddenly to Jamie.

"Great. Good for you."

"Will you tell the others we can talk about our kindness stuff after? I just...just...I need to run." That's all I can manage before I bolt for the door.

29

I run until my legs won't let me run any more. Stupid legs.
I could've run so much further if they weren't so stupid. All
in all, I must've run at least five times around the camp
grounds. I am dripping with sweat. It runs off me like I'm
standing under a shower of it and my muscles wobble when
I walk. But I feel better. Calmer.

And most importantly, ready.

Everyone is gathered outside enjoying the sunshine.

"What you doing out here?" I ask Hannah, who looks
instantly traumatized at all my sweat.

"We're SUPPOSED to be having a meeting that was
YOUR idea," she snaps. "Where have you BEEN?"

"Just for a run."

"You need a shower."

"The sun will dry me off," I joke and step closer to her.

She freaks and holds up her hands.to stop me. "Don't!
Honestly. What's wrong with you anyway? You get us all het

up about saving the world and being kind and then you just bugger off on a run?"

Jamie, who's standing behind her but staying out of it, catches my eye. We share a guilty smile.

"That's not all I did," I say, more to him than everyone else.

Then I notice Lewis noticing us and his eyebrows dive downwards. I feel a blob of guilt that makes me want to run around the perimeter again but I really am sweating and surely Lewis won't be able to guess anything anyway.

"Shall we play Frisbee as a cover?" I ask my little group. "Just give me a moment to shower and then I'll be down."

Hannah curtseys. "Whatever you say, Queen Olive."

"Hey, I thought this meeting was about being kind to each other," Lewis jumps in, defending me.

"I am being kind. I just called her a queen!"

I resist the urge to roll my eyes.

"This meeting will be brilliant. Trust me," I say. And it must've come out charismatically because all of them stop complaining and just sort of smile.

I quickly shower and change but don't bother drying my hair as I jog out onto the lawn. The Prime Numbers are arranged in a little circle, tossing a soft Frisbee to each other that Sophie reliably drops whenever it's her turn.

I hold out my arms. "To me, to me," I call, and Jamie effortlessly tosses it towards me in a perfect throw. I run to get it, feeling that pure euphoria you get when you successfully catch something. I stop for a second to focus on tossing it onto Gabriella and feel hope bubble up in me once more. Yes, this morning was a knock. But I feel much better after my run and zingy and on it.

"So," I ask when I join the circle. "How has Operation Kindness gone so far? Who wants to start?"

The Frisbee stays still in Gabriella's hand as we wait to see who'll come forward first. Hannah puts her arm up.

"Yes, Hannah?"

"I've been kind to you today, Olive, by not getting pissy with you for running out when we're supposed to be having a meeting."

I screw my face up. "Umm, you were quite pissy, Hannah."

"I could've been pissier."

My mouth falls open just as she starts laughing. "Kidding!" she says through giggles. "I did something kinder than that."

The rest of us laugh, me taking a bit longer than the others. "And that was?"

Hannah looks down at the perfectly mown lawn for a moment and, when she looks up, her face has changed, the laughter all drained from it. "I emailed my mum actually. This morning. In computer lab." She pauses again. "I told her I forgive her."

We're all quiet for a second. "Forgive her for what?" I ask softly.

Hannah shrugs. "For everything. I forget you've missed

a week of group. Hey, can I have the Frisbee?" Gabriella gently throws it over and Hannah claps at it to catch it, then hugs it like it's a hot-water bottle. "Well, the speeded up version is that she's a single mum and she spent my whole childhood introducing me to a new boyfriend every six months. Living in whatever shithole the newest twat lived in." I feel shock stir in my stomach. Hannah has such a posh voice, I've always assumed she comes from a posh background. She sighs and lifts the Frisbee over her head, stretching out her arms. "Anyway, it's always been the thing we argue about. I've always had a go at her, told her she's a shit mum, that it's all her fault I'm so highly strung or whatever. But, well, from talking to Dr Jones in therapy, and then thinking about all this kindness stuff, I realized the kindest thing I could do was forgive her." Her plummy voice catches and Sophie reaches out and taps her arm reassuringly. Hannah gulps. "Not just the kindest thing for her, to alleviate her pain and her guilt. But it's the kindest thing for me too. To accept she was just trying her best, that she wasn't doing it deliberately."

"And how do you feel?" Lewis asks.

"Better. Lighter." When she looks up again, she's smiling. "I feel like I've lost two stone."

The goodness of this bubbles in me like a stew being heated. "That's amazing," I find myself saying. "I'm really happy for you, Hannah." It's probably one of the truest sentences I've ever spoken.

She starts to go red. "Yeah, well. As I said, I reckon it's a combination of being here AND this little project. Anyway, that's my go over. What else have other people done?"

Our little circle look at one another. I get the short stab of a feeling. And the feeling is guilt. Guilt that I've not been quite as engaged with therapy as Hannah seems to have been. Guilt that I'm wasting my time here… Then I remember that the incompetent idiots can't even diagnose me and remind myself I'm doing a better job. I'm genuinely glad it's working for Hannah though.

Jamie raises his hand, making all his twiney bracelets and festival wristbands fall up his arm. "I also sent an email this morning," he says, "to my parents." There's a long pause with nothing but the sun shining and the birds singing and the breeze blowing to fill it. We all instinctively leave Jamie with his silence, waiting for when he's ready. "Saying I'm sorry for everything I've put them through," he manages. He reaches out and takes the Frisbee from Hannah. "Right, who wants another go around?"

We all silently acknowledge his need to change the subject and spread out so we can start tossing the Frisbee back and forth. Jamie doesn't talk any more but, like Hannah, he seems to have lost emotional weight. He's smiling as we work out ridiculous ways to throw to one another, suggesting more and more outlandish ideas.

"Let's only use our elbows to catch it. Let's all drop to our knees and try playing like we're really, really short."

We laugh and drop to our knees, and start throwing it with our elbows and none of us catch it and we all laugh harder and harder. Throughout our hysterics, the rest of the group reveal their attempts at kindness.

Lewis chatted to one of the security men because he looked lonely. "It got a bit deep actually. He started talking about his daughter who he doesn't see much."

Sophie and Gabriella both had similar experiences to me – struggling to figure out what kindness exactly meant and how to do it. Sophie ended up complimenting Liv on her lipstick. "It was a real social anxiety trigger, so two birds, one stone," she said, while I glowed with pride.

Lewis is beaming. "This is great," he keeps repeating before dropping the Frisbee on the grass. "Isn't this great, Olive?"

Everyone turns to me like I'm a leader, which I guess I am. And I can't quite tell you what I'm feeling to be honest. I am split in two. Half of me is looking at this little group, kneeling on the lawn, and seeing how they're blooming and growing just from one day of being kinder. This half of me is going YES, YES, YES, THIS IS IT, THIS IS IT, THIS IS IT. I want to air-punch and dance the tango and swan-dive into how right this feels. But the other half is saying…

It's saying…

This is not enough.

That's what I find myself muttering out loud.

"What was that?" Sophie asks, her eyebrows raised in concern.

I shake my head. I stand up. I cannot bear to be on my knees any more. It stops me from pacing, and I really need to pace right now.

"This is good," I'm saying. "This is so good. I love where this is going, I do. I really do. But, it feels like it needs to be bigger – don't you think?"

They are all raising their eyebrows now.

"Bigger how?" Hannah asks, already crossing her arms.

"I don't know. This is a start. It's a good start, but we need to scale it up. Look what's happened in just one day. Look how great it is. Amazing. So amazing. I told you. But where next? Where do we take this? We must think of something. Make it scalable. Then we can do so much, help so much…"

I trail off. None of their eyebrows are left in the usual part of their faces. They are all raised, and all looking at me funny.

"How many coffees have you had?" Jamie asks.

"Three."

"Hmm."

"I'm not being manic!" I counter. "I'm just trying to move this idea on."

They all share a look.

"Come on. If we're going to do this, we should at least do it properly." I try really hard to slow my talking down. I can't have them thinking this is me on a whimsy, not when I feel we're so close to the final breakthrough. "I really think there's a way we can make this bigger, that's all I'm saying. In the meantime, we can just focus on continuing to do one kind thing a day. See how that goes?" There. That sounds reasonable. I am so reasonable. I mean, I'm beyond reasonable. I'm about to finally fit the puzzle pieces together on the world's best jigsaw, I can just *feel* it.

"We can have another meeting in a day or so? And keep our thinking hats on?"

There's a silence where I'm scared I'm going to lose them. I'm swaying from foot to foot, as I watch them, all on their knees on the lawn, trying to weigh up if I'm right or not. (I'm TOTALLY right by the way.)

And, again, I'm surprised when it's Jamie who breaks the silence with enthusiasm.

"Oh, what the hell?" He shrugs. "I did something today that made me feel good for the first time in years. I'm beginning to trust you, Olive. Even if you do act like someone who is on coke all the time."

I beam at him. "How about the rest of you?"

More silence.

"Come on. Show me a bit of kindness by trusting me on this."

The words have the desired effect. One by one, the group nod and I'm lighting up like a slot machine at the joy this brings me.

"Yes!" I lean down and hug each and every one of them, squeezing until they squeal. "So, how do we even START to roll out kindness on a bigger scale?" I ask. Because I don't have the answer, just the question.

Lewis starts to get up off the lawn, still pink from me hugging him.

"That, my Prime Numbers," he says, "appears to be the next puzzle we need to solve."

30

It's another muggy night with nothing to do but pace around my luxe room and try and stop my brain from thinking. Sleep is out of the question. Yet that is not a thought that is bothering me. Quite simply, I don't seem to need it right now. Yes, I'm aware that *chronic insomnia* is one of the things on the you're-going-to-go-crazy list, but it doesn't FEEL like chronic insomnia, if that makes any sense? It feels like my body doesn't need sleep. That my body understands that I'm in the middle of potentially changing the world and is just quietly accommodating the hours of the day that you need to achieve this. But my brain isn't coming up with anything useful about kindness. Despite my run and despite mucking out a giant stable and despite the fact I went for another long walk after dinner, I still don't feel tired.

Dr Jones wheedled up to me at one point, asking, "Are you okay, Olive? Your dad called and told me about his email. I've been waiting for a quiet moment to speak to you."

I told her that I was fine and that I felt fine, even though I didn't. Not really.

"Okay, as long as you're sure. We can talk about it in our session tomorrow," she said. "Now, go get some rest."

But rest is ungettable when my brain is like this and when there is such a big problem to be solved. In fact I start jumping on the bed because maybe the act of jumping will help dislodge whatever needs to be dislodged from my brain. The bed is so new and posh that it absorbs my jumps and I can't really do it properly. I sigh, get down and look at the red numbers on my alarm. It's just gone midnight. Even if I get to sleep now I will only get seven hours before I have to get up for breakfast. And, let's face it, I'm not going to get to sleep any time soon.

Shit. Sleep! I need to swap bracelets with Lewis again. I forgot. Will he be asleep already? Is it fair of me to knock at his door again after what Jamie said today? But the little conscience bird on my shoulder is easily swatted away because getting up and visiting Lewis will be something to do and I really need something to do that isn't padding around my room getting flashbacks of all the traumatizing sentences from my dad's email.

I at least manage to put some clothes on this time. I pull on a light grey sweater and yank my pyjama shorts down so they cover my butt cheeks. I won't linger. I won't go into his room. I won't lead him on if indeed that is what I have been doing up to this point. I will just knock, politely ask if we can swap bracelets, then be on my way. No mixed signals, no being selfish, no, no, no.

Lewis is still dressed when he opens his door. He looks unsurprised to see me. He's wearing a light green shirt with the sleeves rolled up and some longish denim shorts. It's not what he was wearing earlier, and he looks good. The colour suits him. The green brings out the tan he's developed since being here.

"Hey," I say. "I just…"

He holds up his bracelet, smiling. "Want to swap bracelets again?"

I smile. "Do you mind?"

"Not at all." He takes off his bracelet and hands it over. It's still warm from his body. I snatch mine off and hold it delicately so our hands won't brush when we swap.

"Well thanks," I say, slipping his on.

"No problem."

He doesn't go to close the door or say goodnight and we just stand there awkwardly, me moving from one foot to the other, not wanting to say goodbye even though I know I should. Because I don't want to be alone with my thoughts and my brain.

"Umm, you want to come in?" He stutters a bit as he asks. "We could watch a film or something?"

I know I should say no. No, no, no. Be fair, Olive. Be fair. If Jamie is right and Lewis does like you then you should be kind and not go into his room in the middle of the night, especially if earlier that day you were about to have sex with someone else. But I am lonely. So I say, "Sure."

And the look.

The look on Lewis's face. When I say *sure*.

That look

Tells

Me

Everything.

His TV is on, playing quietly. His room looks tidied. Everything is unnaturally pristine and prepared, like he was planning and hoping for this. The only mess is the pages of torn-out notepaper, littering his bed.

"Sorry." He sweeps them into a pile. "I've just been trying to figure it all out."

I glance down at a page littered with maths. The sort of maths that may as well be in another language.

"Me too." I perch cautiously on the edge of his bed. "Though my figuring out looks much less smart than yours. It's just me pacing around my room."

"So, what do you want to watch?" he asks. "There's a movie channel?" He picks up the remote and starts scrolling through.

"Is there anything about setting the world on fire?" I ask. "Maybe it will give us ideas."

He breaks into another smile. "Let's have a look." He plays about with the remote for a few minutes. "Ahh, there's a film here called *Fight Club*. I think that's about setting the world on fire?"

"And it has Edward Norton in it," I say. "Perfect!"

"You fancy Edward Norton over Brad Pitt?"

"Oh yeah, of course." I gesture to the screen where there's a still of Brad Pitt all sweaty and muscly and topless. "Whenever I see a guy with a body like that, all I can think is BOR-ING. I mean, yeah, it looks good, but do you have any idea how dull it is keeping up a body like that?" I sigh and remember sleeping with Rick and how hard his stomach was, but also how boring his conversation was. "All those guys can talk about is their workouts and protein and chicken. They're all OBSESSED with chicken. I sort of dated this guy once, and it's like he needed to eat chicken every two hours otherwise he got PANICKED. You could see it in his eyes. You'd be telling a funny story, but he'd he glancing this way and that, and you knew he was just thinking, *Chicken, I must get the chicken.*"

Lewis laughs and leans back on his elbows. I can see he's trying to do it casually but it still feels awkward, like he's given serious thought to how every single limb should be splayed. He presses play on the film and I settle back and try to ignore the Vibes coming off him. It's hard though. He's like a broken microwave, emitting I AM AWARE OF YOUR PRESENCE waves. It makes it hard to concentrate on the movie. I mean, I'm not in the most concentrating of moods anyway. But the film is good. Slick, dark. It opens on this dude who has chronic insomnia and is all messed up until Brad Pitt turns up and makes him realize capitalism is making him unhappy. But I can't lose myself in it, I'm too busy trying to figure out if it can give me clues. Because Brad Pitt then starts this underground resistance cult called "Fight Club" and it's sparking off all these ideas. It's like we were MEANT to watch this movie. Like it's speaking to me. Like it's cosmic fate that we picked this particular film.

I point at the screen after an hour or so. "This is what we need!" I tell Lewis. "We need an underground movement like theirs. One that speaks to people. One with charisma and charm. We need to CONNECT with people somehow and then let *them* spread kindness for us."

Lewis is quiet for a second. "You know what, that's a good idea."

"Jamie's right," I say. "We can't mend everything ourselves, but if we can recruit people to help us? If we can start a ripple…then who knows where it can go? How far it can reach?"

Lewis rolls over on the bed and I roll over too so we're facing each other.

"We just need to work out the best way to start the ripple." I fill the silence throbbing between us. "And we need to get Jamie enthusiastic," I muse. "He's so cynical. If we can think of something that speaks to him, we've cracked it."

Lewis pulls a face. "Ignore him. He's just in detox…" He trails off. "Is…is…" Then he comes right out and says it. "Is anything going on between you two?"

I try and hide my inner gulp. "I thought I'd already thrown a strop about this?"

Deflecting is not lying by the way. That is a very important thing to note.

The muscles around Lewis's jaw relax. "Of course. Sorry. I forgot. Boys and girls can totally be platonic friends, right?"

I nod. Because I do agree with that. And, actually, I do consider Jamie and I to have a platonic friendship. What happened earlier wasn't feelings or attraction. It was just letting off steam. But I can't help thinking that sex, and everything that surrounds sex, is a much bigger deal to Lewis.

Am I platonic friends with Lewis? I ask myself, as we turn back and snuggle down and get back to watching Brad Pitt build an activist army. I mean, I think I am. I try and concentrate on the movie but, to be honest with you, the act of lying down and staying still and concentrating is a little akin to torture. There is so much life to be had, why do we have to stop and rest when there is so much life to be had? It's a very infuriating social norm and it bugs me that just wanting to live my life to the fullest is called "hypomania" or whatever it is Dr Bower wants to call it. Unable to take much more, I roll over in Lewis's bed to get his attention. The roll means our feet are touching, both of us barefoot in this muggy night. My feet sing and I crave physical contact so much.

He senses the zing though and rolls over too.

"Hi," he says sleepily. His eyes are so squinted they're almost like dash symbols on a keyboard.

"Hi."

I'm annoyed that he's sleepy when I'm so unsleepy. What is wrong with him? How can you be sleepy when you're potentially on the verge of saving the world?

"Are you getting better here?" I ask him.

He lets the question dissolve, taking his time to reply. He raises himself onto his elbows and talks to the telly rather than me. "I'm not sure."

"The...thought you have. Have you had it less?"

His hands now grip the sheet and I feel like I should feel guilty for triggering him but I'm suddenly too keen to know everything about him.

"I think so." His voice is almost a squeak. "I mean, the CBT has been kind of useful. Dr Nada made this terrifying Mind Map that challenged the Thought and it was like having my brain hijacked...in a good way...I think."

We hear a gunshot on the screen and turn our attention back towards it for a while.

"Sometimes I think I'm getting better here," he says after a moment or so. "And sometimes I think I'm just distracted here. By other things." He swallows, then slowly turns his head around to face me. To stare into my eyes. "Better things," he adds.

And I know this is a come-on. A teeny tiny, Lewis-style come-on. A squeak of his feelings, a sentence without a full-stop. A safe, as-safe-as-you-can-make-these things anyway type opener that could lead to A Situation. A situation where I say, "What do you mean by better things?" and he says, "You." Then I lean forward and kiss him and we melt into the sheets but probably don't even get as far as him taking my jumper off. But I don't want to hurt him and I don't think I could stop at a kiss with anyone right now. Not when every inch of my body is on high-alert and wants to feel alive, wants to be touched in every which way.

So I don't roll any closer and I don't ask what better things. I snub out his fantasy of the night and what it could bring. The fantasy he had when he got changed into that green shirt that really does suit him and stayed up waiting for my knock.

It's the kind thing to do.

"What's the point of swapping bracelets if you're going to be up with me all night?" I laugh and hold up my wrist.

He blinks a few times. Dislodges the hope that remains clinging to his eyelashes like sleep. And he laughs too.

"You're the one keeping me up!"

"I should let you sleep. One of us has to, if we're going to come up with a half-decent idea about how to spread kindness." I roll off the bed and onto my feet – feeling the distance between us.

He shrugs and pretends it's nothing and it's easy to go along with because his move really was a very safe one. He crossed no barriers he couldn't retreat back behind. I almost can't believe I'm leaving as I say goodbye with the film still playing. I'm surprised at my self-control. Usually when I feel like this, I have none. I would've just kissed him and probably full-on seduced him, and no, don't think about that, Olive. Otherwise you will end up just knocking on his door. Any door! I wonder if I can go swimming at this time of night? If the pool is open this late? Oh, that would be nice. To submerge myself in the cool blue water. To stretch out my limbs in the weightlessness of it. To push my body to beyond tiredness, so that when I do eventually fall onto my pillow, I'm too tired to think about Lewis and the feelings he evokes.

Yeah, the pool.

I'll go find the pool.

31

I am in trouble.

The bracelet swapping hasn't fooled anyone.

"Olive," Dr Jones says. "We really think it's time we discussed your medication again and consider putting you on a mood stabilizer."

Dr Bowers nods ferociously next to her. "I agree. I heard you were found in the swimming pool this morning. Is that correct?"

"I can't BELIEVE you *swapped* bracelets with another client. It's bad enough that you want to endanger your own recovery. But someone else's?"

I stare at both of them with contempt because I'm still pissed off about being dragged out of the pool if I'm being honest. It's not like I was hurting anyone! Yet they're acting like I peed in it! I mean, well, I did pee in it a little, but everyone pees in pools a little, don't they?

"I was swimming," I tell them. "Why does that mean

my mood is unstable?"

"Because it was two a.m.!" I'm surprised by Dr Jones's tone. She sounds a tiny bit hysterical. Like she's worried. Like I'm getting to her. Which is not allowed to happen, I don't think. They have to absorb all the time like the soles of expensive running trainers.

You see, in my head, it's not the STRANGEST thing to be swimming at two a.m. if there is a pool there and if you're not sleepy. That's what I find hard about this whole clinical diagnosis stuff. Everything you do or say gets put into this filter – like a "crazy" filter you can pick out on Instagram that makes everything you do look weird. If they didn't think I had bipolar, and if this was just a five-star hotel rather than a five-star clinical mental health facility, and I was sixteen and had gone swimming in the big posh pool in the middle of the night – they'd have sighed and said, "Teenagers!" But no, I have a big fat "loony" label stamped on my forehead and can never swim at night-time.

"Are you even listening to us?" Dr Jones asks. "Olive? You're looking out the window."

I'm not looking out the window either. I mean, it looks like I am, but I'm actually just thinking.

"I'm listening," I tell them. "I can listen and look out the window. I'm a girl. We're good at multitasking, aren't we? Although, I mean, if gender is on a spectrum, then does that mean we're all on a spectrum of multitasking? And, what if women aren't better at multitasking at all? What if, like, actually, it's just we HAVE to multitask more than men because we have to HAVE IT ALL...?" Where has my mind gone? Am I saying this aloud? It really is a good point actually.

The doctors look at each other and talk using only their eyes. Bollocks. They think this is mania. Maybe it is. But, even if it is, that doesn't distract from the fact I've just made a really good point!

The thing is, I don't want to take this mood stabilizer because I don't trust them. They have no idea what's wrong with me; they're just guessing. And I'm not going to swallow down some random drug that alters my ENTIRE MOOD based on a whim. I know I'm not an expert, but I can tell that's a bad idea. I'm better at their job than they are.

But I need to give them something so they go away.

"My dad's email really upset me," I tell them. "I think that's why I got stressed and went swimming, and sorry I swapped bracelets with Lewis. I just didn't want anyone to worry. I was just really upset. My dad told me all sorts of stuff about my childhood."

And if there's any word that distracts a psychotherapist, it's the word *childhood*. Dr Jones's face jerks up, like she's a zombie who just got their first whiff of brains. It could be a fun game actually. Get a room full of psychologists to all lie down and do a relaxation exercise or something and then shout, "CHILDHOOD." Or send them all off to play golf, and the moment they're about to swing, shout, "CHILDHOOD." Or sing them a song but secretly change some words to "CHILDHOOD" and see if they notice and start twitching. I mean, after all my research, I get it now.

Childhood is where a lot of the stains are smudged onto us. Where a lot of the scars start as cuts. Still though, it's funny. I'm funny. I'm hilarious!

"That's very interesting," she says neutrally, even though her eyes are letting her down. Going, *DING DING DING, breakthrough*. And Dr Bowers looks slightly redundant. "But, maybe if we continue this conversation about your meds first, and then…"

"My mum went crazy after I was born," I blurt out and holy moly that gets their attention. "That's what my dad told me in his email. She had a really bad birth with me, because I was in this dickhead upside-down position, and we both almost died and then she went nuts for years afterwards and has refused to have any more children."

They are sharing a look again, like they're not sure what to do with this development.

"It makes me feel confused," I garble on. Because I know that was going to be the next question. *How does it make you feel?* "And I'm angry," I say. "Because why didn't anyone help her? Because maybe all of this could have been avoided and I wouldn't even be sitting here if only some stupid doctor had done their job better." I blurt it all out. All of it. All my feelings and emotions. And though I'm mainly doing it so I can dodge the medication issue, it does feel good. Dr Jones kicks into psychologist mode and asks me all these interesting questions while Dr Bowers looks on uselessly. I feel triumphant, even though I know, really, he's only trying to help.

There's another reason I don't want to take the medication...

Because part of me kind of likes my brain like this. Yes, it's been like this before and it has not worked out so well before, but I wasn't getting help then. And I'm not doing anything too mad. I showed self-restraint around Lewis last night, didn't I? I don't think hyper-not-in-an-institution Past-Olive would have been capable of that. So maybe I don't NEED the meds as long as I'm being looked after properly. And then I can be Super Olive. All the goods from the high without all the shit from the low? Like a superhero, like an X-Man, like a Prime Number. Yes, maybe I'm a little bit wound up but look at what that is achieving. Look at what I've figured out with my brain like this. I have found a potential formula to help my sanity! And now I'm using all that knowledge to find a way to make the world a better, kinder place. I need this brain. This brain is good. This brain is special. This brain is better. This brain is me.

So on and on I go, letting it all out. Everything that email triggered in me. Anger and guilt and shame and confusion and it's like playing "Words psychologists like to hear" bingo. But I do feel lighter and clearer and my tummy is uncoiling slightly from its twist and I keep going and going until there's an actual knock at the door saying we've gone way over time.

"Gabriella is waiting outside," Grace says to the doctors.

And after finishing some things off ("Olive, you've missed your last two CBT sessions, why did you feel the need to do that? Olive, promise me you won't swap bracelets any more. Olive, it's great that you've opened up about all this, but we still need to discuss medication") I'm being shooed from the room.

Dr Bowers is flustered. "We'll pick this up tomorrow," he tells me, with a smile on his face but a threat in his voice.

"Of course, of course." I am sweetness and light. I am butter-wouldn't-melt.

Dr Jones wiggles her finger at me. "No more late-night swims!"

I beam. "I promise."

I'm bored of the idea of swimming anyway.

32

I actually can't think of anything worse than having to make it through mindfulness right now, but I have to behave and tick all the boxes and show progress to keep the doctors off my back.

"Meeting afterwards?" I whisper to the Prime Numbers, as we file into the room and pick up our mats.

"What's the point?" Hannah whispers back, dragging a mat behind her. "We don't know what we're going to do yet. All we've got is 'be kind'."

"ATISHOO." Gabriella sneezes so loudly, half the room jumps. "Sorry," she says to everyone. "My hay fever has just kicked in." She drops her voice so only we can hear. "We'll come up with something," she says cheerfully, before sneezing again.

Nick and Maggie, two clients who struggle with germs, visibly flinch and move their mats away.

"It's not contagious," she calls at them, laughing.

"Quiet now, please," Elizabeth says, and we all manoeuvre ourselves onto our backs so we can be mindful.

It's almost painful lying on the floor. Staying still. Trying to relax. It's such a waste of me when I'm like this.

But here I am, spread-eagled on the ground. A cushion under my butt to help my spine. We fan out on the wooden floor like a rock pool of starfish. Eyes closed. Hair spilling out to the sides of our heads. Feet twitching...

Though maybe that's just mine.

"Now, I want you to just gently rest your hands on your stomach and feel how they rise up and down as your breath goes in and out," Elizabeth says.

I put my hands on my stomach. They do indeed go up and down with my breath. Whoop de fucking doo.

"Now I want you to really notice the weight of your body on the floor. Focus on where your feet touch the ground. Do your muscles feel heavy or light today?" Her voice is like a soothing lullaby. "Remember, there's no right or wrong, just notice it." You can hear the smile in her voice.

There's a moment in mindfulness class where you can actually feel the room has let go. The energy shifts as, one by one, we slip into our own heads, we are lulled by Elizabeth's voice, we go to where we are supposed to go. It's super irritating when you are not one of the people letting go. A bit like when you're SO TIRED and you're in a room full of sleeping people and you're just glaring at their smug unconscious faces, knowing they'll wake all perky in the morning, and yet you can only stare at them with envy.

I feel it now. The collective restfulness. A room full of busy brains quietening down, like all the lights have gone down in a beehive.

My brain is not happy. My brain is not restful.

This floor is too hard and I can't stay still and I'm thinking about kindness.

Because I don't know how we're going to spread it, and I really need to figure it out because I really feel like this is what's going to mend me. *I* need to be taught how to be kinder, because *I'm* not a very kind person. That's why I don't have many friends – not because of my illness. I do horrible, selfish things, and, yeah, at the time, I don't feel in control of that, but maybe I will. Maybe this project will help me and then I can help others and that will feed back into helping me, but bloody hell we need to come up with something. Time is running out. I only have a week and a half left.

"Now, count with your breaths," Elizabeth coos. "Count on the in breath, one, two, three, until you get to ten, and then start back at one again."

God, listening to other people breathe is annoying. Gabriella's head is near mine and I swear she's over-egging the breathing. IT'S NOT A COMPETITION, I want to yell over at her. I try and focus on my breath but it's not coming out that evenly, and this is annoying now.

"Now, if your mind wanders, just realize what's happened, make a note of it, then let it go and focus on your breath again."

Elizabeth was banging on about mindfulness the other day in one of our theory classes. She said once you've got the basics you can go on extreme mindfulness courses. "Where you sleep out in the open, without even a mattress. You learn to get comfortable with discomfort." And, again, it seems like a good idea. The world is uncomfortable. It's gnarly with sharp edges and you can't run your hand down the side of it without cutting your finger in some way. I GET that, to some degree, we need to learn to cope with that. We need to be IN THE NOW and RESILIENT because the WORLD ISN'T FAIR. Yadda, yadda. God, I'm really supposed to be focusing on my breathing but my brain is not complying. It's not interested in my breathing, it's interested in knowing why we're told to just accept that the world is full of dickheads that make life harder. Because that isn't acceptable. I don't want coping strategies for how to handle a horrid world, I just want the world, and everyone in it, to stop being horrid. To start being kind to each other. But how…

"A-a-a-TISH-OOO."

The whole room jerks at Gabriella's giant sneeze and the collective trance is broken.

"SORRY," Gabriella says. The room ripples with laughter.

"Come on, everyone, back to your breath." Elizabeth tries to lull us back but I can't go back…because…because…

I'm not contagious, Gabriella said.

But what if she was?

Oh, my.

This is it.

I knew it. I knew my brain could do it. God, I'm clever. God, this is going to work.

It

HAS

To

Work.

I am lurching up like Frankenstein's monster because I cannot lie on this damn floor any more.

"Olive? Is there something wrong?"

I see the fluttering of other eyelids.

"I have to go," I announce.

Elizabeth smiles, even though she must be pissed off that I keep ruining her sessions. "You don't have to stay, remember, Olive? But it would be nice if you did."

"No!"

I'm out and I'm up and I want to drag the Prime Numbers with me, but only Lewis is being unmindful, leaning up on his elbows and shooting me *Are you okay?* looks.

"I've got it," I mouth over to him.

His eyebrows wrinkle in confusion for a second, until he realizes, breaks into a grin and makes a subtle a-okay sign with his fingers.

Elizabeth gently ushers me away and I cannot get out of this room fast enough because there's too much glitter and I'm too clever and I can't wait to tell the others and I need… I need…I need a run to get this all out.

33

The run helps. Because, okay, I'll admit it. I am maybe a little bit too hyper at the moment. I can feel it. And it's, frustratingly, a lot like how it felt last time. And last time everything went to shit. But, that's because last time I was being selfish and not trying to be kind and only focusing on myself, and last time I wasn't running miles and miles like a loon, and it really does help. After ten laps of the grounds I feel cleared out. Like someone has held me upside down and shaken out all the unreasonable. But I still feel uber sharp, just how I like to feel. And I'm so excited to tell the Prime Numbers my idea. So, so, so excited.

They're waiting for me on the steps and I run into them and draw them into a hug.

"I'VE GOT IT!"

Hannah squeals and jumps away, upset that I've got sweat on her. The rest of them rigidly let me embrace them, and I realize I need to tone it down somewhat if I'm going to convince them of my rightness.

"Why did you run out of mindfulness?" Jamie asks, detaching himself from my hug and leaning back against one of the marble pillars.

"Because I've figured out what we need to do." I lean forward to tell them, but just as I do, Darrell and Kieran come out holding a Frisbee.

"Wanna play?" Darrell asks us.

"Thanks, but not now, maybe later," I say, smiling back before whispering to everyone. "We need to go somewhere private. Lewis and I have a clearing," I tell them. "We can sneak off there?"

The others share a look at the mention of my and Lewis's clearing but no one says anything.

My legs ache as I steer the group into the trees. When we arrive, the fallen logs form the perfect circle and we perch on them, facing in on each other. The sun's already dried my sweat into my dungaree dress.

"So, what's the brainwave?" Hannah asks, looking unimpressed before I've even told her.

"It's you actually, Gabriella, you gave me the idea." I turn to grin at her and she smiles back, snuffily, her hay fever in full stream.

"What have I done now?" she asks.

"It was your sneeze," I say. "That's what we need to do. We need to infect people with kindness. We need to make it contagious."

My eyes find Lewis's. They are bright and blue and

shining and he just beams at me, a grin that needs sunglasses. A smile that lets me know he's already got it.

"We start a virus," he says, reading my thoughts exactly, extending his beam to the whole circle so we all bask in his sunshine. "We start a compassion virus."

34

Emotions are contagious.

That is what I realized, in this big old brain of mine, when I heard Gabriella sneeze.

If you're super duper happy, people notice. They smile at you more. You radiate it out and they are warmed by it. If someone is really, really laughing, then you cannot help but laugh. And, of course, if someone is down and depressed and like Eeyore reincarnated – it drags you down too. So does being around anxious people. Their twitches make you twitchy. We are lemmings in that way. Colliding into each other, catching one another's bad moods and giggling fits, and raging at whatever it is that's set someone off that day.

"Don't you see?" I say to my group of brilliants, who are half sitting on the logs, half sitting on the dusty ground. "That's the quickest way to spread kindness as far and as wide as we can. We infect people with it, like it's the flu. We infect Gabriella with compassion and get her to sneeze on everyone."

Gabriella sneezes right on cue and we all laugh.

"Cheers for that."

"You're welcome."

"But then they'll be infected, and they'll be contagious, and they'll metaphorically sneeze and the kindness will spread and spread and then maybe people will stop being so awful to each other. They'll start looking out for one another, and standing up for what's right, and voting for governments that really take care of people, and, with the world being nicer, people will be less likely to get mentally ill."

Lewis slaps his head. "Of course," he says. "Biochemistry! Why didn't I think of that?"

All of us raise our eyebrows at him at exactly the same time, but Lewis doesn't notice. He's now frantically drawing on the ground with a twig.

"So we can make and release a virus. There's a maths to viruses," he explains, almost to himself.

"Oooo, what a surprise. Maths!" Jamie starts saying, then remembers we're trying to be kind. "Sorry…"

Lewis nods, too lost in maths to be bothered. I let him take over. I've played my part for this moment, I've got us this far.

"Right, so. Viruses aren't just germs that give you horrible colds or flu – they're more defined by being a contagious thing – whether it's a type of bacteria, or even just an idea, that embeds itself in a host and spreads rapidly." Lewis's smile is warmer than the sun spilling through the gaps in the trees. "What Olive wants to start is officially called a 'social epidemic'. And that's just a posh word for a craze. Like, umm, the ice bucket challenge. Or the mannequin challenge. These crazes seemingly come out of nowhere, but they NEVER come out of nowhere, they've always been started by something." The dusty ground now resembles many graphs and strange symbols. "So, we need to somehow 'infect' people with kindness – a really contagious strain – and then we'll hopefully get to this thing called the Tipping Point. This is one dramatic moment where the kindness will become an epidemic. People copy. They respond to how everyone around them behaves. So, if we make kindness the biggest, bestest, most normalized thing ever, then people will fall in line." He looks at me and smiles. "Like really kind lemmings."

I smile back, so wide.

"It's all there," he adds. "We just need to start it."

All of us are stunned, digesting how very smart Lewis is. I want to stand closer to him all of a sudden. I want to reach out and grab his fingers between my fingers. I want to breathe in the air he has just breathed out. I'm not sure why but that's what my body wants and so I find myself stepping right up next to him and declaring to everyone, "This is brilliant." Because it is, it really is. Then I reach down and lace my fingers with his and it feels just as good as I knew it would feel. In fact, electricity tingles up my arm and now just holding his hand isn't enough. But it's going to have to be because Lewis is looking down at our entwined hands in both shock and wonder and, slowly, he squeezes my hand back. This would be marvellous except Jamie has noticed. I see his eyes move from our linked hands up to both our faces and he gives me a sad little smile and a tiny shake of his head.

No.

He's reminding me. No. This is an impulse I should not act on. Also, WE ARE ABOUT TO SET OFF A KINDNESS VIRUS and that is VERY EXCITING.

So I

Reluctantly

Drop

His hand.

"Don't we need to define what kindness actually is?" Hannah says. "I mean, I've been thinking about it since we started doing this, and our definition of kindness is a bit vague."

Jamie puts on a boomy God voice and says, "DO UNTO OTHERS AS YOU WOULD HAVE THEM DO UNTO YOU." Then he smirks and says, "If Jesus couldn't infect enough people, why do we think we can?"

Hannah crosses her arms. "Umm, I think you could argue Jesus did *infect* a lot of people. Christianity is kind of a big deal."

Everyone laughs and I laugh too, even though Lewis is looking right at me, with a confused look on his face. One that is asking, *Why have you dropped my hand?*

Sophie timidly puts up her hand, like we're in class. But we all get it and let her talk. She glows red but says, "I've been thinking about this since our last meeting too." She stops to draw breath and I'm careful not to look at her too much, in case it makes her feel exposed and panicky. "And I was thinking that true compassion is more than just 'trying to be nice to people'. I reckon most people try to be nice anyway, or at least think they're nice, but something is still obviously going wrong." She steps forward and the sun hits her pale face, making her shine almost translucently. "I think real kindness, real compassion, is having the strength to stop and try and see where another person is coming from. To try and work out why they're being the way they're being. It takes time and patience. It's not as easy, but that's real kindness."

There's a moment's quiet as we reflect on what has just been said. All of us silently agreeing with her. I feel fizzy on how well this is going, on how smart we are, on how much this is going to change things and make everything better and make me better and yes, yes, yes.

Gabriella draws a heart with her twig. "So, how do we get people to understand what real compassion is?" she asks. "And then how do we get the kindness virus to reach tipping point? Do I have to go sneeze on a million people or something?"

"Sort of, yes!" Lewis replies.

I can feel him fizz next to me. *Fizz, fizz, fizz.* I'm the pack of fizzy sweets and he's the bottle of Coke and together we're exploding in such a good way.

"We need to make kindness as contagious as a yawn. Yawns are perfect examples of social viruses. If I yawn, you will almost certainly all yawn. In fact, I don't even have to yawn. Just me saying the word 'yawn' right now is probably making your mouth need to yawn."

As he says it, my mouth waters. Gabriella breaks rank by being the first to yawn widely and openly. It's too much. We all yawn after her, which is hard to do when you're laughing.

"See!" Lewis says when he's finished yawning. "We need to come up with some kind of message that reminds people to be truly compassionate, one that's contagious and makes people want to share it. Then we have to try and infect as many people at the same time as possible."

"And that will help the world?" Jamie says, deadpan, leaning against a tree again.

Lewis narrows his eyes at him. "It might. We may as well at least try."

Sophie, already on a roll, surprises us by speaking up again. "Jamie, kindness isn't just about other people. It's about yourself too. It's about understanding your own pain, your own suffering. I've found it so reassuring to be in this group and start to accept that my illness is not my fault. It's helped me be more compassionate towards myself. To stop and think about why I am the way I am, and be kind about it, and more understanding, rather than beating myself up. Like you always seem to do."

He opens his mouth to interrupt but she, miraculously, cuts him off before he's even started.

"But just because it's not my fault I'm the way I am, it's still my responsibility to do something about it. Only I have the power to change my life, only I can take the harder steps to hopefully give myself an easier life. I get what you've been trying to say. We can't just dodge all responsibility. I owe that to myself, and I owe that to the world around me too. So, I'm going to try and..."

I don't hear the rest.

Because, oh my, it's like my brain is exploding into fireworks.

"THAT'S IT!" I yell. "That's it! You've got it. I've got it. We've got it, Sophie."

Everyone looks at me like I'm crazy which is somewhat annoying because they should be used to me by now. I pick up Lewis's stick and scribble out all his maths.

"Hey!" he says but I ignore him and use the space I've cleared to write in big letters on the ground:

WHAT HAPPENED TO YOU ISN'T YOUR FAULT, BUT IT IS YOUR RESPONSIBILITY TO DEAL WITH IT.

Everyone peers down at it like we're at the edge of a well.

"I like it," says Jamie quietly. The first positive thing he's ever said about this whole thing. There is a flurry of nods as the others agree.

"We can come up with more messages," I gabble. "We can write them on little scraps of paper and make, like, kindness fortune cookies for everyone to open that remind people of compassion and how important it is. Then we can stand somewhere high or something and set them all free. Let's say only one in ten people get infected, they'll still be contagious and spread it onto others. And they could infect more people, then those people will go on and infect more. Just like any virus, some people are immune to kindness, but think of all those who aren't!"

Lewis grins across every inch of his face. "It's a nice idea, Olive."

"I think so," I say confidently.

"I know how to fold origami," Gabriella says. "I can teach everyone? Then we can make loads of them."

Hannah is scowling. "How are we supposed to fit this around all our therapy too?"

"We'll make time," I assure her. "Surely this is more important?"

"For you maybe," she says pointedly.

Sophie moves us along before we fight. "Where do we go to infect lots of people in one go?"

I point at her. "Good point," I say, then I get excited because I said the word *point* at the same time as actually pointing and it makes me happy. "What day is it? What do we have coming up? Any big events?"

"Exam results," Sophie half-whispers. I get a mild flip-flop. Bollocks, I'd forgotten about those. By *forgotten*, I mean *wilfully repressed*, which is always a healthy thing to do, but I don't have time to worry about that now.

"Shall we stand outside a school and infect a load of students?" Hannah suggests. The sun hits her face just as she bites her lip. "Actually, on results day I'm sure I'll need all the kindness I can get."

"I don't think hitting just one age group is enough," Lewis says. "And one school isn't big enough… There must be something coming up? Somewhere we can go where there's loads of people."

"Notting Hill Carnival," Jamie says. He steps away from the tree. "I go every year. It has over a million people at the weekend."

"That's perfect," Lewis admits almost reluctantly. "We want people who are easy to infect, and the sorts of people who go to the carnival will be just that. Tolerant, liberal. That's a great place to start the virus."

Hannah is counting the days on her fingers. "But that's next weekend," she points out. "We're still here next weekend. How are we supposed to get to Notting Hill?"

Jamie shrugs. "We break out."

35

Things are exciting.

Things are coming together.

We have been a HIVE of activity and we've been buzz, buzz, buzzing and I almost can't contain my emotions I feel so GOOD about it. The plan has come together effortlessly. Each Prime Number has come up with some brilliant part of the mission and I just want to hug them all for ever because we're going to help the world, we're going to, we're going to.

The days are hazing into one another and results day is so very nearly here. But I can't worry about that right now, we're too busy making origami helicopters.

They were Gabriella's idea. She figured they were the best way of spreading the virus and has taught us all how to make them. We've written *YOU HAVE BEEN INFECTED BY THE KINDNESS VIRUS* on the outside, and then, when you open the coloured folded paper, we've made a selection of contagious phrases:

WHAT HAPPENED TO YOU ISN'T YOUR FAULT,
BUT IT IS YOUR RESPONSIBILITY
TO DEAL WITH IT.

EVERYONE IS FIGHTING A BATTLE YOU CANNOT SEE
ON THE OUTSIDE, SO BE KIND.

BE BRAVE ENOUGH TO SHOW COMPASSION.
TO OTHERS, BUT ALSO TO YOURSELF.

The distribution of the virus is solved by Jamie, whose brother's friend lives in Notting Hill. Even better, this friend's flat overlooks the main carnival route.

"It's all set," he announces over dinner one night. The cafeteria has put on a Chinese night, but all the dishes are super healthy and fresh and non-monosodium-glutamatey. "I told Grace I was calling my parents but called Jim. He says his flat even has a roof. The building has a party up there every year, so he's invited us and we can set the virus off over the edge." He twizzles noodles around his fork and shovels them in. "I mean, we'll probably get kicked out of the party the moment they see us emptying a ton of origami over the edge, but the virus will've been activated by then."

Escaping the camp is another hurdle Jamie solves. "I just called and booked us all a cab when I finished talking to Jim." He shrugs. "It's not like we're sectioned or anything. Though we should probably scale the wall, rather than walk right out past the security guards."

Lewis is totally distracted, doing calculation after calculation. Trying to figure out how contagious the kindness virus will be, how many origami helicopters we need to release to have a chance of making a tipping point. I sit next to him in art therapy and hear him muttering things like, "If only one in four helicopters get opened, and the message only infects a further one in four, then the odds of contagion are…"

"So how many helicopters do we have to make?" I ask. I see him open his mouth and realize he is about to bulldoze me with formulas and equations I can't keep up with. "In English," I add.

He smiles back. "The official number?" His smile is all gum and charm and makes my stomach bubble, but then again, my stomach is bubbling a lot at the moment. "A hell of a lot."

And that's what our spare time has been dedicated to – making the virus. Every spare second has been spent folding paper and trying to hide the virus wherever we can. I've had no time to follow my personalized sanity formula. But that's fine. I don't need it. Because I'm going to change the world and that will mend me. I've only been able to keep up my self-portrait project because it would look shifty if we *all* took an intense interest in paper folding in art therapy. So we gather in corners and fold helicopters and stuff things into our pockets. We wait until the hallway lights have been dimmed at night-time and then patter to one another's rooms and fold into the night.

I keep going to Lewis's room.

I'm not sure why I keep going to his room, but I do.

He waits for me, the door open before I've even finished my gentle knock. He is always clean and changed and smelling good and we smile at each other shyly but then just get to folding, a movie playing quietly in the background. We talk about maths and sanity and the universe and grilled cheese sandwiches. But I don't lean over and kiss him or touch him or do any of the things my body wants to do because I care too much for this boy to hurt him. So we talk and fold and plot and plan until the dawn creeps in around the gaps in his drawn curtains.

I've not really slept in days but I don't mind – I don't feel it. All I feel is excitement in my stomach and this brilliant clarity in my mind. That this is the right thing.

Gabriella is cheating at Monopoly again, but all of us are pretending not to notice. She's also trying to convince me that mood-stabilizing drugs aren't so very bad after all.

"Lithium's great!" she tells me, as I see her pick up two one-hundred-pound notes as change rather than one. "Why don't you want to be on lithium?"

Hannah, who is the estate agent, hands over the card for Bond Street. "You still think you're a special snowflake who doesn't need drugs?" she asks me, with a raised eyebrow. The comment has the desired effect and I feel irritation lace my blood.

"No!" I snap back. "I just don't trust that they know what they're doing. And aren't we supposed to be trying to be kinder? HANNAH?"

She giggles and passes the dice over to Lewis to throw.

To tell you the truth, irritation is something I am really struggling with right now. One, because Dr Jones brought up medication in my one-to-one AGAIN earlier today and was all about the mood stabilizers. "I know you're unhappy with the idea of lithium, but your symptoms are concerning us, Olive," she'd said, while I crossed my arms and looked as unimpressed as I was. "Look, I'll be honest. Ideally I'd like us to see how you do just with changing your medication to another 'type' of antidepressant rather than a stabilizer. See if that works? You're still so young and we still don't have a definite diagnosis and…"

"I'm feeling better," I blurted out. "I get that you think I'm a bit hyped up, but I feel so much better. I'm running and I'm being creative and I'm making friends and everything is fine."

She bites her lip. "I understand what you're saying, Olive. But a typical side effect of hypomania is feeling euphoric, but it's not *real* euphoria, if you understand?"

I rolled my eyes. "Who says it's not real? You? Some diagnostic book?"

She ignored my dig. "So, I've talked it through with Dr Bowers and we agree that, if you're really unwilling to try a stabilizer, let's reduce your dosage and see if that helps with your energy levels." She smiled. "And I'm not saying your happiness isn't real. I'm so pleased this camp is helping you feel better. It's just if it *is* mania, Olive, well, you might have a crash. We don't want that, do we?"

I'm also irritated because we're supposed to be having a Prime Numbers meeting in the games room but Darrell and Liv just WON'T LEAVE. They're playing snap and Darrell keeps yelling "Snap" way louder than necessary and I want to stand up and rip the cards out of his stupid hands and tell them to bugger off and go outside like everyone else, but that would be a bit too ironic considering the meeting is about kindness.

"Lithium made me fat though," Gabriella adds as Lewis rolls himself into jail and groans. "I was, like, three dress sizes smaller than this before I started taking it."

"You're not fat," Sophie, Hannah and I all chorus at exactly the same time. Because girls have been trained to say that instantly, the moment a girl says she's fat.

Gabriella cackles in reply. "Tonight is all about kindness, yeah, but not bullshit."

Eventually, when Grace comes in and announces Magnums are available in the canteen, we are left alone. We leave the half-finished game of Monopoly out as a decoy, but all of us reach into the bags we've brought and tip out the contents to make more kindness origami helicopters. We transition from Passing Go to Saving the World perfectly, all of us so good at folding these things quickly now. Sophie, Hannah and Jamie start by writing the messages and passing the squared paper onto me, Lewis and Gabriella, who fold them. Then we'll swap in twenty minutes so we don't get too bored.

My irritation has vanished now that we're back on task and I fold in a frenzy, the writing team hardly able to keep up with me. I keep holding my hand out for more, excited to make as many as we can while the coast is clear.

"Oh, by the way," Hannah says casually. "I've figured out how we can get all these virus helicopters to Notting Hill Carnival."

We all stop what we're doing to look at her. This was the one problem we've been struggling to solve. Lewis calculated we needed to make several thousand, but they weigh too much for us to carry them all the way to London.

She shrugs and carries on writing. "I told that sad henchman about our idea."

"WHAT?"

She sees me freak out. "Relax, Olive! He's not going to tell anyone. He's just a private contractor. He doesn't care." My heart is still going berserk but she waves my distress away. "I just asked him what was the kindest thing anyone's ever done for him, to soften him up. And then he got all soppy, and started talking about his daughter getting him football tickets for his birthday, and how great it was because they never get to spend time together. So, I told him all about kindness, and that we're planning this art project, and he offered to post our boxes to Notting Hill for us."

My mouth is open. Half annoyed, half not believing she's fixed such a vexing problem.

"I told you, it was nothing."

"Does this mean—" I start, and she cuts me off.

"That everything is sorted? Yes. Well, we've got one more stack to make, but then we're done. The virus is ready."

There is only one fly in our otherwise delicious ointment: Dr Jones's continued obsession with my apparent hypomanic state.

"You're still not sleeping," she says at my one-on-one. "I'm worried, Olive."

"I feel fine!" I insist. And I'm not lying, not even a little bit.

"A sustained lack of sleep is dangerous." She ignores my protest. "You will crash, and I don't think it will be good for you to crash."

"Well, you're changing my meds, maybe I'll sleep soon?"

"I don't want to wait that long. I've been talking to Dr Bowers about potentially giving you some sleeping tablets. Just to get you rested for a few days?"

Ergh. The thought is like someone has dropped a ton of sludge into my stomach. I don't want to sleep. Not when I'm like this. Not when we're only DAYS away from releasing the virus and spreading kindness everywhere like a really good version of Spanish super-flu, that maybe, just maybe, will stop people from getting so goddamned sick in this horrid world. I can crash afterwards. Part of me KNOWS I'm going to crash. Because this is what happened last time and what comes up must come down, but you know what?

If that happens, I feel like I'll be fine because at least this time around I'll have done something. I'll have tried to do something good. I'm not always a bad, terrible, awful, selfish person. I have tried to understand the pain and suffering of others and the pain and suffering in myself and that is what compassion is. So maybe if I crash it won't be as hard because I'll have that to hold onto? But, in the meantime, I need to get through until the weekend. So I nod and say, "Okay, I'll try some," to shut her up and make her smile and feel like she's helping. And, to be fair, she is helping. She's been really good at discussing Dad's email with me, and how it made me feel and how angry I am about so many things. That they never really told me, that Mum never got help and allowed her sadness to seep into me. Which I know isn't fair, but the good thing about therapy is you can say stuff which doesn't make you sound very likeable and therapists actually really like those bits.

"So, how you feeling about results day tomorrow?" She changes tack all of a sudden and I almost jerk back in the chair.

"Okay," I lie.

She picks up some notes and scans through them. "You get good grades in school from the looks of things?"

"Mostly."

"What do the results mean to you?"

I squirm and I wiggle and even wish we were talking about medication again. "I mean, they're just exams, aren't they?" I say. "They don't define you."

She raises an eyebrow. "You don't have to impress me, Olive. You don't have to pretend you don't care if you do."

I let out a long breath. "I'm scared I messed up my English exam and I need it for college," I admit. "I sometimes think I'd like to be a photojournalist, you know? Combine taking pictures with writing or something. So I really need English, but I was in a bit of a...way at the end, and that was my last one."

"And how do you feel about that?"

It's like my euphoria is a balloon and she's just taken out a sharp tack and punctured it deliberately. I feel my mood sour; I feel darkness and anger come tumbling into me. I suddenly feel very, very tired. And sad, it seems. Because when I put my hand to my face, I realize I have started crying.

"Like it's not fair."

"That what isn't fair?"

"Everything. Life!" I fling my arms out. "I mean, I revised really hard and I do my best in school despite everything. So, if I've messed it up, when I couldn't help it, that fucking sucks. It's not fair. I should be able to write a note at the top of my exam sheet and say, *Hey markers, look, I'm potentially going through a manic episode right now and that's not my fault so can you take that into consideration when you're marking me?* But they won't."

There is a silence as she lets me calm down.

"You said something interesting just then, Olive." Her voice is hot water and lemon with a spoonful of honey.

"I did?"

"You just said it wouldn't be your fault. That's the first time you've admitted that since you've come to camp."

"Admitted what?"

"That none of this is your fault."

Something inside me melts at her words. What they mean. Where there was ice, there is now a small puddle of melted emotions.

"Is that true?"

She nods. "None of this is your fault, Olive. I know you feel guilty about all the ways you may've hurt people, but it's important to know it's not your fault you're here. It's not your fault you're unwell."

The tears slosh down my face because I believe her and I never thought I'd ever believe anyone who told me my messes were not my fault. That maybe I am a victim of circumstance rather than a terrible person. That maybe I've had bad luck rather than bad bones. But it cannot stop here. This cannot be where the story ends. I've learned there is so much more to this than me. The mess is bigger than me and I have to help clean it up.

"I agree with you that it's not my fault." My voices catches in my throat and I swallow the emotion down. "But, isn't it my responsibility now to try and make sure I don't let any more hurt come from this? Like, yeah, it's not my fault I'm like this, but isn't it my responsibility now to know myself and contain myself? And, well, stop hurting people?"

Dr Jones nods her head and then shakes it. She chews on her lip and takes a while to reply. "I guess, to some degree it is," she eventually gets out. Then she raises both eyebrows. "But part of not hurting people is looking after yourself properly. And, Olive, you have been more resistant to treatment than most of the other clients here. There's only a week left. Maybe really focus on you for a bit? So, you might want to think about taking those sleeping pills. Maybe get some rest? Look after yourself? I'm a professional and I'm telling you to look after yourself right now, Olive. Especially as we're still not in a comfortable place with your medication. Looking after yourself is the responsible thing to do."

I walk away with a tiny little sleeping pill in a tiny little plastic bag. And now it is late and I'm supposed to be going to Lewis's room to finish off the last of the helicopters, but I'm also supposed to be taking this sleeping pill with a big glass of water. I can't decide where my responsibilities lie. I'm not tired. I don't feel like I need sleep. I'm also so wired up about results day that I don't trust the pills to be strong enough, to be honest.

Do I have a responsibility to myself first, or to the world?

I'm pacing my room. My noise machine blasting.

No.

I cannot stay in this room. I cannot swallow this pill. I need to kick back against the world that made me like this in the first place. The world that is noisy and selfish and crowded and quick to judge and unkind and underfunded and under-resourced and backward. I will not numb up my brain. Not now. Not when it's firing this well and rallying the troops and inspiring sick people to fight for the first time. The cause is more important than me. The cause needs me and my brain. I am on fire but I will not burn out.

I will not burn out.

I will just burn.

Brightly.

I will, I will, I will.

…

God, Lewis's smile as he opens the door.

36

Today is the day.

Not *that* day. Although the virus is made and we just sent it off. But today is results day. The day when I find out how much I messed up my own life.

It is so depressing when the main thing sabotaging your life is yourself.

Lewis and I stayed up until one, folding paper and chatting brilliant nonsense and then he fell asleep. Cutely, on his side. All balled up like a really cute woodlouse. I watched him sleep for a while. Not in a creepy way. More in an intrigued, envious way. Because it is always fascinating to watch people who close their eyes and drift off. I managed to grab an hour and a half between five and six thirty this morning. Then I got up and ran three times around the place and it still hasn't been enough to calm my tummy.

The atmosphere at breakfast is quiet and tense. Most of us are in Year Eleven, so most of us will get our results today.

Only Jamie and Gabriella got their AS results last week and both did okayish.

"You don't need good grades to be in a kickass band, anyway," was all Jamie had said about the matter.

Hannah and Sophie are already sitting down, picking porridge up with their spoons and then dribbling it back into the bowl. I grab a banana that I know I won't eat and join them.

"Hey."

They hardly look up. Sophie's hand is shaking so much on her spoon that the porridge is slopping all over the place. They mutter "Hi" back.

"I feel sick," I announce, and they nod. "How did your exams go?"

"I only made it to three of them," Sophie whispers. "I had a bad week, because of the stress of them, and found it really hard to leave the house. But they let me take those three in a special little room so I'm hoping I passed them..." She drops more porridge off her spoon. "I guess I'll have to retake the year to get into college."

Hannah reaches over and squeezes her hand and Sophie manages to put the spoon down. It clatters against the hard wood of the table.

"How about you?" I ask Hannah.

She gives a wince of a smile. "I'm hoping I did okay. I mean, there were no drains near the exam block... You?"

I shrug. "I got predicted good things, but I'm not sure how well I did when push came to shove. I got a bit...wound up in my last one." I close my eyes as the memory of my English exam flashes up, uninvited, into my subconscious. Oh God, please don't have failed English. I need it for college.

"At least there's a party later," Hannah says. "I heard the promise of cake."

I do not eat my banana. I cannot stay in the canteen long. I wave to Lewis and the others as they arrive and decide to go on a nice calming nature walk in the woods to make me nice and calm and calm and nice. But walking is too slow so I speed up and do this weird jog-skip-walk thing, following forest paths at random. I think about everyone from school and how different their day will be. They will get to go into school and open the envelopes themselves. They will probably dress up to look nice and hug each other and say how much they've missed one another over the summer. They will squeal as they line up for their envelopes and open them in corners of the hallway and, if they do great, they will jump in the air and if they do badly, they'll know it was because they didn't revise enough or had a bad teacher. They will not have to ring their parents and get them to open the envelope for them. If I do badly today it's because some evil twin part of me let me down.

I'm not sure how I will deal with that.

And so I start to run again.

When I get back, sweaty again, and all red in the face, I find everyone gathered outside Grace's office.

Darrell emerges and greets everyone with an air punch.

"ACED THEM," he says and everyone cheers and whoops.

I find the Prime Numbers huddled at the back. Sophie is past white at this point. Lewis is giving me a look. One that makes me feel like he doesn't mind that I'm covered in sweat. Not even for a moment. I feel shy all of a sudden and smile back at him.

"So, what's going on?"

"We're taking it in turns to ring our parents and find out how badly we've done," he says.

I push him playfully. "Like YOU'VE done badly? I bet you get straight nines."

"No. I really panicked in my biology exam."

Grace comes out of her office and beckons Hannah in. She makes a freaked-out face and follows Grace inside. I turn to Sophie, who's turned from white to green.

"Hey, Soph, it will be okay. What's wrong?" I ask, keeping my voice down so no one can hear.

"I'm actually not that nervous about results," she says. "I mean, I only took three. I'm going to have to retake the year anyway. But I've started to think a lot about Saturday. I've been trying to be brave and not say anything but..." She gulps. "Olive?" she asks. "How am I going to get on a train? And then the Tube? How am I going to cope being in those giant crowds?"

"Aww, hon, you should've said something," I say, putting a sweaty arm around her. "But you may be fine. I mean, you'll be with us."

"A million people, Olive! I get scared being around more than one."

I try and think about what I would want to hear if I was her. I try and use KINDNESS to figure out where her pain is coming from and if I can alleviate it.

"What are you scared of? Having a panic attack?"

She nods and wipes away a tear before it has the chance to fall from her cheek, so I steer her away from everyone into a quieter corner.

"What if I mess everything up?" she says. "What if I freak out and ruin it? You'll all hate me. You'll think I'm weak and that I've let everyone down."

"But it's us, so we won't!" I reassure her. "We get it, Sophie. We know how hard it will be for you. And you know what? We won't judge you or be annoyed with you if you can't come. At any point, if it's too much, you can say 'Stop' and we'll just be grateful that you helped us up until this point. Doesn't knowing that help?"

She sniffs and nods. "People always SAY it's fine but I can tell it isn't fine. They say it's okay, but I can see how annoyed they are. I don't want you guys to look at me like that."

"Am I too sweaty to hug you properly?" She shakes her head and I envelop her. She's so tiny and fragile beneath my pongy arms.

I let go and hold her shoulders. "You KNOW we won't look at you like that," I tell her. "Because we get it. We've been there. That makes such a difference. We know it could easily be one of us who has the bad day and needs YOUR support. Now, if I suddenly get so manic I totally forget about the virus and take all my clothes off in the woods

344

and dance to Queen, will you judge me?"

She laughs through another tear being shed. "No."

"See! Because we get each other. Because we're here for one another. Look, we can't start a kindness virus if we don't practise what we preach, can we? Whatever happens on Saturday, I promise you we will treat you with compassion. We love you!" I give her another small shake. "Now, are you feeling any better?"

Sophie wipes under her nose with her finger. "A little, thank you."

"Any time."

We walk back into the crowd just as Hannah bursts out of the office, her eyes glinting.

"THREE SEVENS AND NINE SIXES!" she yells and we all cheer. The Prime Numbers yelling the loudest for her.

I want great results. I deserve great results. Oh God, please let me get great results. When will it be my turn? I feel sick, I feel so sick. I hardly catch Sophie's voice as Hannah makes her way back to us, pure happiness bleeding over her face.

"What's that?" I ask her.

Sophie tilts her head at me over her glasses. "I just said, it goes both ways, you know? All of us are here for you too. None of us are in this alone any more."

And I don't have time to take that in properly because Grace walks out and finds my face.

"Olive, it's your turn."

37

Grace's office door must have thick glass because the hubbub of outside dies to a dim murmur as she shuts it behind her.

"How are you feeling, Olive?" she asks, all smiles and hope-for-me in her eyes.

"Like I'm walking to the electric chair."

She lets out a burst of laughter. "And there I was thinking you would be overdramatic. Now, the phone's over there. I can wait in the other office if you want to be alone?"

I nod. "If you don't mind."

"Of course not." She goes to leave, then stops. "Remember, grades on a page don't define you, Olive. No matter what you get, you're still you."

"Me, with a lifelong job flipping burgers if I mess them up."

"There are worse things."

She retreats to the adjoining office. I'm left with just me

and the phone. Me and my future. I drum my fingers on the desk. I whisper, "Come on, come on, come on," to myself.

And then

I pick

Up

The phone.

Mum's voice greets me before the first ring has even finished ringing. "Olive?"

"It's me. Your daughter. On judgement day."

"IT'S OLIVE," she calls. There's a clattering down the line and Dad's voice joins us.

"Olive, how are you doing?"

Hearing both their voices sets off a freight train of emotions in me. I've not spoken to either of them since I got Dad's email. I just feel this huge gushing of love pouring out of me. Warmth and love and forgiveness. Because whatever went down, whatever caused me to be the way I am, it wasn't their fault. I love them, they love me and none of it is anyone's fault. But my gush of compassion is short-lived.

"I'll be better when you open that envelope," I try and joke.

"It's here in my hands," Mum says. "We saw Ally when we picked it up from school. She says hello and that she misses you."

"How did she do?"

"Really good. Five eights and four sixes."

I grin, though I don't have room to be happy for Ally right now. Maybe in a minute. Once I know.

"That's great," I shrill. "Umm…so, are you going to open it?"

"I guess."

There's a ripping and then a pause. "Are you going to be okay, Olive?"

"I'll be fiiiiiine." My voice isn't mine. My fingers won't stop drumming on the desk. They make a satisfying noise as I do it.

Frlump, frlump, frlump.

There's further ripping followed by the scrunching of paper and then a gasp and…

"Olive, you got sevens in Biology, Chemistry, Photography and French!"

Sevens. I got multiple sevens! That is good! My brain is trying to tell me that is good.

"What else? What else?"

"And…well…you got sixes in practically everything else, Olive! That's amazing."

"Congratulations," Dad says.

But I'm not having it. I'm not buying it. Not even for a moment. I can hardly get my breath out.

"What do you mean by *practically*? What are my other results?"

Mum's answer is rushed and coated in a thick layer of crystallized sugar. "Well, umm, you got a two in your English paper, but, Olive, let's focus on the positive here. Four sevens and five sixes – that's INCREDIBLE. Especially after everything you've been—"

"I've FAILED English?"

I'm tangling my fingers in the phone cord, I'm struggling to hold up the receiver. A two. I thought maybe, just maybe, my crazy theories into the characterization of Dill would be amazing rather than the ramblings of a madwoman.

I was wrong.

"Honey, these are great results," Dad says. "I'm sure your college will let you retake English."

"We're so proud. And happy!" Mum says. "Aren't you happy? Olive, considering everything, this is a good result."

And maybe I'm overdramatic and maybe I'm not counting my blessings and maybe I need to see the bigger picture but all I can think is, I failed English. And I failed English because I couldn't get a handle on my stupid fucking brain, and I thought I was better than the exam paper like a stupid fucking egomaniac and this is what life will always be. There will always be that no man's land between what my life could and should be, and what my life is because of my stupid mental health. They are cooing down the phone, Dad is saying they're going to open some champagne. The word "proud" is used so many times I wonder if they took shares out in it.

"I have to go," I announce. "Everyone is taking turns with the phone."

"Are you okay?" Mum asks. "Try not to focus on English. Focus on all those shiny sevens instead."

"And we're seeing you next week for family therapy,"

Dad adds. "And, when we get home, we'll go for a big meal out to celebrate."

I say thank you and I say that sounds great and I tell them I miss them and reassure them that yes I am fine and then I say goodbye and I hang up and I'm left just me and my thoughts and they are not in the best of moods if I'm being honest with you. Not in the best of moods at all.

Grace must've heard me put the phone down because she pushes through the door.

"How did it go, Olive?"

I must not let it show. Whatever I'm feeling, I need to not let it show. Not just yet. Not until I've worked out what it is. Because, right now, I feel like screaming until I puke up my guts. I feel like trashing the office. I feel like picking up every single breakable thing in the universe and throwing it at a wall. But I can't fall apart because in two days I will do something bigger than my GCSEs, bigger than my exam results, bigger than me.

So I smile and say, "Great! Four sevens and five sixes," and nod and smile while she says, "You go, girl." Then I push back out into the reception and tell everyone the same collection of numbers and let them congratulate me. I want to run away, right now. From this moment. From this faux euphoria. It feels like a disease that is sinking into my skin. I have to wait for Lewis though.

I have to see how he does.

I have to contain it, just a little longer, for him.

So I let the Prime Numbers hug me, and I listen to them

get excited about tonight's party. And I hug Lewis so, so tight before he goes in to make his phone call and I hug him even tighter when he emerges glowing like sunshine, with all eights and nines against his name and an air of swagger that I've never seen in him until now. We have downtime all day before the party starts at the not-very-cool time of 3 p.m. Everyone is arguing about what to do around me. They are asking me and I want to scream, "I DON'T CARE." But all I do is say I need a shower and I'll see everyone later.

I go back to my room and I turn on the hot water.

38

I wash and I wash. God, the showers here are amazing. All like being in a rainforest, not like I've ever showered in a rainforest, but you know what I mean.

You know what's the opposite of amazing?

Me.

I want to scrub off my shame. Loofah off my disappointment. Failed English. Failed English. Because I couldn't keep myself under control. Because I thought I knew better. Such a stupid, stupid, weak, idiotic MESS of a person. I lather rinse and repeat and repeat and repeat. I never want to leave this shower. It's nice here. Maybe I can just stay in it for ever. The hot water feels so good as it pummels my shame-ridden skin. I try to think of good things. Happy things. I try to do what they tell you to do and focus on the positive. I passed most of them. I passed most of them well. But all I can see as I close my eyes is the fail. I open my mouth and scream into the water. It runs in and

I gag and cough the water back up but scream some more. God, screaming feels good. Everyone should scream a bit more. I yell and scream and I stay in there until all the hot water runs out and still I stand, shivering, not wanting to leave this lovely safe shower where I can pretend I'm in the rainforest. But soon every part of me is freezing and my lip's wobbling so I switch off the tap and step out and wrap myself in a towel and go and look at my stupid self in the mirror.

I think the term you would use is: *hot mess*. But without the hot part.

For the first time in a long time I can see why Dr Jones is worried. The bags under my eyes are so huge that I'd get charged extra for taking them onto a plane. And yet my eyes themselves are big and wide like I snort coke for breakfast. I've lost the weight I'd gained back. I've got myself into a state again. I'm doing it all over again. But I think maybe it will be worth it. If this kindness campaign helps change the world it will be worth it. Not just for the world, but for me. It will be a way of proving to myself that I have worth, that I'm not awful, that I can be good, that I can do good things and clear up messes rather than just creating them all the time. But holy moly I have sacrificed so much to get here. Because apparently I can't be healthy *and* useful. I can't be sane *and* revolutionary. I don't want to look at my face like this. This is not the face you need when you're trying to inspire a bunch of mentally-ill teenagers to change the world. I empty out my make-up bag into the sink and get to work giving myself a face that can be followed. I smear under-eye concealer over my bags. I curl my eyelashes until they pop and layer on a thin coat of mascara. I rub lip stain onto my mouth until it's a small, red, attractive bud. I tip my hair upside down and blast my bob into voluminous submission. When I look up again, I look pretty. I smile. I rummage in my suitcase and take out a flower clip. I pin my hair to the side of my head and look at myself.

Even better.

I mean, I'm completely naked. I guess I have to deal with that too.

What to wear, what to wear? Not jeans, not that skirt. Ahh, look, here. My strappy summer dress that I packed at the last minute. When I came here with such hope. Such a naive longing that four weeks of posh bedrooms and telling a group of strangers about my childhood would somehow mend my mind. It only has a few creases in it and I pull it over my head without putting on a bra or knickers.

I know what I'm doing this for, by the way. I know. Because I'm too sad not to do it. I'm too weak right now to be strong. I need kindness and I need to feel like I'm okay and also my body is wired and singing and I can't ignore it any longer. Maybe it's not right but I don't care and I'm not even sorry that I don't care.

I just need to.

See.

Him.

And the way he smiles at me.

One last look. *Banging*. That is the word I will use to describe how I look right now.

From hot mess to banging.

Not that he would say no if I still looked like a hot mess. Because he is kind like that. Because he's seen me look worse and I could still sense the love. Like standing with your back to a radiator on a cold day. The glow of his heat, the steady rays of his love or adoration. I need it. But I need the radiator turned up now.

39

Lewis looks surprised as he opens the door.

"Olive?"

It takes all the effort in the world not to kiss him right away. I ask if I can come in and he stands to one side, letting me into the familiar room. It's messier than normal – very different from my evening visits.

Okay, I'm in. I can't hold this in for much longer.

"Umm, everything okay? I'm just getting changed for the party."

"Do you like me?" I blurt out, stepping backwards to give us physical space. Because if I step any closer I'm just going to jump on him and I care about this boy and I feel like he will want some kind of vaguely-romantic narrative before we do what I really hope we're going to do. He turns red instantly, his mouth open in shock.

"Yes, like that. Do you like me like that?"

I watch his face, how it changes. It is beautiful. Part of

me wants to savour each expression, how it evolves as he decides what to say. As he weighs up the outcome of each word, putting every response into a formula he's devised out of nowhere, looking for the answer that makes the most sense. He blushes more, he lets out a "Well…" before stuttering back into himself again. Finally, he looks up, full of resolve but fear very much in his eyes.

"Yes, Olive. I like you like that. To tell you the truth, it's very hard not to."

He may as well have thrown a lit match at me, because I am a tank of gasoline and his words have just exploded me from the inside out. I cross the space between us, lean in, and kiss him. I know I should go slower but I can't. It's his lips. It's Lewis's lips. And they're warm and nervous but enthusiastically responding. He lets out this sort of moan into my mouth and it's all I can do not to take his top off. Although I really plan to take his top off.

He isn't the best kisser. I sense that maybe I could even be his first kiss. His tongue plunges in and out of my mouth without any delicacy but it's still good. It's still great. Because it's the energy coming off him that is what I need. I can feel how much he likes me, how much he wants me, how much he feels I am a good person who tries their best. I break off, just to hug him. To hug him so tight. I squeeze and squeeze, inhaling the smell of him, loving the feel of his arms, how they are squeezing me back just as hard. They're so potent, these moments. These moments when you cross the boundary of not being able to touch someone to finally both jumping across that line together. A line there is no coming back from. But why would you ever want to come back from crossing a line that feels this good? Okay, the hug isn't enough any more. I need to kiss him again. And so I'm kissing him again and he's getting better already, just by my gentle guidance. I manoeuvre him backwards onto his unmade bed. As he falls back, the distinct smell of boy erupts around me. But it's a nice Lewisy smell.

"Olive?" he asks, uncertain.

"It's fine," I murmur and I pull him on top of me and he falls clumsily, squashing my legs. I have to steer him up onto his elbows as we melt into the kiss once more. My eyes are closed and every goosebump on my skin is savouring this moment. This moment where there is nothing but feeling – all thinking gone out the window. Where it belongs. Because where has thinking got anyone, really? And now kissing isn't enough. I never thought it would be. I push Lewis's chest and tug at the bottom of his *Doctor Who* T-shirt. Again, he looks nervous but he still shrugs it off. He's so skinny and his chest has no hair, but all that skin. Bare skin. In this context, it ignites me even further. I go to kiss it and he closes his eyes, smiling, like he can't believe any of this is happening. It makes me feel strong and powerful and good and I am good, I must be good if a guy as good as Lewis can look at me like that. My body is craving further touch and so I take his hands and lead them to where I want them to be. I think he's going to explode when he realizes I have no underwear on. He starts off uncertain but it's not like I'm not going to show him how so he relaxes into it and he touches me and I touch him and we're doing things I'm sure he's never done before but I've done plenty of times but it feels great but it's still not enough…

So, of course, I pull off my dress.

And that's when he freezes.

"Woah, Olive," he says, not looking at my body. Why isn't he looking at my body?

"What is it?" I try not to come across as irritated but I'm really damn irritated because I cannot handle this stopping right now.

He gulps. He looks at me again, his eyes bulging at my nakedness, but then looks up at my face. "This is…going too fast. I'm not…ready."

"Not ready for what?" I smile innocently, shifting back, exposing my body more. Because maybe just maybe I can turn this around. Maybe we just need to talk things through first, which is a pain because I am so, so, so horny but it's also the fair thing to do. What Lewis needs.

His face goes red. "You know what," he mumbles.

"I have no idea what you mean." I smile again. God, I'm cute. There is no way he can say no to my cuteness, surely? But he is not breaking into the mischievous smile that I'd envisioned. Instead he's scrambling up so he's sitting cross-legged on the bed and he is handing me back my dress.

Handing.

Me.

Back.

My dress?

"Olive, please. This isn't funny, this is serious. You really want to…" Oh bless, he can't even say it. "Right now?"

I don't have much brazen left. All the confidence he gave me is blowing around the room like a released balloon, making fart noises.

"You don't want me," I say small-ly.

"What? No! Come on. But, this is very fast. I've never… Can we just talk?"

"About how you don't want me?"

"No! Olive. Please. What's going on in that head of yours? Let's talk, please."

I cannot talk because humiliation has just hijacked my body and is steering me off a cliff into nothing, nothing, nothing… I'm disgusting. I'm a slut. I'm a repulsive slut. I am not good enough for Lewis. I'm not good enough for anyone or anything. I pull my dress over my head and tug it over my body.

"Olive, where are you going? I didn't mean to hurt your feelings…Olive…"

I am out of the door. The door is slamming shut behind me. I can't.

I can't.

Can't.

There is nowhere for this energy to go. This energy of shame. This energy of disgust. It pumps around me and there is nowhere to let it out. I hate myself. I really hate myself. There, I said it.

I finally said it.

I.

Hate.

Myself.

Because, come on, if you were me, wouldn't you?

40

Where am I? Oh, outside. The sun is hot and beating down and someone might've called my name but I'm not sure if I'm totally honest with you because all I can think is what a stupid, weak, disgusting, horrible slut I am. It's all my thoughts are. Insults hurling themselves from one side of my brain to the other.

I don't deserve kindness.

I thought maybe I did, but I don't.

I deserve every bad thing that has ever happened to me.

Ouch. That hurt. I trod on something sharp. Because I'm running, running through the woods. I don't remember crossing the lawn but I must've because I'm now running in the woods and thinking I need to get this out. This poison of insults in my head. I just need to tire myself out and I don't know why I'm not tired because it's not like I've slept for the last week or anything and I've hardly eaten but I'm not tired because the energy I have, this energy of hate, for myself, for the world, but mostly for myself, well it is strong. You don't need sleep when you're high on hating yourself.

Lewis's face.

Failing English.

My mum sick because of me.

The world sick because of everything and me being stupid enough to think I could change that.

When I can't

Change

Anything.

I only

Make

Things

Worse.

Thump, thump, thump through the trees. I don't even have shoes on but it's okay, I'm managing and I'm sure I can stop soon. I'm sure I will get tired enough soon. To tell you the truth, my heart is kind of…hurting. Not just in a metaphorical way, but, like, in a genuine biological, hey, maybe I'm having a panic attack way, but I can't be having a panic attack because I'm still running and I'm quite sure you can't have a panic attack and run at the same time but

I'll tell you what

It hurts to breathe too. It's getting harder and you really need breath when you're running as fast as I'm running but I can't stop because the shame and the hatred is still hot on my tail.

God, it hurts.

My heart it hurts, lungs
Hurt.
All hurts.
Oh God, hang on, I can't see and now there is blackness.
And now
There
Is
Blackness.

41

I feel myself wake up, but no.
    I do not want to open these eyes of mine.
    Because I have crashed
    And burned.
    And it's back.
    Oh boy.
    It's back.

42

43

It is later and Dr Jones is annoying me.

"Olive, I know you're awake. Can you open your eyes, please?"

I ball up and huddle on this bed which isn't my bed. I'm not sure where I am and to tell you the truth I'm not sure I care.

"I don't want to."

It is hard to get those words out.

I do drift off then. Into something that isn't quite sleep, but a sweet quilt of darkness. One that wraps itself around me, beckoning me in.

I like it here in this blackness.

I don't have to think about what I've done.

44

45

Dr Jones is here again and I suppose I have no choice but to open my eyes. I blink the room into focus and find her face.

"Hello, Olive." She says it with neither kindness nor sternness.

I don't say hello back.

So I look around and try to work out where I am and how long it's been.

"It's Friday morning," Dr Jones tells me. "You slept all through the night, though you were sedated. You're in our medical room."

It definitely has more of a hospital than hotel vibe. My arm is attached to some kind of drip hooked up to a machine.

I can't think of the word.

"We found you collapsed in the woods. Your blood sugar was dangerously low. You're exhausted, Olive."

Exhausted.

That, I am.

Finally a diagnosis I agree with.

"We've let your parents know what's happened…" She goes on but I don't hear it because now they'll be freaking out. And thinking, *Oh God, she's still crazy, we don't want her any more.* Blah blah blah. I can't blame them for not wanting me.

I don't want me.

"I think today should be about resting, and tomorrow I've blocked out some time for us to have extra sessions. How does that sound?"

I shrug.

"Well, you've got some magazines and the TV, and someone will be popping in on you once an hour." She gestures to my side and I guess she wants me to look at where her hands are but I can't be arsed to move my head. "The phone's right there if you need anything. But, mainly, try to rest for today, Olive. We can discuss what's going on tomorrow when you've had more sleep."

I can tell you what's going on, by the way.

It's pretty easy.

I'm an awful person.

A terrible, weak, selfish, awful person.

I tried to be kind and I couldn't. Because I'm so inherently bad I just turn everything to sludge.

I'm a horrible person and I'm never going to get better because I don't deserve to.

And that is the only thought I have as the sun travels across the sky, as the shadows move from left to right, as the air outside turns slightly cooler. I just stare and think. And not much of what I'm thinking is very good.

In fact, none of it is.

I have a little mantra, that keeps me going through the day.

It goes like this:

I hate myself, I hate myself, I hate myself.

Catchy, huh?

46

At some point later in time, there is a knock on the door.

I ignore it.

But they bloody knock again.

"Olive? It's us. Dr Jones said we could visit."

They don't bother waiting for my reply. The Prime Numbers pile through, each of their faces doing a comedy jaw-drop when they see the state of me.

I stare back at them.

"Woahhhhh." Jamie is the first to step forward. "Look who crashed."

"Shut up," I murmur. I'm trying to catch Lewis's eye. He is here but he won't look at me. He is staring at my toes sticking out from under my scratchy blanket.

The rest of them shuffle in. Sophie's mouth is a small O. Hannah looks suitably unimpressed. Gabriella sits herself on the end of my bed without invitation and crushes my foot but I can't be bothered to tell her it hurts.

"You okay, bubs?" she asks. "You look like shit."

I can hardly even be bothered to raise an eyebrow.

"What are you all doing here?" I manage to get out.

They look at one another nervously, deciding who's going to be spokesperson. Lewis's face is beyond red. He is even redder than my toenail polish that he is staring at.

"We just wanted to double-check what to do about tomorrow?" Gabriella asks.

I very slowly close my eyes and very slowly open them again.

I hold up my wrist. "I'm on a drip."

"Yeah, but if you're better by tomorrow…"

I shoot them all A Look.

I open my mouth.

I say what I feel.

"I don't want to come any more," I tell them.

I feel somewhat guilty as I say it, but mostly I just feel glad for them. That they don't have to bother having me there, ruining it all.

Everyone apart from Jamie is shocked.

"But it's your idea!" Hannah says. "You really don't want to come?"

I start playing with my blanket, pulling it out so I can turn away from them. I curl up on my side, my back to their faces.

"You can still go," I say. "I don't know what good it will do, but you can still go." Because people can't change. I couldn't change. And I really wanted to. What's the point of trying to make things better when humans are just so very awful and the world is just so determinedly awful too?

"FOR FUCK'S SAKE." Hannah has lost her temper.

How. Very. Hannah.

She starts talking all loudly and I can feel her using her hands a lot as the air swishes around them. Words like "piss-take" and "let-down" and "joke". I wait until she's out of steam then murmur, "Are you finished?"

"Yes, I'm finished." Her footsteps storm away and that's a relief.

Though

There's

Still

Quite

A few of them

Here

To get rid of.

"Look, guys, please can you leave me be?" I ask quietly.

Gabriella pats my foot and removes her butt from my bed. Jamie mutters, "I hope you feel better soon." There is a squeak of Sophie's voice.

"Olive?" she says to my back. "Ignore Hannah. She's just being Hannah. I listened to what you told me. And, if this is where you have to stop in this project, it doesn't mean we think you've failed. You came as far as you could, and we'll carry the torch for you. Tomorrow, you'll still be with us."

A tear leaks from my eye and falls down my cheek, seeping into this uncomfortable pillow. I don't want to turn over and have her see me cry.

"So, thank you for showing me kindness," she continues. "I'm going to go tomorrow and be brave, because you're not well enough to. And, in return, I hope you will try and show some kindness towards yourself."

Another tear.

And another.

Plip plip plop.

The pillow catches them and goes soggy.

"See you soon, Olive."

I hear her footsteps leave and, even though she was being nice and all, I am relieved she's gone. Because my eyes are so heavy, my brain is so foggy. I just want to go back to sleep, where I can escape into unconsciousness, away from all the thoughts that are telling me how awful I am.

There's a cough.

I summon the energy to turn and see who it is. Even though I already know. Because my heart is racing and my mouth is dry and every single inch of me is embarrassed.

"Hi, Lewis," I say, unenthusiastically.

He doesn't look great, although probably better than me. There are huge bags under his eyes and his hair looks unwashed and unruly.

"Hi, Olive." He says my name all formally, like we're both in a job interview or something.

I blink a few times.

Slowly.

Trying to figure out if I have the energy to deal with this right now.

He coughs again. "I'm really sorry," he stumbles. "If I...
You didn't give me a chance to explain. I never meant to
upset you... You just ran off...and now you're here."

"Lewis, this has nothing to do with you." It comes out
harsh and mean. Maybe it was supposed to. I don't know.
He flinches.

He visibly

Flinches.

"Right. Okay." He pulls at his fingers, one at a time, his
hands scrunched into his torso, like he's trying to keep them
a secret. "Well, still, I'm sorry."

I shake my head. "I get it. You're sorry. Thank you or
whatever."

I'm just in the process of turning onto my side again.
Because I want to sleep. I don't want to deal with this.
When...

"You know what? Fuck you, Olive!"

I'm so shocked I turn back, to see his face is red raw and
his whole body quivering.

"Fuck you!" he repeats. "I say I'm sorry for something
I shouldn't even be sorry for and you just throw that shit
at me?"

"I'm not in the mood for this," I sigh.

"Well I am! And you know what? It's not always about
you, Olive. It's not always about YOU. Do you have any idea,
ANY idea, how big a deal for me yesterday was? I have never
liked a girl who might like me back. I'd never even KISSED
a girl, okay? And, you what? Because I didn't want to do

everything exactly on your terms, you piss off? You shut me out?" His voice cracks; he's almost crying.

I am blinking because it is all I can do. Blinking like my eyelids can be bulletproof shields, bouncing his words off so they don't embed in me and blow me open. "Do you even like me?" he asks. "Do you even like me like that at all? Or have you just been using me this whole time?"

Blink.

Blink.

"Answer me!"

"I…I…" I scramble for words in my fug. His emotions are only making me more tired. "I…don't know."

His face falls in on itself, his fists unclench. He visibly deflates. He sits on the chair at the end of my bed, and his head bows down so he is staring at the floor. "Right."

Blink.

Blink blink.

"I can't trust my brain, Lewis." It is worth trying to explain. If I can manage. It's worth trying not to break this boy's heart, if I can possibly help it. All I see in him is pain. Pain I've caused. Simply by being me. Because I'm a terrible, awful, shitty, selfish person who fucks up everything she touches. "I can't trust my feelings, or my emotions. They are not reliable sources of information."

Blink.

Blink blink.

Why is talking so hard? "I can't tell love from lust. I can't tell head from heart. I can't tell up from down, wrong from right, truth from lie. My brain is…fucked. I am fucked. I can't be sure because nothing I do makes any sense. I never know why I'm doing anything but I know that anything I do tends to hurt people."

That's all I have, that's all I can manage. I want to cry again but the numbness is coming in quick. I think Lewis might've triggered it earlier than normal. It's creeping up my toes like I'm standing in a box quickly filling with icy water.

He sighs and puts his head down between his legs, giving himself a moment. I think about getting out from under this scratchy blanket and going over to pat him or something but I can't be bothered.

He raises his head and stares right at me. "You know what?" he says. "You came in here and you were all about rejecting labels. You didn't want to know your diagnosis, you thought you were better than the words other people gave you. But, it's pointless because you've been giving yourself a label this whole time. You think you're a horrible person, Olive. That's the label you've chosen to give yourself. And, guess what? You're not very nice, no. All this kindness bullshit…" He laughs and scratches his neck. "You're not kind to yourself and therefore you're not kind to others. You think, *Oh, I'm a shitty person*, and therefore you behave like one. Because you've got to make your label make sense."

Blink.

Blink

…blink.

He is using far too long words for how tired I am right now. I'm trying to get them to deflect off me, but a few are sinking in. And the few that are sinking in are doing some serious damage.

"I can't help it," I say. "I'm sick. I don't WANT to be like this, but I keep being like this."

He shakes his head, unimpressed. "Bullshit! Yeah, of course you don't want to be like this. I don't want to be like this! Do you want to know what my bad thought is, Olive?" He's crying now. He's doing the crying for both of us; he is so generous in that way. "My bad thought is…is…that no one loves me. That no one ever will. That's why I'm here. Because that thought tortures me, every moment of every day." Tears splash off his face and he doesn't make any effort to wipe them away. "It's why I'm so good in school; it's why I'm so good at maths. Because you can control numbers – they make sense. Whereas people…people make no sense. None whatsoever. They can hurt you and chew you up and spit you back out again and ignore you even though you're trying your hardest to be nice and not even care about the damage they cause. You…yesterday afternoon…" He dissolves then, hiding his head completely, and I really don't know what to do.

A very dim voice in me is thinking, *Woah, Lewis is crying.* But more than anything I'm just kind of wanting to go back to sleep because this is too much and my brain is constantly jabbing an *eject* button.

He looks up, tears smeared everywhere, no shame in

them. "Do you have any idea how triggering last night was for me? You've essentially done everything I'm scared someone will do. But you know what? I've listened to my therapist and I'm working through my emotions because it's not my fault I'm like this, but holy hell it's my responsibility to not let it mess up my life. I'm the only one who can change things for me. But what about you? You're acting like you're not responsible just because you feel it's your default setting to be a bad person? I don't CARE about your brain chemistry, Olive. I don't care about your childhood. It's not your fault you are the way you are, but you still have a fucking responsibility to wake up each morning and try not to be the label you've given yourself." He stands up, runs his hands through his hair. I've never seen him like this. So angry, so alive. "You know what?" He shakes his head and looks at me like he hates me. "I'm wasting my time trying to talk to you when you're like this. See you whenever."

He storms out of the room. I watch him go.

He has done what I wanted.

He has left.

I am alone and it is quiet in here and I can be alone with my thoughts. My thoughts about how terrible I am. Which is exactly what I wanted.

But now maybe I don't.

"I like you," I whisper at the door. It comes out like a tiny squeak. "I do really like you."

47

Sleeping when you fall into darkness is such a sweet relief. Such a blessing. To be able to turn off from the world, like hitting the red button on your remote. All the despair, all the confusion, all the worry worry worry hate hate hate why why whys vanish.

If only for a while.

If I could sleep for ever, I would. But I know what sleeping for ever is.

I know what wanting that means.

And so, I am here again.

In the dark place where blankness is preferable to anything else

The

World

Chooses

To offer me.

But Dr Jones is determined to not let me sleep.

48

"Wakey wakey, rise and shine."

The lights come on hard, and it hurts my eyes even though they're still closed.

"Come on, Olive. Dr Jones needs to speak to you urgently."

I flicker my eyes open, which is hard because they are crusted together with gross morning juice. Rather a lot of it. I must've been asleep for a long time. It does not feel like that though. All my muscles ache and I just want to find oblivion again. I shut my eyes tight.

"No, no, no," Grace says, moving around the room. "We need you up."

I groan and put my arm over my eyes before I open them, shielding the worst of the summer sun streaming through the curtains, highlighting dust flecks that dance and cartwheel under the golden beams coming from the window. Grace's face is tight, her mouth a small thin line.

Oh God, what have I done now?

"Come on, Olive. We've not got time for this. Up and dressed." She claps her hands and, oww, it rips me open. "NOW!"

"Okay, okay." Where did nice Grace go? Smiley Grace? I yank my limbs off the bed and stumble to the bathroom. There's a shower but I don't bother having one. I just pee and emerge to find her still here.

"Ready?"

"For what?"

"I told you, Dr Jones needs to speak to you. Urgently."

My candyfloss brain can't compute why. What could I have possibly done in my sleep? Why won't they leave me alone? I collapsed! Surely that means I'm allowed to be left alone for at least a year? Though I notice I don't have a drip in me any more. When did that happen?

"I need to get dressed," I manage to say.

"I'll wait outside. Five minutes."

Some clothes have been taken from my room and are folded neatly on the chair where Lewis sat and cried and told me it's my own fault I'm a terrible person. I wiggle into my jeans and flop the T-shirt over my head. Wondering what feels weird about today, trying to put my finger on it...

Then I remember.

Today is the day we're releasing the virus.

I look up blearily at the clock and see it's gone 10 a.m. Oh. They must've already left. The taxis were due to pick us up from the gate at 7 a.m., before breakfast, so it would take a while for people to know we are missing.

I'm not missing.

They've gone without me.

Oh well.

I push through the door and tell Grace I'm ready. She makes no small talk as she leads me to Dr Jones's consulting room, even though I know where it is. She's walking too fast and I want to tell her to slow down but talking requires too much effort so I just hate myself and hate her as we walk along. She doesn't even say anything when we get there, just points to the door.

Dr Jones looks just as pissed off as Grace so I'm guessing they've noticed the others have gone. I crumble into the leather chair.

I blink.

Then I say, "They've gone to Notting Hill Carnival."

Because it's always

Less

Exhausting

If you just tell them first.

Both her eyebrows shoot up in panic.

"It's fine," I say. "They'll be back later."

"Olive, it's very important you tell me what's going on."

I blink.

Blink again, and keep my eyes closed for a little while because it's nice in here, when the world is black.

"Olive!"

"I told you, it's FINE."

But that's not enough and so I sigh and tell her everything that I can be bothered to. It takes a while and I really try to hurry it up but speaking really isn't something my body feels like doing so it's slow and sludgy. I manage to tell her about the algorithm and the kindness virus and our plan to set it off at the carnival.

"Don't freak out," I tell her. "You've always said we can leave whenever we want."

"This is very serious, Olive." I can hear a quiver of temper in her voice. "Five highly vulnerable people are heading into London into a crowded festival. Do you have any idea how this makes us look? How DANGEROUS this is for them?" I see her try to regain her temper.

I'm a jerk.

I wish she would just shout at me.

Jerks deserve to be shouted at.

I watch as she struggles to calm herself, smoothing her suit down like it will smooth down her reaction.

"Olive, if you go get some late breakfast in the cafeteria, I'll come speak to you again soon."

"I'm not hungry."

"Olive! You need to eat." She takes a deep breath. "Grace?" she calls and Grace appears at the door. "Olive knows where they've gone. I need to make some calls. Do you mind taking her to the cafeteria and trying to ensure she eats at least something?"

49

So we trudge to the cafeteria so I can shove calories down myself so they can be reassured I'm healthy. The thought of eating turns my stomach. Grace hardly speaks to me. Just tells me porridge will be "easier to get down". I dribble it into my mouth like a baby bird, coughing a few times because I can't be arsed to swallow. I finish and Grace gets up and makes us both a cup of tea. We sit and sip in silence.

Sit and sip.

Sit

And

Sip.

There are happy voices as other campers make their way from one activity to another. An echoing of laughter through the halls. *I missed the party*, I think, for the first time. I wonder what happened there?

I miss so many things by being me.

* * *

After an hour or so, I hear a clip-clopping of heels and Dr Jones appears. I can tell she's got her shit together, her face is more relaxed. She even manages a smile.

"Thanks for waiting, Olive."

"I didn't have much choice, did I?"

She ignores my jibe and looks over at Grace. "Thanks for watching over her. Did she eat?"

"I am still here, you know," I grumble as Grace says, "Some porridge."

"Good. Ready, Olive?"

"For what?"

"Let's go have a chat, shall we?"

I have no choice but to lumber after her, dragging my body along like it's fighting against the basic rules of physics. We go back to her room and I wilt into her chair once more. This morning has exhausted me, yet she's not letting me go.

"Are they in trouble?" I ask.

Dr Jones picks up her notepad and pen. "Trouble isn't the right word. I wish you'd told me what was going on."

I stretch up and yawn. "You'd have tried to stop me. Have you sent people after them?"

"I don't want to talk about them right now, Olive. I want to talk about you. What's happened?"

Such a simple question.

What's happened?

It doesn't have a simple answer though. Because so many things have happened. Good things and worse things and seemingly inconsequential things and can't-be-helped things and could-definitely-have-been-averted things and some of them have led up to what's happened and some of them haven't but you can't ever really know for sure. Not even with the best maths formula. Life's just a complicated mess with absolutely no purpose.

"You're exhibiting signs of a depressive episode. Do you agree?"

"I guess."

"Can you tell me what you think led to this happening?"

I throw my head back towards the ceiling. "Nothing. Everything. I've just been an idiot."

"An idiot?"

God it's so boring when she just asks question after question. "Yes, an idiot!" I shout. "Because I was deluded enough to think I was getting better, and I obviously wasn't. I let myself get all wound up, even when you told me that wasn't good, and I ignored you because I always think I know best, when I obviously don't and now look at the mess I'm in. I just HURT everyone. I'm STUPID and BROKEN and even over three weeks with all this help hasn't changed anything. I tried to be a better person, and I thought that's what could make me better, but all I've done is make everything worse because I'm a DICKHEAD."

She uncrosses and recrosses her legs. "Did you think coming here would change something?"

"No," I deadpan. "I just came for the food."

"Olive…"

"Yes, of course I did."

"And you don't feel like you've begun to understand yourself any better?"

"I…I…guess so…but look at the state of me. It's not like it's helped. I mean, I get why I may be like this now. And, I told you, me and the Prime Numbers, we've figured out all the bad things in the world and how to help. I understand it, but I'm still not better. Am I?"

Dr Jones puts down her notepad and I think, *Oh, here we go*, sensing a big speech. I am right.

"Firstly, it's worth pointing out that you've not exactly been making full use of the 'help' that's been on offer here. Have you, Olive? Compared to the other clients, you've missed a lot of therapy sessions, and you've also refused our recommendations about your medication. So in terms of you wishing you felt better, I would like to point out that you might very well be if you hadn't regularly overridden our guidance and support."

I cross my arms. "Rub it in, why don't you?"

She smiles rather than gets cross. "You know, Olive, you're right," she continues. "About this little project of yours. The theory behind it is right. Mental illness isn't all in your brain. And I admire you for looking outside of yourself, for looking out at the world and all the other things that cause pain and suffering. I mean, if you'd asked more about the data we collected, I could've told you that this is a key part of Camp Reset. We were on the same page as you… though we're not trying to set off any virus…" She smiles again. Like the virus idea is stupid. It probably is, because I came up with it and everything I do is stupid. "We are just at the beginning of understanding how data can help us with mental illness. It's very early, but very exciting days. We're getting there, but these things take time. Plus, there's only so much we can control. We can't always control someone's childhood, or how poor they are, or how they're treated in life. We can help them make sense of what happened to them, and empower them to make more positive choices about how to cope with it, and that is proven to help. But we accept our limits, Olive. You may want to think about accepting yours…"

I open my mouth to protest but she carries on.

"Look, I know you're not your biggest fan all the time. As I said, it's admirable that you have taken an interest in helping others, but does that have to mean you stop helping yourself?"

"What do you mean?"

Her smile is as gentle as a flower opening. "You don't have to stop looking after yourself just to help the world. In fact, sometimes it's better for the world if you put yourself first. That's not being selfish, in fact, looking after yourself is the greatest act of kindness you can give the world. Loving yourself first is the best way to spread love. You've tried so hard to be kind, but you've not started with you, and maybe that's where it's gone wrong?"

I blink.

And blink.

"What are you saying?" I ask, though I'm getting there.

Even in this sludge I am getting there.

Dr Jones looks me right in the eye. "I'm saying that you should attach your own oxygen mask before helping people with theirs, Olive. You ignored our professional advice because you thought you needed to be in that state to save the world. But look what happened."

I'm a selfish, horrible person and, in trying not to be, I've turned out to be a selfish, horrible person.

"So the answer is to just stay selfish all the time?"

"Selfish isn't always a bad thing, Olive. It gets a bad rep. Being selfish can sometimes be the most selfless act there is. It gives you the strength to *really* help. Sometimes you need to put *you* first and get fit and strong so you can go out and save the world when you're in the best shape to."

I blink.

Blink.

"So, what do I need to do to put my oxygen mask on first?"

She breathes in slowly, exhales even slower. "Listen to us. Trust us. Consider letting go of the belief that 'you know better'. It would be a good idea to at least think about the medication Dr Bowers has suggested. See how it goes? If we can balance you out, it might help. If we can balance you out, you might be better equipped to fight for a world where nobody needs medication. It's up to you. But have a think about it."

And I won't be able to come up with a yes or no.

Not right now.

It would be good not to do things like I did to Lewis ever again.

But I'm so tired right now.

So, so, so tired.

All I can say is, "I will think about it."

"Good. And, in the meantime, Olive?"

"Yes."

"Please be kinder to yourself. Life is hard enough, and recovery is hard enough, without you beating yourself up for being you."

50

I don't have to muck out the alpacas.

I mean, for every cloud, I guess there's a silver lining.

I'm allowed to go "rest" in my room.

I wish I could say I feel enlightened by Dr Jones's chat but I don't.

I wish I could say this is the start of something good but it might not be.

I wish I could say all of this will never happen again but no one can make that promise.

And, if I didn't feel so numb and exhausted, maybe that would make me sad.

I shuffle through the corridors, looking down so no one talks to me. Though I can feel their looks. Everyone has noticed who is missing. They must know I have something to do with it. I just want to close the curtains and block out the world and shut my eyes and hope I sleep so I don't have to deal with today any more.

I hold my card against my door and it opens.

I'm just about to slump onto the bed when I almost slip on an envelope on the floor. A big one. With my name on the front.

I pick it up, turn it over in my hands. I'm not sure if I want to open it, if I'm being honest, because I'm emotionally just...not. I take it over to my bed and lie flat, holding the envelope at arm's length.

Am I supposed to feel something?

Because I don't feel anything.

That is how depression works.

I cannot change how it works for the sake of a fairy-tale narrative. Plus, it may just have *FUCK YOU* written on it and be signed by Lewis.

I put the envelope down and get on with the important business of

Lying flat

On my bed

Looking at the ceiling

And thinking I'm a terrible human.

Maybe lots of time passes, maybe it doesn't. When I close my eyes I feel worse, so I just keep them open. Blink.

Blink.

Blink.

Then, eventually, I roll over onto my stomach and rip open the envelope.

A collage falls out. A photo made of dozens of me's. The Prime Numbers have arranged all my self-portraits into chronological order, taken a photo of them together and printed it off. My face and my face and my face and my face. It's my photomontage. It's me. Day after day, it is me. And, though the print is small, I can still see the differences in each version of my face. How it changes and adapts, over the twenty-five portraits. On the days I felt steady, on the days I felt euphoric, on the days I felt helpless – it was all me. All of those emotions are in me, and I am a collection of all those emotions. My face changes, the moods change, but I am still me. Sometimes I am happy, sometimes I am sad. Sometimes I am good, sometimes I am horrid. Sometimes I do things because I can't control myself, and other times I really should've tried harder. All of it is me. The kind and the selfish.

Me is what I am stuck with.

And I'm just about to think about how terribly depressing that is, because I really do think I am quite the arsehole…
but

I turn

Over the

Sheet of paper.

The message is written in big black pen:

BE KIND TO YOURSELF FIRST

It is signed by all of them.

Even him.

I look at it for a very long time and then I put it down on

my bedside table. Then I stare at the ceiling some more.

I start to swirl with dangerous thoughts. Thoughts that I have been taught how to manage since I came here. So I do not go out into a greenhouse and kick in a window. I do not run to a cliff edge. That is progress. A baby step forward. Maybe I am not cured. Maybe my problems will be enduring. But last time I felt like this, I wanted to die. And I still think that life in this world seems relentlessly hard in this moment, but I don't want to die.

Wanting to live is more than just a baby step, I guess. And babies grow bigger and their steps get steadier. They wobble and they fall over but, in time, and with nurture and guidance and love, those steps get bigger and turn into strides.

Not today though.

I need to distract myself from myself so I reach over to the remote and I turn on the TV.

It pings on and I surf through the channels. I cannot cope with one channel for more than five minutes. So boring. So nothing. Some news anchor is wearing a blue suit and telling us all about loads of people trapped in rubble somewhere far enough away that no one cares too much about it. Then some lady wearing red lipstick talks us through the country's finances and says that all the banks are due to get even more money, then she interviews someone who cannot afford to eat saying it is not fair. And I'm about to change the channel when

When.

"And, finally, for some more uplifting news. Reports are coming in from Notting Hill Carnival, saying that a group of young activists have set off what they're calling 'A Kindness Virus'." The anchor smiles straight into the camera and the smile goes right up into the creases of her eyes. "Thousands of motivational messages have been set loose from a rooftop onto the carnival. Each one claims the receiver has been infected with kindness and compassion, and urges people to treat one another better. So far, it's unclear who is responsible for this wacky campaign but, from what we're hearing, the message is being well-received."

The TV switches to mobile phone footage of thousands of our origami helicopters floating down like happy drizzle. People hold their arms up to catch them. There are shots of strangers hugging each other, of people in the parade opening them up mid-march and smiling and shouting "BE KINDER" into the crowds.

I don't watch any more, because I don't want to.

I switch off the TV. The black screen replacing the smiles that I created. I lie back down on my side, hugging my legs up to me.

I am numb.

I don't know how long I will be numb. But somehow...

Somehow...

I smile.

A LETTER FROM HOLLY

Dear Reader,

Do you lose a lot of your life wishing you could be different? Why can't I be calmer? Or happier? Why does everyone else seem to find life EASIER than me? Will my brain always be like this? I wish I could be like that person over there…they seem so sorted, so confident, so…so…sane!

Thought so.

I'm hoping this book will help people realize that your misbehaving brain is actually a totally appropriate response to the life you've had up until now. And we don't have to put up with it. If we fight back, if we campaign, if we don't accept the ways things are, I really believe we can create a world that's kinder. One that doesn't make people ill.

But kindness starts from within. You have to be kind to yourself first. So, please, if you take anything from this book, may it be the lesson to be less hard on yourself. To forgive yourself for being "the way you are". To know that everyone struggles, all of us are having a hard time on this crazy little planet.

You're so much stronger than you think. There is no one else like you in the universe. You really are a special snowflake. But, together, snowflakes do create avalanches. And, with more kindness to ourselves, and to each other, together I really think we can create a world that stops making people sick in the first place.

#KindnessIsContagious

If you have been affected by the issues raised in this book, the following organizations can help:

Samaritans are available round the clock, every single day of the year. You can talk to them any time you like, and in your own way, about whatever's getting to you.

Call, free, any time, on 116 123

Or email jo@samaritans.org

Visit – find your nearest branch on

samaritans.org

The Mix is here to help under 25s get to grips with any challenge they face. Anywhere and anytime, online, over the phone or via social media.

Helpline: 0808 808 4994

themix.org.uk